NOBODY'S GHOUL

ORDINARY MAGIC - BOOK 8

DEVON MONK

ODD
HOUSE
PRESS

Nobody's Ghoul

Copyright © 2021 by Devon Monk

ISBN: 9781939853233

Publisher: Odd House Press

Cover Art: Lou Harper

Interior Design: Odd House Press

Print Design: Odd House Press

NOBODY'S GHOUL

Police Chief Delaney Reed can handle supernatural disasters. With gods vacationing in her little town of Ordinary, Oregon, and monsters living alongside humans, she's had plenty of practice.

But trying to handle something so normal, so average, so very *ordinary* as planning her own wedding to the man she loves? Delaney is totally out of her depth.

When a car falls out of the sky and lands on the beach, Delaney is more than happy to push guest lists and venue dates out of her mind. The car appears empty, but someone has slipped into Ordinary with stolen weapons from the gods. Someone who has the ability to look like any god, monster, or human in town. Someone who might set off a supernatural disaster even Delaney can't handle.

*For my family, and all the Ordinary dreamers
out there*

(Oh, and Megan? Gan and Moosh!)

CHAPTER ONE

Okay, so the truth was things had gotten a little out of hand. Tell one god about an under-planned, under-decided, not-even-scheduled-yet wedding, especially if that god was Crow, and suddenly another god wanted to know when they're getting an invitation. And then another god. And then a dozen.

I'd muted my notifications and refused to look at that message string for weeks. Things were better that way. Well, not for the wedding. Or the gods. Or my fiancé, Ryder Bailey, who was doing all the heavy lifting on the wedding planning. But it sure made me panic a lot less if I didn't have to look at the invitation list growing by the minute.

"How many gods, Delaney?" Ryder asked over piles of paper strewn across the breakfast counter. He'd been dragging his fingers through his light brown hair, and now it stuck up sideways away from his ears.

I shook my head like I was lost in cooking breakfast. "Oh, you know," I said, going for vague.

He narrowed those green eyes. "Delaney?"

"Gods?" I asked, like I'd never heard of such a thing. I poked at the white part of the egg hoping I looked really busy.

"Most of them?" he asked.

I made a noncommittal noise and clicked the hood fan up a notch.

"All of them?" he said over the noise of the fan. "Did you invite *all* the gods in Ordinary to our wedding?"

"Technically, no." I clicked the fan up one more notch.

"I need a list," he shouted over the jet engine roar. "Gods and, you know, everyone else. All your people. You said you'd get me a list. Hey. Hey, Chief Reed, I know you can hear me."

I leaned in and frowned harder at the egg. It had gone brown at the edges surprisingly quickly. It was starting to smell, and I wasn't sure it was a good smell. I dug at it, trying to get the spatula under before it burned.

My sister, Myra, had taken pity on me (again) and walked me through breakfast (again): eggs over easy— and if that failed, scrambled—sausage in a different pan, and toast.

Add some fruit and coffee, and I could officially claim I knew how to cook a breakfast.

I wanted to do this right for once, for Ryder. He'd been doing all the wedding planning since I'd been putting in extra hours at work.

And by "putting in extra hours", I meant I'd been

hiding out at work so I could avoiding planning the wedding.

I didn't know why, but every time I worked myself up to do something for the wedding: flowers, food, guest list? I just froze and all the worst-case scenarios of every possible choice ran through my head like a video stuck in fast-forward. A minute or so of that was traumatizing enough to make me back away from making even the smallest decisions.

Ryder had put up with it for six weeks before he pulled all the neglected tasks to his side of the To Do list, told me he had it under control, and that was that.

I knew I wasn't pulling my weight on the wedding. Breakfast was my attempt at an apology, and now even that was going up in smoke.

I jiggled and scraped, flipped the spatula upside down to get some leverage and pushed harder. The egg popped free, half of it soaring over the edge of the pan before landing with a plop onto the burner.

"Crap!" I yanked the pan off the burner but there was so much egg everywhere. On the burner, down the side of the pan, in the pan. Egg goo stretched, more of the whitish-yellow snaking across the burner and going black in an instant.

Smoke plumed in a ropey spout, a tiny reverse tornado, the stink and greasy gray of it sucked up by the fan. The sausage wasn't doing so hot either. It curled in on itself protectively, exposing pink on the top, purple-y on the sides.

I was pretty sure Myra's sausages hadn't been purple.

I could fix this. I could do this.

"Oil!" I grabbed for the green bottle by the toaster, and realized I'd forgotten to push the bread down and smacked at the lever with one hand. I picked up the oil with the other, ready to pour it over the eggs to unstick them. But instead of pushing the bread down, the toaster bucked and clanged over onto its side.

"Crap!" I lunged for the toaster. My shirt caught the handle of the egg pan, ramming the whole thing into the sausage debacle like bumper cars going ninety.

I slapped at the toaster and grabbed for the pan.

Strong, steady hands stopped me. One on my hip, holding me in place, one reaching for the pan but catching my wrist instead.

"The eggs," I said.

Ryder made some kind of noise I could barely hear over the fan roaring above us. He stepped into me, his whole body fitting behind me. Then his mouth was at my ear and his low, sleep-smoked voice rumbled, "I got this."

I hesitated. Sure, *he* could do this. He was good at everything. But I could do this too. Making breakfast was easy. Anyone could do it.

"Laney," he coaxed.

I thought about pushing it. Insisting I could deal with a very normal-world, regular-person disaster that lots of people dealt with every day. But his body was strong and warm against mine, tensed and waiting for me to let him jump in and take over. I relaxed against him and held my hands up in surrender.

He moved the egg pan toward the unused back

burner, flicked off the front burner, and did something with the sausage to make the breakfast meat stop rocking so wildly. He shifted sideways, moving me into the curve of his arm, practiced as a dance move.

I went with the motion, and he quickly got everything settled: smoke put out, pans arranged, toaster righted. He switched the fan to a lower speed, and finally off. The silence in the kitchen was suddenly very large.

"Hey," he said quietly, still holding me, his lips inches from my ear.

"Hey," I said, defeated.

"How about I take over breakfast, and you take Spud out for a bathroom break?"

"I can do this."

"I know."

"I'm capable of doing normal things like normal people," I said quieter.

His chuckle was low and warm. He planted a kiss on my temple, and his hands on mine lifted, tugged. Then he was twirling me out of the kitchen.

I huffed a laugh, and my mood lightened. How could it not, when I was in the arms of the man I loved, looking up into his sparkling eyes?

We came to a stop in the little hall space between the kitchen and living area.

"Hey," I said.

"Hey," he said back. "It's all going to work out."

"I know." I knew *we* would work out no matter what.

It was other things I was worried about. I didn't have a problem dealing with the big stuff.

The god, Mithra, tying Ryder to him even though Mithra pretty much hated me? No problem. Demons fleeing to Ordinary from and angry king of hell who might aim all that anger at us? Can deal. The only Valkyrie in town somehow even grumpier about being short-handed for her community events? Got it under control.

But some things, easy things, *normal* things like the wedding or the guest list situation seemed bigger than me somehow. And so much harder to solve.

"How about you take Spud for his walk, and when you come back, we'll have breakfast?"

"I can cook, you know. I am a normal person. I can do normal cooking."

"Obviously," he said. "You are a very normal person capable of cooking so very normally."

I smacked his hip.

He grinned, and I liked that smile on his face. Liked everything about him, really.

"See you in ten, yeah?" He dipped is head a little and raised his eyebrows.

"I can..."

"*So* normal," he interrupted. "Got it. And yes, I know you can." He pointed at the door. "Your espresso's gonna go cold if you don't hustle."

The promise of espresso waiting for me put a jog in my step. I hopped into the entry hall and lifted Spud's leash from the hook by the door.

The jingle brought our border collie/chow chow mix galloping down the stairs and across the living room in a flash.

Right on his heels was our dragon pig. Dragon pig was actually a dragon who liked to run around in the shape of a cute baby pig. A cute baby pig who ate cars for breakfast.

"All right you two," I said, "let's get some fresh air."

Spud dropped into a sit, his fluffy tail wagging and wagging, his mouth open in a happy smile. I latched the leash to his collar and plucked up Ryder's old gray hoodie, shrugging into it.

Spud and the dragon pig bounded out the door with me. We spilled into the front yard and then down the sidewalk to the little footpath that rambled between weeds toward the shore of the lake.

I took a deep breath of air that smelled of clean water, green moss, and dusty sand, then let it out in one big rush.

Dragon pig grunted and looked up at me, its pointy little ears flopping back.

"I've been a little stressed," I said, as Spud sniffed around for a good pee spot.

Dragon pig grunted in agreement.

"It's just...the wedding planning. All the details and decisions. People asking me what date to save, and where it will be, and how formal they should dress, and if there's going to be an open bar *and* free weed, or *just* free weed. Then the gods keep dropping hints, and I can't tell if they want to officiate, or just want better seating options. It feels like everyone is more excited about it than I am. That's not normal, is it? Feeling like the wedding is a performance we have to put on for everyone else? Feeling this kind of fight or flight or freeze over my own wedding?"

Dragon pig squeaked and trotted toward the water, startling a couple crows up into the sky. The crows landed in the trees behind us and called out their displeasure. Dragon pig made a pleased sound. Spud finished his business and galumphed toward his buddy, his leash dragging behind him.

"Five minutes," I called after them. "I want that espresso hot. I mean it this time. No long walk. Just a shorty stroll."

Dragon pig grumbled at me and followed the water's edge, Spud splashing through the shallows beside him. They both stopped to sniff around a rock, and the dragon pig swallowed it whole before moving on.

My shoes sank in the dry sand and little reedy grasses slapped at the hem of my pants. The wind was cooler by the water, but the sun poured down a soft, early summer morning heat.

Bertie, our local Valkyrie, couldn't have chosen a better week for the annual talent show. With any luck the outdoor stage would be dry this year and no one's picnic lunches would be ruined.

I knew she had upped her firework budget, and lured a bunch of food vendors to offer treats. It was going to be a hit, because, really, almost everything she touched turned into a tourist magnet.

Tourists meant money, and our little town always needed funds.

I made a mental note to remind everyone on the

force I was going to need all hands on deck for the event.

We still hadn't hired someone to take over Roy's position at the station since he'd retired. We'd been rotating front desk duty, which worked for a stopgap, but was putting a bit of a strain on our small department.

We only had five full-time officers: Me, my sisters Myra and Jean, and the two cops we'd nabbed from Tillamook just north of us: Hatter and Shoe. Our reserve officers: Kelby, Ryder, and Than helped part time, but they all had full-time jobs on the side.

I needed to hire someone else full time, but had been holding off until things settled down. The only problem with Ordinary was that things never settled down.

Spud was working on a stick, biting each end of it, then the middle, then each end again as he tried to decide how he was going to drag the thing back to the house. Dragon pig had found a pile of rocks someone had stacked, and was currently perched on the top like a king.

Or a like dragon on a mountain. Or a pig on a pile of rocks.

Mostly that last thing.

The crows muttered and clucked in the trees, and a trio of seagulls piped across the sky, cruising for forgotten French fries or bits of bread.

I tipped my face to the sky. Clouds rolled and shuffled like foam churning at the wave-edge of the heavens. My gaze ticked west, following the blue out and out for miles.

Dragon pig growled. Spud dropped his stick and *woof*ed.

The crows suddenly went silent and took wing eastward, fast.

The waves on the lake, the wind, the buzz of insects all stilled. As if this moment was stalled between the *tick* and *tock* of time.

Something magic was happening. Something supernatural.

"Holy crap," I breathed. "Spud, Dragon pig, come on. Now." I shot off toward the house, my gaze on the horizon.

The westward sky wobbled like someone had stuck a soapy finger into oil, forcing the blue out to form a ring around a glossy golden disk in the sky. The disk flashed with blue fire and then...

"What the...?"

...a car tumbled out the sky and hit the beach a couple miles north.

A seagull called out, the wind picked up, *tick* followed *tock*, and the day once again seemed like any other day in Ordinary, Oregon.

CHAPTER TWO

RYDER TOOK one look at my face and dumped the espresso into travel mugs. He grabbed the toast, hooked both mugs with one hand, and shrugged into his Carhartt Jacket. I got Spud off his leash and told the dragon pig to stay and look after him.

"What happened?" Ryder asked as we jogged to the driveway.

"Magic, I think. Big magic."

He slid into the passenger side of my Jeep. I took the wheel and got us moving north.

"What kind of magic?" He settled the cups into the holders, balanced the toast on his knee, and reached for the police radio.

"Hole in the sky."

"Got it," he said, taking the supernatural weirdness of our town like a champ. There were days when it was hard to remember he'd only found out about the monsters and gods and magic of this place a couple years ago.

There were days when it was hard to remember he used to be part of the Department of Paranormal Protection, a governmental agency that hired people to hunt monsters. People who could do a lot of damage to our town.

But there wasn't a day when I wasn't thankful for Ryder finding out just how un-ordinary Ordinary was, and then immediately quitting the DoPP. He'd taken our side and had become an important part of keeping our secrets safe.

"Jean and Myra?" He switched from the police radio, which was monitored by a handful of mortals who didn't know about magic, to his phone.

"Yes."

"North?"

"I think 50th Street. Tell Myra to sweep the beach from 40th up, and Jean to..."

"Delaney's here with me. You're on speaker," Ryder said responding to the call he'd answered before the phone even rang. "Jean," he told me.

"Something fell out of the sky," I said.

"I know." My youngest sister, Jean's voice buzzed with excitement.

"You saw it?" Ryder asked, handing me toast.

I wasn't hungry, but knew better than to turn down food before rolling into something like this. I took a bite and grinned. He'd put butter and honey on it. Even scrambling to check a possible disaster, he had his eye on the details, and had made a quick breakfast of toast and coffee something special.

"I was at the beach when it happened," Jean went on. "I had a feeling..."

Jean's family gift was knowing when something bad was going to happen. She called it her Doom Twinges, and she had been trying to get better at sensing the incoming "wrong" before it happened. It meant paying attention to the slightest niggle of wrongness she felt, instead of only paying attention to the big, possibly life-ending stuff she usually noticed.

I didn't envy her gift, nor her quest to improve it. If I had to second-guess everything my intuition told me, or worse, believe every change in my mood, every random thought I had might be something more than just a mood or thought, I'd go out of my mind.

"I was parked right above the beach access. A hole opened in the sky, then time stopped—*boom, fire*—a car plops out of the sky."

"Where did it land?" Ryder asked.

"On the beach. No one was around. No injuries."

That was good, but we needed to make sure no one else had seen it fall.

"Do not approach the vehicle until we get there," I said.

"Oops."

"Jean," I said.

"What did you want us to do, just stand here are stare at it?"

"That's exactly what—who's 'us'?"

"We're on the beach right below 50th," my other sister, Myra said.

Myra's family gift was always being in the right place

at the right time. So of course she was at the newest weird event. "We didn't see anything or anyone exit the vehicle," she said. "No one's reported seeing anything strange. No one's nearby."

"Good." I felt a little better knowing Jean wasn't poking at the thing alone. I trusted both my sisters, but I was glad they had each other's backs. "We'll be there in five."

Ryder thumbed off the call. "Anyone else?"

"No, we're almost there."

"Drink your espresso."

"Why, did you spike it?"

"No, should I have?"

"Ask me after we figure out why cars are falling out of the sky."

"Car. Only one so far."

"Optimist."

"To the grave, baby." He toasted the cup and took a big swig.

I shoved the rest of the toast in my face and chased it with coffee. "So good," I mumbled. "Honey's amazing on this."

"Blackberry and clover," he said.

"Where'd you get it?"

"Gan and Moosh came by the station with samples."

Gan and Moosh had returned to Ordinary after being away for several years. Gan was the god Ganesha, and his son Moosh was Mooshak. They were in the process of opening up their tea shop again, only this time they would also sell flowers.

"And I didn't get any samples?"

"No complaining. I saved it for breakfast, and it was...?"

"Delicious," I agreed.

I finished the last of my drink and plunked the cup in the holder next to his. "Ready?"

He nodded, and I pulled over onto the gravel and dirt pullout with a clump of trees between it and the beach below. A little foot-worn path jagged down through those trees to the beach.

Ryder and I swung out of the Jeep. I paused at the top of the path, glad I was still wearing his hoodie in the gusty wind. It smelled strongly of salt and seaweed mixed with sweet pine, a scent that would always be home to me.

I scanned the beach.

The vehicle was impossible to miss.

The baby-blue muscle car, something along the lines of a classic GTO, had landed on all four tires, high above the water line.

Myra and Jean were several yards away from it, Myra in her uniform, since she was pulling the morning shift today. Jean wore a flowing yellow skirt over light-green leggings, her bright pink hair propped up in ponytails. The whole thing made her look like a flower.

I put my fingers in my mouth and whistled.

Myra waved. I waved back, and meandered down the path, watching my feet for the first part where roots of trees stuck out like knobby knuckles, then looking southward down the beach.

The beach was empty, which wasn't all that strange this early in the morning. About five miles south, I could

make out one big tunnel kite—a huge wind sock spinning slowly— anchored to the beach by bags of sand.

Northward was a curve in the hillside, no people, no
kites, just bare brown stone tufted at the top by tough
grass.

"Didn't Than tell you he was closing shop for a few
days?" I asked Ryder.

"Yup."

"Then who has the big kite out today?" Than was
the god of death, but here in Ordinary, he ran a kite
shop.

"The Persons have one of those. I think the Wolfes
do too."

The Persons were a family of shape shifters, and the
Wolfes a clan of werewolves. "I thought they only bring
out the big kites on weekends," I said.

"I can call Than and see if he's back from his *amble*."
I didn't look over my shoulder but I could hear the air
quotes Ryder implied.

"Oh, gods, is that what he called it?"

"He said he wouldn't have a phone with him
because it would interfere with his "rumination", which
sounded about right for a man who *ambles*. It'd be nice if
he *ambled* back and picked up his next shift covering the
front desk."

"It's a volunteer position, Ryder."

"So's mine. I show up for my shifts. And his."

"That's because you're engaged to the boss and want
to make a good impression."

"That's one reason."

"What's the other?"

"I look damn good in a uniform. Also, my fiancé has a thing about men in uniform."

"Man," I corrected. "Your fiancé has a thing for one man in a uniform. Or out of it, for that matter."

He chuckled, pleased with himself.

The wind cut off as we descended the trail, and for a few steps it was suddenly summer, hot as August, instead of the warm June day. Then the wind picked up, spooling away summer's heat and it was June forever again.

"What's the story going to be for this one?" he asked as we continued down the path.

"High winds, I think."

"That doesn't sound very convincing."

"No, it's easy. Listen: There was a microburst, just hit one spot, right where this car was on the beach, picked it up, then dropped it flat."

"Microburst."

"You know. Tiny powerful wind phenomenon. It's a real thing, but no one's really seen it. One knocked out a three-block swath of trees up near the pass a few years back. Flattened a strip of the forest like a giant fly swatter had smacked all the trees beneath it with one whack. The trees on the edge of the microburst are still standing like nothing ever happened."

"Might work. Depends on how many people saw it drop."

"We'll make it work, no matter how many people saw it, because we are amazing that way."

"Does it ever bother you?" he asked. "Lying to people about this stuff?"

"Yes," I said honestly. "I know it's part of the job. I know it's important for everyone to stay safe and I need to do everything I can to keep them safe. If the outside world knew gods and the supernatural myths and fables all hung out among mortals here, it would be...chaos. Maybe even destruction.

"Gods have powerful enemies. World leaders have bombs. It would be..." I shook my head, not wanting to give more thought to the nightmare scenario that had plagued me since I was a child.

"I love Ordinary. I love the mortals here—well, most of them. I love the supernatural people—again, most of them. And I love the gods. Okay, most of them too." I threw a grin over my shoulder.

Ryder had that thoughtful look on his face. Like he was working through something. Something serious. Like he was contemplating asking questions I wasn't sure I wanted to answer.

"I see the lies as a protection." I ducked one last low branch that crossed the path. "A way to keep our town safe. A way to keep the world safe. Because if a god gets angry? Universes explode. Frightened people facing something they don't understand, something they fear might have power over them? Those people, for right or wrong, do some horrific things."

He scratched at the side of his neck and nodded. "Back when I was part of the DoPP, I was thinking those same things. What if we really found a supernatural? What decisions would we make? I knew what the regulations said. Capture, but don't harm. But I knew the people I worked with too. Some were fanatical. They had a drive to capture, to win, even if that meant killing the thing they'd dedicated their life to find."

"Lots of movies about that," I noted.

"Never ends well for the monster."

"Or the humans."

I strode down onto the sand, dry and squeaky under my tennis shoes and followed the easiest path between rounded rocks and driftwood.

Ryder pulled up on my right, matching my strides.

Jean broke away from Myra and headed our way. "Car falling out of the sky was not on my bingo card," she said happily. "But look at that thing."

I shifted my gaze away from my floral-colored sister to the car.

"No one's in it?"

"Not that we can see."

"No one got out of it?"

She shook her head, ponytails bouncing. "Unless they're invisible. Which, you know, is possible."

"Was it a Doom Twinge?"

"It was..." She chewed the corner of her lip and shoved her hands in her skirt pockets. "...not bad? I mean I knew something weird was going to happen, but it didn't feel like death and destruction. Not like the other times. But it felt like I should come out here and...watch."

I squeezed her shoulder. "That's good. You're really getting good at this stuff."

"Thanks." She beamed. "That's what happens when you live with a hot boyfriend who is into all the weirdo powers in town."

Hogan was indeed hot. He was half Jinn and could see a person's true nature through any disguise or illusion. He was also an amazing baker on whom my sister had a huge crush.

"You know," Jean went on, elbowing me as we staggered slightly through the heavy soft sand toward the car, "like Ryder."

He snorted, and when I looked over at him, he was grinning. Sexy. Smug. Happy.

I liked seeing him that way: happy. Happy to be a part of this town. Happy to make his home here, to become a part of the handful of beings who kept everything running as peacefully as possible, for mortals, monsters, and gods.

"You do know, don't you, Delaney?" he asked, that grin smoldering. "What it's like to have a boyfriend who's into all the weirdo powers in town. A hot boyfriend?"

"No," I said archly. "I do not."

He *tsk*ed. "Liar, liar."

"I don't have a hot boyfriend. I have a hot fiancé."

And oh, how that smile grew. He was hot. He was the kind of man who could stand in the middle of the grocery store debating what cereal to buy and turn heads. But when he smiled like that, it transformed him into something bright and wonderful.

How had I'd gotten so lucky to have a man like that—someone kind and smart and curious and hot—fall in love with me?

"What's that face for?" He moved toward me, seemingly unable not to. "Penny for that thought in particular."

"You'd need more than a penny for what I'm thinking."

"Oooh," Jean cooed. "Look at you two lovey-dovies. Bet the wedding planning's been a lot of fun, right?"

Mood ruined.

Wedding planning had not been fun. Ryder's wince showed me he was thinking the same thing.

He'd been trying to pull it together all on his own, and I felt guilty about it. But if I tried to help, he pushed me away. It had happened enough I'd given up and stepped back.

Like way back. No matter how much he said he could handle it, I knew he was drowning. I could see it, I really could. But I didn't know how to get back into the ring and tell him to tap out.

The few times I'd tried, he'd firmly refused my help.

But I'd caught him staring into space like he had a hundred plates he had to keep spinning on a hundred sticks and he knew there was no chance he was going to get through that without plates toppling and breaking all around him.

Or I'd catch him pacing, one hand running up the back of his hair over and over as he talked to someone on the phone, or grumbled over a list, or pulled out his sketchbook to draw little rectangle tables.

I'd peeked at his sketches. The tables sometimes had flowers and streamers scribbled everywhere, or sprays of sparkle lights. Or one time, something that looked like chain-link fencing and prison bars.

"Yeah," Ryder said, filling the silence that had gone on too long. "Planning's been…fun."

Fun.

"So, no one in the vehicle," I said, all cop voice, which was not lost on Jean, if her eyes darting between the two of us was any indication. "And no one exited the vehicle."

"As far as we can tell." Myra nodded toward the car. "We've identified ourselves, but haven't gotten close enough to look inside."

Myra was shorter and curvier than me, and wore her hair in a page boy that brushed her shoulders. Her eyeliner, and whatever else she put on this morning to make her look like a pin-up dream, was flawless. Over her uniform she wore a bulky coat with the stitched emblem of the Ordinary Police Department.

Her phone was in her hand, and the footprints in the sand showed she'd circled the car while taking pictures of it.

"Did you catch it falling?" I pointed at her phone.

"No, but plenty shots of it. How do you want to handle this?"

"Let's spread out. Ryder, stay back and watch for anything strange. Myra, take the backseat, Jean, the trunk. I'll take the front."

Everyone got into position, Ryder stationing himself closer to the strip of harder, wet sand. It was a smart choice. If someone took off running, Ryder wouldn't be fighting soft dry sand at the start of the chase.

We moved in on the car as one, no weapons drawn. "This is Chief of Police Delaney Reed," I said, loud enough to be heard over the waves. Seagulls drifted overhead, arcing toward the shallow waves. "We're here to help. Are you injured?"

Myra chose the ocean side back door. Jean stood ready at the trunk for me to pull the trunk release lever in the front. I glanced in the driver-side window.

Empty and clean.

Most vehicles showed their use. A forgotten straw wrapper. Dust on the console. Smudges on the edge of a window.

Not this vehicle. It looked like it'd just rolled off the factory floor, the black leather clean and supple, the carpeting pristine, and everything else shiny and new.

I caught Myra's eye over the top of the car. She nodded and we both tried the handles. The doors opened smoothly without even a squeak.

"Boss?" Jean asked.

"Yep." I popped the trunk release under the dash to unlock the trunk for her, then leaned into the space, checking for signs of…well, *anything*.

"Myra?"

"Nothing. It's clean."

"Very clean," I agreed. "So someone just dropped an empty car out of the sky?"

It wasn't the strangest thing—by far—that happened in Ordinary.

Maybe a spell had gone wrong. Kids messing with magic they didn't understand and couldn't control. Somehow poked a hole in the sky. Somehow stopped time. Then pushed a car out of the heavens.

Wielding that kind of magic would take some real

supernatural muscle. It would set off all sorts of warnings with all sorts of people in town. Someone would have caught that spell before the last *abra* was *cadabra*ed. It would have been smothered.

I glanced at the odometer. The mileage was one. Just one mile.

I had no idea what that meant.

"Okay, so we've got—" A scrabbling scratch from inside the car shut me up quick.

There was something in there. Something under the front passenger seat.

"Come on out," I said. "We're here to help." I shifted my weight so I could keep a hand on the door, glancing quickly at Myra to make sure she was getting into position on the other side of the front seat.

A flicker of movement drew my attention to the space under the seat. Whatever was under there wasn't human—there was no space for a body under the seat. But there were a lot of tiny supernatural beings.

"It really is okay," I said more gently. "Come on out. You're safe here."

Whatever it was moved out from beneath the seat *fast*. I jerked back and sucked in a breath.

"Crab!" I yelled.

The little Dungeness crab was about the size of a glazed donut. It scuttled in a circle on the floor like it didn't know how to work all its legs yet. Something fell out of its mouth, then it rounded on me, waving both claws threateningly.

"Hey," I breathed. "Hey, there little guy. How'd you get in here?"

It jerked right, left, right. Then made a run for it.

Right at me.

It shot out the door, dropped like a rock, and quickly scuttled under the car.

"Incoming," I shouted to Myra. "Tiny crab."

Myra stared at the sand. "This our perp?"

"It's a crab," I said.

"I see that. Did you want me to cuff it, Danno?"

"Shut up."

She grinned. "Too small to eat," she noted. "Probably just crawled in there for a nice nap and then you scared the shell out of it."

"Ha. Ha." I joined her near the front fender. The little crab was running as quickly as it could toward the water.

Unfortunately for it, the seagulls noticed its escape. Four gulls swooped down, but the little crustacean waved its claws again, giving the tough guy act all he had.

One seagull grabbed for him. The crab squatted, dug, and the next wave covered him up. When the wave pulled away, the crab was gone.

"Nice getaway," Jean noted. "That was just a crab right? Not something…" She wiggled her fingers.

"Looked like a crab to me. Myra?"

She frowned. "All the windows were rolled up."

"Yeah," I said.

"The trunk?" she asked Jean.

"Empty. No holes under it I could see. But maybe under the seats?"

"So," Ryder said wrapping his arm behind my back,

his fingers catching the belt loop on my hip. "We're thinking the car landed on top of the crab and it crawled up into it through a hole in the floor? That sounds likely."

None of us said anything because it did not sound likely.

"So…we go after it?" Jean asked.

"It's gone," Myra said, echoing my thoughts.

"Okay," she said. "What's our story?"

I leaned my head on Ryder's shoulder for just a minute, then leaned away from him.

His hand dragged across my low back, a gesture of such casual familiarity, my heart jumped.

"We're going with microburst," I said. "Myra, you're on phones and community outreach. Get Hatter and Shoe to explain things in person if anyone saw it and needs convincing."

She started up the beach. "Got it."

"Jean…"

"Already ahead of you. Tow the vehicle so we can go over it for evidence." She lifted her phone to her ear. "Hey, Frigg. You got a truck that can tow a muscle car stuck on the beach before high tide?"

She turned north, laughing at something the goddess said in reply.

"You want me to check in with the kite people down the beach or the houses up on the hill?" Ryder asked.

"You're not on duty today."

"I know." The wind tossed his hair, stirring amber and gold into it.

"Then, no, we've got this. Are you working your regular job?"

"I'll probably stop by the office. We have a couple projects on the hook. See if we can reel them in."

"You keep up this pace and every remodel and new build in town is going to be a Bailey special."

"That's the plan. Think of all that sweet cash. We're going to need it. For the wedding." He moved in, closing the gap between us. "And the honeymoon."

His fingers pressed the side of my chin, moving my face up toward his so he could kiss me.

And kiss me, he did.

He tasted of coffee and burnt toast and sweet blackberry honey. He tasted like love.

He tugged on my bottom lip, making me groan a little before he stepped back.

"Go get 'em Chief. If you need me, you know my number." He turned and jogged up the beach, his long legs eating the distance, catching up with Myra to mooch a ride.

I watched him for longer than I should.

"Delaney?" Jean called.

I reluctantly turned. "You got Frigg lined up?"

"Yep. But you should see this." Jean stood in front of the door I hadn't closed, scanning the interior.

I strolled over.

"What?"

She pointed. "Does that look like a shell to you?"

I dug around in my jacket, and Jean handed me a pair of latex gloves without me asking.

"This must have been what it spit out. You get a picture of it?" I asked.

"Yep."

I leaned in, one hand on the seat, the other carefully plucking up the object.

"Is it a crab claw?" Jean asked.

"Looks like. It's been chewed on." I turned the claw which had an obvious chunk missing.

"Crabby buddy was interrupted in the middle of a meal?" she asked.

"I guess." Crabs were scavengers and would eat anything. Including other crabs.

But something told me that wasn't the whole story. Something told me there was a lot more to this. The car, the crab, this claw.

I just didn't know what it was.

CHAPTER THREE

I WAS RUNNING the make and model through the databases, and Myra was at her computer looking for any supernatural connection to the car that had fallen out of the sky earlier today.

It was just the two of us in the station, and the quiet was a nice change. Good weather, especially early in summer, drew people outdoors and away from calling the station complaining about things like missing welcome mats and X-rated chalk art.

My phone rang. I picked it up without looking at the screen.

"Chief Reed."

"Delaney, how delightful you finally answered your phone," the only Valkyrie in town said.

My eyes went wide, and I wondered if I could get away with "fumbling" the phone and "accidentally" hanging up on her.

"Hey, Bertie." I pitched my words toward Myra who

ignored me. "Sorry about missing your calls. It's just been so busy."

I pulled a yellow pad out of my desk drawer and wrote HELP ME in big block letters on it.

"Has it?" she pressed.

Any answer I gave her was a trap.

I covered the phone with my palm. "What's that, Myra?" I threw my pencil at Myra. It hit her shoulder, and she finally looked away from her screen.

I waved the pad at her and mouthed *please*.

Myra just shook her head at me like I was being childish and went back to her work.

The big meanie.

"No, Myra," I said. "You're not getting that time off you wanted because we are so *busy* here."

Myra flipped me the bird without looking up.

"Sorry about the interruption," I said to Bertie. "Where were we?"

"I do not have an assistant."

"Oh-kay?"

"This season I will be three times as busy as usual. But I do not have an assistant. I have a standard to uphold. I alone deal with every detail of every event. Did you know that, Delaney?"

"Yes?"

"Did you know my time is not limitless? There are only so many 'missed calls' I will tolerate."

Crap. She was angry. I opened my mouth to give her a real apology, but she cut me off.

"I need you to do something for me."

Oh, gods. This was what I'd been avoiding. Bertie

was in charge of all the community events, festivals, and fundraisers. She'd been doing it almost longer than Ordinary had had its name. She always needed volunteers.

"I *have* been busy. I'm not sure how much help I can be, other than what we usually sign up for."

I always helped with the events. The whole department worked to keep an eye on crowds, help lost kids find their parents, make sure no out-of-towner was stomping through someone's flower beds. We handled fender benders, traffic management, de-escalated arguments before fights could break out.

Saturday's festival was coming up fast. Flyers plastered every window and bulletin board in Ordinary. Colorful flags and banners had been pulled from storage and installed in front of shops. Flowers were planted, watered and trimmed. The big event was pulling together without a hitch as far as I could tell.

"As you well know," Bertie went on, as if we'd just started the conversation, "we have a very important festival this weekend. It begins Saturday."

"Yes."

"Saturday is day after tomorrow."

"I'm aware."

"Are you also aware the Ordinary Show Off is an event residents mark on their calendar months in advance?"

To avoid, I mentally noted. "Yep. Yes. Talent show. It's on my calendar too."

To avoid.

"It is much more than a talent show, Delaney Reed.

31

It is a chance for everyone to come together and reacquaint themselves. It is vital. Lifeblood. If anything were to stop it, Ordinary would be a shell of itself, gasping for air."

"I don't think Ordinary needs CPR, Bertie."

"Of course it doesn't. We have the talent show for that."

"Is this about Boring?"

Bertie had always been a bit militant about Ordinary's events. But ever since she'd found out her sister Valkyrie, Robyn, had nested in Boring and was going directly head-to-head with Bertie for the tourist dollars by throwing identical festivals at identical times, Bertie had been a little extra-extra.

"This is about a favor I need from you," she snapped.

Okay. Boring was a touchy subject. "I can't."

"You haven't heard what I want."

"But I know it's a talent show. I can't. I won't."

"Being crowned this year's Ordinary Show Off is a great honor."

"Didn't Phil Lambert win the last two years?"

"He was a crowd favorite. Of course he won."

"He played the "Ride of the Valkyries" with armpit farts."

I could hear her inhale through her nose, as if she were trying very hard not to shout at me.

"The year before that it was armpit-fart "The Blue Danube" wasn't it?"

"No," she said through her teeth. "It was Vivaldi."

What could I say? Ordinary liked weird stuff. Like big sweaty bald guys armpit farting the classics.

"Three wins in a row would be very unlikely," Bertie said. "Unless you are suggesting our current Ordinary Show Off hasn't earned his crown?"

"No. No. Phil's great. I just can't."

"Can't what? I haven't asked for my favor yet."

Bertie was right. The events she put on were important. They kept us together, created our traditions. They let the outgoing among us thrive and tempted the hermits to join in.

It was good. The talent show was cheesy as all heck, but it was *good*.

However, the idea of me standing on that stage doing *anything* in front of all those people had me sweating hard.

"Delaney?"

"I can't be an Ordinary Show Off."

Bertie's sigh was long-suffering. "I wouldn't ask you to. You don't have any talent. Not a single dramatic bone in your body."

"Hey, I can do stuff."

Myra snorted and clicked away at her keyboard. I threw another pencil at her. She didn't even move.

"You want to perform in front of the entire town?" Bertie asked, scenting blood on the battlefield.

"No."

"Then what makes you think I would force you to do something you abhor?"

"What about the rhubarb, Bertie? Do you remember

the rhubarb? Because I still have nightmares about the rhubarb."

"I stand corrected," she said dryly. "You do have a dramatic bone in your body."

"Myra can ride a unicycle," I said sweetly.

Myra stopped typing. Her head swiveled slowly toward me, her eyes hard.

"I know what Myra can do. I want you to tell Ryder he should participate."

"Ryder?"

"Yes."

"Ryder Bailey?"

"Yes."

"You want Ryder to get up on stage and be a Show Off?"

"Is there something wrong with your hearing?"

"No, it's just….What do you think Ryder's going to do?"

"I've seen his art. I believe he took piano lessons when he was young."

"Oh, gods." I had forgotten that. "You want him to play piano?"

"I want him to be the last person on stage before the judging. What he decides to do doesn't matter to me. I'm sure he'll come up with something wonderful. Encourage him to accept my invitation."

It should have sounded like she wanted me to just give him a friendly nudge.

But I knew this was a threat.

"I don't know, Bertie. He's been really busy too."

"Planning the wedding, yes, I know. The community

center is open third Thursday next month, two Fridays the month after, possibly half a Sunday. All the other dates after that are booking up fast."

"Uh..."

"You have chosen a date, haven't you? And a venue?"

"Um..."

"I can't keep the calendar open indefinitely, Delaney. If Ordinary is to remain the queen's jewel of small-town festival destinations in Oregon, then every date has to be leveraged for optimal impact."

"I'll keep that in mind."

"See that you do. Now, I have an appointment I can't miss."

"Wait, before you go. Did you hear about the car falling out of the sky?"

"I saw it when I was coming back from my second walk of the morning."

"Overachiever."

"Thank you."

"Do you know anything about the car? Did you see anything odd?"

"Other than the sky broke open, caught on fire, and time stopped?"

So sassy.

"Other than that, yes."

"No."

"A crab crawled out of it."

The silence was very judgey. I didn't know how she managed to do that over the phone.

"Is that all, Delaney?" The words were an ice floe.

"Yep. Yes. That's it. That's all. You have a good day, Ber—"

The call disconnected.

I thumbed off the screen then threw three more pencils at Myra. "Thanks for nothing."

"If you can't handle the Valkyrie, stay off of the battlefield," she said mildly.

I dropped my head on my desk, *thunk*ing my forehead.

"Why. Me?" I whined to the scratched wood.

"You don't have to be here," Myra said for the seventh time since I'd come into work. "I told you to stay home. It's your day off."

I fake screamed with my mouth open, but no sound came out. It didn't make me feel any better, so I rolled my head, pressing my cheek against the desk.

The wood was cool, and everything looked sort of fun-housey from this angle.

"I have work to do." I stretched and pushed the stapler to the edge of the desk, straightening the base with my finger until it lined up perfectly.

"Uh-huh." Myra was back to typing again, the *clickity clack* loud in the quiet station.

"Any luck on the car?" I asked.

"Nope." She kept right on typing.

"Are you on one of those secret auction sites that sells old magic stuff?"

"No. I don't look for magic items at work. Also, nothing good has shown up on those sites in months."

"Think we could get some money for a car that fell out of the sky once?"

"Nope."

I lifted my head a little to try and see more of her screen.

"Bertie wants Ryder to be in the talent show."

"I heard."

"She remembered he used to play piano."

Myra tipped her chin up just a bit and took a deep breath. "Okay, we're doing this now?"

"Doing what now?"

"Moping about the wedding."

"I don't mope."

She tapped her mouse a few times, then pulled on the bottom drawer of her desk and lifted a paperback out of it. "Fine. Since you're going to be like this, I'm taking a break."

She opened the book and leaned back in her chair.

"I thought you liked reading on your E-reader."

She didn't lift her eyes, but she pointed at the device on her desk with the cord plugged in and charging. "This is my back up." She jiggled the book. "Which I need today because the reader is charging. You know what back up I don't need today?"

Now her gaze flicked up, and the blue, lighter than mine, held me pinned. "Any idea what back up I don't need today, Delaney? Any idea at all who I might not need around here," she spun her finger in the air, "interrupting me all day when they aren't even supposed to be working today?"

"I don't want to leave you short-handed if there's another emergency."

"If there were another emergency, you know I'd call

you. We've been working together for years. You know this. So why are you really here?"

I shrugged.

She shook her head and went back to reading.

I tried to stay quiet, really I did, but it felt like I had electricity popping under my skin. I was on edge, wishing there was something I could do to settle my nerves, but I didn't even know why I was so jumpy.

Okay, that was a lie. I was jumpy because a fricking car had just fallen out of the sky.

My wedding was coming up, maybe, probably, if we picked a date. But—and for reasons I couldn't fathom—I was dragging my feet. "I don't know what's wrong with me."

"Mmm-hmm." Myra licked a finger and turned the page. Loudly. Like maybe she was hoping I would get the hint.

I would not get the hint.

"I know I should be happy. I love Ryder. I want to be with him. Spend my life with him, but everything feels wrong."

She closed her eyes and tipped her head down for a minute before gamely lifting her head again and going back to reading.

"I don't know why I feel like this."

The muscle at her jaw tightened.

"What should I do?"

"Go home." She glared at me, waited a second, then went back to her book. "I will call if I need you." She lifted her mug of tea that smelled of lavender and orange and took a sip.

"I just…wish I could figure out the mess in my head. I keep thinking in circles. Some of it is the car falling out of the sky. Some is that we now have three demons living in Ordinary.

"I know they're hiding from the King of demons. But they signed our contract. Just because they had a hard past, doesn't mean I can turn them away when they're seeking asylum."

She sighed. "Delaney."

"Do you remember Bathin's brother showing up when Ryder proposed to me?"

She licked her finger one more time, turned the page, then placed a red silk ribbon down the center of the book, leaving part of it hanging over the spine.

"Okay, now we're doing this?"

"Doing what?"

She turned her chair and faced me. "You are avoiding working on the falling car situation, while avoiding planning your upcoming wedding situation by thinking about our demon situation. And the question you're asking me is if I remember Bathin's brother appearing out of thin air during your engagement and stabbing Bathin with a sword while I was standing there beside him?"

I winced. "I know you remember it."

"I thought he was going to die. Yes. I remember it."

I didn't know how she could sound so calm about it, but that was part of how Myra handled things. She compartmentalized and intellectualized.

Unlike me. My emotions got in the way. Oh, not at work. I was all logic when it came to enforcing the laws of Ordinary. But when it came to personal hard stuff, my emotions were all over the place. I'd get them sorted out, but I had to work through them. I had to process.

"Why are you even worrying about the demons?" she asked.

"You know, maybe we should just get back to work."

"We should, actually, but I'm not letting you out of this now. What does Bathin getting fake stabbed by his asshole of a brother have to do with anything?"

Okay, maybe she had a few emotions to work through too.

"He chose that moment—my engagement—to tell us a war is coming."

"I remember. But we've been hearing that one way or another from a lot of people over the years."

"We've had bad things happen."

"Sure. We have. We've gotten through them."

"And I keep thinking, his warning is just like the other warnings, the other things that have happened, and they all turned out fine."

"Not without injuries," Myra said. "Not without deaths."

"I was only dead for like a minute."

"That is never going to be something I can joke about, Delaney."

I nodded. "Fair. What if this war with the king of demons, old what's his name..."

"Brute of All Evil," Myra said.

"What?"

"It's one of his names."

"That's a terrible name."

Myra shrugged. "Demons. They come up with the weirdest titles and names."

"I'm going to ask you how you know that someday. But what I'm getting at, is we've been told the Brute of All Evil," I rolled my eyes, "is power hungry and wants to destroy Ordinary because he wants to destroy all the world, and Ordinary might stand in his way."

"We do like the world," Myra noted.

"Maybe he's not after Ordinary. Maybe he wants something else."

"The king could be targeting Ordinary because Bathin is here," Myra said. "He's next in line for the throne. Or because the queen of the demons and her recently escaped consort are here too. If they left, we wouldn't have this problem."

"He's not leaving," I said.

"I know."

"Myra, I won't let Bathin leave."

She studied me for a minute. "You couldn't stop him. No, don't get all puffed up about it. He's a demon. He can transport himself to any place in the universe in a second. He can control the inner spaces of any stone in the worlds. If he wanted, he could transport into a pebble on the top of Mount Everest, and that would be that."

"He loves you," I said one-hundred percent sure of that and wanting her to know it. Bathin had possessed my soul for over a year. In some ways, it had been a two-way connection. I knew him—the real him—maybe better than anyone. "He won't leave you."

"If it meant saving me from a war?" she asked. "If it meant drawing war away from Ordinary?"

"He doesn't get to break your heart just so he can be a heroic martyr."

She blinked and for a moment she looked younger, vulnerable and afraid. Myra hadn't had a lot of relationships in her life because she guarded her heart very carefully.

But when she gave her heart to someone, she gave it all. It was just the way she was made. That was why she had been very, very careful about falling in love.

It would be absolute hell on her if he left. Even if he thought he would be saving her, he would be doing the opposite.

That was not going to happen. Not on my watch.

"You were talking about your engagement. What does that have to do with demons and kings of hell and war?"

"A demon showed up when Ryder proposed to me. Do you think that's a coincidence?"

"I don't think anything is a coincidence."

I spread a hand in a *there-you-go* gesture.

"So...let me see if I'm following your logic here. You think if you get married, what? You're going to start a demon war?"

"No. I don't think my marriage means anything to the demon world. But the whole wedding thing is making me…"

"Neurotic?"

"Hey."

"Whiney?"

"What the——"

"Stupid?"

"Go back to the first thing."

She took a moment to really look me over. I didn't know what she saw in my blue jeans, belt, and black tank under Ryder's hoodie. I didn't know what she saw in my slouch, or my hair pulled back in a low ponytail.

But she saw something. And it made her narrow her eyes.

I folded my hands in my lap and picked at a thumbnail.

"No," she said.

"No what?"

"You cannot hide out here at work worrying about a war that might not even be a thing just because you're avoiding wedding planning."

I scoffed. "I'm not hiding out." But the words sort of dried up under her slow blink.

"Delaney Reed, I cannot believe you just lied to me. About work and about your wedding *to the man you've loved since you were eleven*."

I picked at my other thumb and muttered something under my breath.

"What was that? What did you just say to me?" she demanded.

"Six and a half. I've had a crush on him since I was six and a half. And that's not what this is."

She waited. No rustle of the page being turned, no squeak of her chair springs. The phone had been silent for two days, ever since the weather went mild, so no help there.

"Want to try that again?" she asked.

"Maybe I'm hiding out a little. Not from Ryder."

I wanted to get married. I'd loved Ryder since I was so young I didn't even know how big, how wonderful, love could be.

Even then, when I'd been a tiny human with a whole world of experience still ahead of me, I'd known he was it. Ryder was the curiosity I needed to understand. Ryder was the one person I needed to see with my eyes. His voice, his laughter, the sound I needed in my ears. And the smell of him—which had changed over the years and yet somehow remained familiar, becoming more than a deeply ingrained knowledge of *Ryder* and becoming more, becoming *home* and *joy* and *love*—was what I wanted around me at all times.

But a wedding, oh, that was change. A big change. My life would never be the same after, and I had a pretty great life right now. Maybe the best it had ever been.

I met Myra's gaze. It wasn't judgement in her eyes, it was…well, not quite pity. Maybe understanding? It was one of those sister looks I only ever got when I was being a dumbass about something.

"He loves you," she said.

"I know that." I did. So much so that my heart started pounding faster just hearing her say it.

"He wants to marry you."

I nodded, slouching further into my chair.

"He wants your wedding to be special." She dipped her head to catch my gaze. "You know that's what he wants, right? For your wedding to be wonderful. Perfect?"

"Yes." But the word was quiet.

"Delaney."

"I know. I know he wants it perfect." I blew out a breath then squared my shoulders and straightened. I reached back and split my ponytail in two to tighten the rubber band.

"I know he loves me. I know I love him. I know how lucky I am to be right where I am. With him. Together."

"Now you're going to tell me what the problem is."

"I'm scared."

"You're scared. Of what? Ryder?" There was a little less sister and a little more cop in her tone.

"No. He's not…. You know he's wonderful. I just… things change."

"What things?"

I shrugged. "Things." Then after a moment, "People."

"Mom?" she asked. Her voice was almost a whisper.

We didn't talk about our mom much. We'd been pretty small when we lost her. But I remembered Dad before mom had left us. I remembered Dad after she'd left us. He'd never been the same after her death. Our house hadn't been the same. Our family.

"I think about her sometimes," I said just as quietly. We were both leaning in toward each other, like we could hold this memory, this pain between us. So we could keep it from spreading like a bruise we'd never stop feeling, the memory of her, the pain of her aching and swelling into the rest of our lives.

"I do too," Myra said. "Sometimes."

"Dad was…different when they were married. Do you remember that?"

"I remember him laughing a lot. Singing."

"They would dance…" I stopped, the memory of Ryder and I dancing in the kitchen catching like a knife in my chest. "They were really happy," I said. "Really in love."

Her eyes ticked back and forth, searching me for something, maybe for the memories that were stronger for me, since I was the eldest.

"It's change," I said. "I know life always changes but this is big. I like the life I have, Myra. I don't know if I'm ready for it to change."

Myra took a breath to argue, or hey, maybe to agree with me at the exact moment the front door banged open.

"What the hell is this about?" shouted the god Odin, who went by the name Odin while vacationing in town because he had an ego as big as Zeus'.

Nothing about Odin said graceful, refined, or artistic. He stood, storm-tossed, his gray hair sticking out in all directions, his good eye, the one without the patch, sharp and accusing. He had on a black T-shirt that really showed off the muscles he usually hid under baggy flannel while he was living the life of a slightly wild unskilled chainsaw artist.

He pointed a blunt finger our way. "Did you do this?"

We leaned back from each other, and Myra was on her feet, slow, but easy.

"Do what?" she asked.

We'd known Odin since we were kids running out in the forest around his cabin, trying to pick out which tree he should use for his next work. Grumpy uncle on the outside, kindest, fiercest heart on the inside.

"This." He pulled out the box he had tucked under his arm. It was just a regular plain cardboard box. Long. More like a document tube than a box.

"I didn't give you a box," Myra said. "Did you give him a box?"

I shook my head. "Someone sending you presents in the mail?" I teased.

He strode to the counter that separated our desks from the tiny lobby/waiting room, slammed the box down and flipped up the lid. "This," he said, "should not be here."

Both Myra and I were on our feet now. She got to the box before me, and I saw her whole body stiffen. I peered down at the contents.

"It's a spear," Myra said.

"I know it's a spear," Odin growled. "I didn't come here for you to tell me it's a spear."

"Why are you angry about someone mailing you a spear?" I asked. "Is this a threat of some kind? Do you think you're being threatened?" I could hear the excitement in my voice, but I couldn't help it. Things had been really quiet around here.

"Of course I'm being threatened, all the powers help whoever's behind this," he said. "That's my spear."

He crossed his huge arms over his wide chest and that condescending look belonged on a prosecutor who had just produced the bloody fingerprints, damning documents, and gotten a confession to nail shut the big murder case.

And yeah, I could feel the power just pouring off of it.

"When did you receive it?" Myra asked.

"This morning."

"In the regular mail?" I asked.

"It was left on my front step."

"Who did you leave it with?" I asked.

"I don't loan out my weapons, Delaney."

"This is a part of your godhood, a part of your power which means it can't just be picked up and passed around by everyone in the world. Who had access to it?"

"No one."

"Has it been in town?" Myra asked.

"No."

I was starting to catch on. "This was left...behind? In Valhalla or wherever you hang out when you're godding instead of vacationing?"

"Yes. None of us bring our weapons to Ordinary. We never have. Look at it again—really look at it."

The spear was too short to be a functioning weapon, although the longer I looked at it, the more I knew I wasn't seeing all of it. The head was black heart stone of an ancient universe, razor-sharp and silver-shot. The shaft was jade and umber, twisting with golden runes that burned and flared, pulsing in and out of existence as if a cosmic breeze slowly blew across the eternal fire kindled there.

I was sensitive to god power—it came with my family gift of being the Bridge, the one who allowed gods to put down their power and vacation here. My dad had been able to see god power when he'd held the job, but now that I was the Bridge, I heard it too.

And oh, the power in this weapon. It sang out in a clarion of exaltation, a soul-aching call of something beyond, something deep and hot and thirsty. This was brotherhood, sisterhood, shoulder to shoulder and step to step; heartbeat to heartbeat. This was a rush of raven wings, a howl of wolves, a roar of hope.

This was battle.

This was victory.

"Oh," I said, hearing my voice break. "Oh," I said a little clearer. "Yes. Um, yes, I can…I can see it."

"Are there any markings on the box?" Myra asked.

"Just this." He turned the whole thing over like it weighed nothing. I was pretty sure that box—that god weapon—would be too heavy for a mortal to move. Even a mostly-mortal like me.

On the back side of the box was a red, stamped circle with a horizontal line bisecting it, and a stamped red feather.

"Do you know what that means?" I asked.

Myra was frowning, the crease between her eyebrows gone deep. "The circle is the alchemical symbol for one of the three primes: salt, or the body. I don't know what the red feather means."

"It means someone has access to a weapon I have made a point of keeping hidden and locked away," Odin grumbled.

"And that's bad," I said.

Odin ran his big mitt over his beard and it sprang

back even more wild. "Yes, Delaney." His words were quieter, the anger banked and something else filling them. Something like dread. "That's very, very bad."

"Are you going to take the weapon back to where you usually keep it?" Myra asked.

Odin shifted his weight, squaring off to her. "I'd rather not."

"Because you'd have to go be a god and stay out of Ordinary for at least a year," I said.

"Which I've done recently and do not intend to do again for some time."

"So what do we do with the spear?"

"Gungnir," he said.

"Gesundheit."

That earned me a scowl. "You know Gungnir is the name of my spear, Delaney."

"Right," I said trying to hide a smile. "So what do we do with Gungir? The safe here at the station won't hold it, and I don't like the idea of leaving it in the magic jail unguarded."

"The library," Myra said. "I have a vault in the basement, well, an entire room. It's equipped with every spell, lock, ward, and sacred circle in the books. No one can go in the library but me, so it won't be stolen. If anything happens while it's there, Harold would tell me."

I raised my eyebrows at Odin, waiting for his reply.

He thought it over for a minute. "The foundation?"

"Oldest part of the library," Myra agreed. "Set there by all the gods as one."

He nodded. "That will do."

"Good," I said, glad to at least have part of the situation under control. "Myra, I'll leave you to take Odin to the library. I'll stay here and deal with," I waved my hand at the quiet station, "everything else. Good thing I came into work today, isn't it?"

She didn't say anything but she didn't have to. The finger she flew behind her back as she followed Odin out the door worked just fine.

CHAPTER FOUR

THE PROBLEM WITH AN ANCIENT, powerful, dangerous god weapon being smuggled into town without either myself, the god, or anyone else knowing about it, was that we had to put together a list of everyone and everything capable of doing such an act.

Making lists was an everyday part of police or investigative work. But making this list might be a lot easier if my fiancé weren't in the middle of a very heated argument over brie.

"It won best in the world. Of course we're going with Umpqua's blue cheese," Ryder said into his phone as he paced from one desk to the other. "Why would you think I said brie?"

I tapped my pen on the pad and read the list again. On one side, I'd written the name of everyone with enough power to actually smuggle Odin's weapon into town. After I'd listed all the gods and goddesses, I'd added Bathin, Xtelle, and Avnas. I'd put little question marks after their names because I had no idea if a demon could transport a god's weapon.

On the other side, I'd listed everyone in town who had a complaint about Odin.

Unfortunately, that list was even longer.

So now I was compiling a new column titled: Likely To Do This Now and Why. I started with the complaints I'd heard over the last six months or so.

Zeus insisted Odin's chainsaw art cheapened the aesthetics of the town. Chris Lagon, our local gilman, wanted Odin to shower before he came into the brew pub because he was driving away customers. Crow complained Odin had handed him a pile of fir twigs instead of the display stands he'd promised for Crow's glass shop.

I'd already handled all the complaints. No one had taken things to the next level.

Unless stealing his spear from under god lock and key was the next level.

"Well, you didn't say it was on sale," Ryder put his hand over the bottom of the phone his gaze searching me out, as if I'd wandered off since the last time he'd tried to share cheese information with me two minutes ago. "They'll do a deal," he whispered.

I smiled and nodded.

"Cheese." He frowned at me. "The good cheese, Laney."

I gave him a thumb's up and went back to my list.

"Well, screw you too."

I widened my eyes. "What was that?"

He yanked the phone away from his ear and scowled at it while punching it with his finger several times.

"Coupons?" he snarled. "They're gonna give me a 5% off coupon if we order the cheese now? I can find a 30% coupon on one of those online Big Deal pages. You know what? I'm calling the Better Business Bureau. This is my wedding we're talking about here, and I'm not going to let some...some...*cheese squeezers* in bullpuck Oregon rip us off."

Myra looked up from where she was going through the security video Odin had given us from his property. I hadn't known Odin had cameras installed. They covered most of his front porch. Too bad the package had been dropped on the other side of the bush next to the porch, just out of the camera's range.

Myra stared at Ryder, who was red faced and making a sound in his chest somewhere between a growl and a snarl. She mouthed: *What the hell?*

I made I-have-no-idea eyes, and stood away from my desk to go over to him.

"Hey," I said, like I was approaching a snarling land-mine. "Hey, honey. Hey, there big guy. Hey. How about," I put my hand on his wrist, "we just put the phone down for a second."

He stopped dialing and glared at me. "What?"

"We don't have to get worked up over cheese."

"Worked up?" It came out loud, and I just gave him a look.

He exhaled. "Okay, I heard that. That was...a little much."

"A little," I repeated. "Just a little worked up."

"But this is cheese, Delaney. Did you hear what they said? Five percent off? For crappy brie and second-rate blue cheese?"

"I thought it won awards."

"It's obviously not the quality it used to be."

I was really putting some pressure on his wrist now, and he was fighting it, the phone still clamped between his fingers.

"Okay. So we'll find a different cheese."

"But I liked this cheese. You liked this cheese."

"Did I?"

"You said you liked it," he insisted.

"I've never eaten Umpqua cheese, honey. Ryder, my love, my everything. Can you let go of the phone now? Just relax your fingers and…There you go. That's good, I got it now."

"Five weeks ago. On a Thursday. You came home from work late, and I had dinner ready. The charcuterie board. You ate the cheese. Don't you remember the cheese?"

I did not remember the cheese. I didn't even remember the charcuterie board. "Was that the one where you paired everything with chocolate or with beer?"

"I paired it with tarts, Delaney."

"Tarts," I said. "That's what I meant to say. I remember they were so…fruity?"

He squinted at me. "You don't remember any of it do you?"

"You've put together so many wonderful dinners lately."

"I told you I'd handle the food. The food is important."

"Yep. And you're doing a great job. But this," I held up the phone. "Fighting with an innocent cheese factory? Don't you think that's being a little much? You know I'm going to be just as happy if we get married in a shotgun shack with nothing but saltine crackers and spray cheese."

He gasped and placed his fingertips against his chest as if I'd just said the most offensive thing he'd ever heard.

"Saltines and spray cheese?" He said like it was, well, like it was saltines and spray cheese. "*That's* the kind of wedding you want? That's what you think our love deserves? Spray cheese?"

"Well, not the cheap stuff. I mean I'd expect brand name."

He leaned toward me, his face inches from mine and grinned. "You're not funny."

"I'm a little funny."

"Give me back my phone."

"No. You're going to harass the poor *cheese squeezers* in bullpuck Oregon." I stretched away from him on tip toe, which wasn't going to do me much good because he was just that much taller than me and his long arms could out reach mine.

"Still think you're funny. That's a main stage act you got there, Delaney. Real Show Off material."

"The cheese, Ryder. Think of the cheese!"

I was chortling now, and couldn't seem to stop it.

Ryder had had enough, so he put that big body of

his to use and charged forward, backing me into the wall, catching both my wrists in his hands.

I still had his phone, but it was now up above my head.

I could get out of this hold. Could get out of it half a dozen ways. Instead, I stilled.

But as the seconds piled up and ticked away, as our breathing settled down, as I got my laughter under control, something else happened.

Ryder slowly, slowly lowered himself toward me, erasing the space between us.

I shifted so that my stance was wider. He took the invitation for what it was and slotted his legs and hips into the space I made for him.

"Hey," he said, and it was heat and sex, and I was straw under a magnifying glass, catching fire.

I swallowed hard, my throat dry. "Hey."

"You know we're going to get married."

"I've heard something about that. There's going to be cheese."

The flash of annoyance in his eyes made a corresponding wash of heat flood my chest. I liked it when he was riled up. Liked what it did to him. Liked what he did to me.

"I promised you. You agreed. We agreed I'd be the one to take care of this stuff. Catering." He leaned down and suddenly my breathing had gone thin.

He pressed a soft kiss on the side of my throat, followed it with just enough teeth I had to press my lips together so I didn't embarrass myself in front of my sister who was sitting at her computer typing away and pointedly ignoring us.

"Venue. Decoration. Cake." Each word was delivered with another nip, bite, or kiss. I was getting a little dizzy, my knees gone soft.

"And cheese squeezers," I gasped.

He lifted back, doing a very slow push up with his fingertips since his palms were still around both my wrists against the wall. It made his forearms flex, his biceps flex, and even though I couldn't see them, I knew his pecs and abs were tightening too.

It was sexy as hell. He knew it, and he knew I knew it.

"That's right," he said in his bedroom voice, "and the cheese squeezers."

I was nodding, but my mind was nowhere near the wedding part of the wedding, or the reception part of the wedding, instead veering toward the after party.

Sex. My mind was on the sex.

"You aren't taking any of this seriously." He pulled the rest of the way back, releasing me, and I made a noise of protest. I grappled for his hips, fingers hooking into his belt.

"I'm taking some of this *very* seriously." I tried to tug him back toward me.

"No," he said archly, turning his head to one side like a spurned debutante. "You've mocked my cheese."

"C'mon. Just…let me make it up to you, babe. I'm *super* serious about cheese. You were trying to get the Gouda, right? That sweet, sweet Gouda."

"It was blue cheese, and you are a terrible liar."

He kissed me on the tip of my nose then took another step back and held out his hand. "Phone please."

"Promise me you won't go ballistic on any more cheese factories today."

He took a moment to consider. "Fine. Today."

Myra snorted.

"I'm going to make this the best wedding of your life, you know."

"Since it's going to be the only wedding in my life," I said, "that's a pretty low bar."

He looked over at Myra. "Tell your sister to take this seriously."

Myra didn't look up, but she waved a hand like she was trying to fend off annoying bugs. "I am not getting in the middle of this. I have a crime to solve."

"*We* have a crime to solve," I said.

"Yeah, well, *I* have a wedding to plan," Ryder said.

"Before you get on with all that," a voice said from the door, "I want you to know this isn't what it looks like."

We all looked over. Crow, who was actually the trickster god Raven, stood in our lobby, holding a headless penguin.

CHAPTER FIVE

"So you aren't holding a headless waterfowl statue?"
I asked, as I strolled over to Crow.

Ryder was on his phone again. He thought he was
being quiet, but I heard, "cheese master" and "complaint."

"Delaney. Boo-boo. Have I told you how lovely you
look lately?" Crow was full-blood Siletz, his short hair
heavy and black, his eyes full of mischief. He had been
an uncle to me all my life.

"What's up with the bird?"

"I think someone is hunting me," he said.

"Is it Mrs. Yates? Because apparently you have
beheaded her famous penguin statue, and she's gonna
kill you for stealing her cash cow to fame?"

"This isn't her penguin." He held up the body, then
dug around in the messenger bag slung below his hip.
"This is one of the spares I made. I mean one of the
statues I kept when you made me clean up that penguin
mess that had absolutely nothing to do with me, and it

was unfair of you to make me clean up so many concrete penguins, by the way. I didn't put them in her yard. I've told you that, right? I'm innocent?"

"You've been telling me you're innocent since I was five and caught you eating the center piece you'd cut out of the brownie pan."

"That was the best piece."

"The brownies weren't for you, Crow."

"I'm sure you're wrong about that."

"No, the brownies were a housewarming gift Dad was going to take over to the Persons when they moved in. I remember because I wanted a piece of brownie and couldn't have one."

"I offered you a bite."

"I know."

"I offered you half if you wouldn't snitch."

"I know."

"You ratted me out to your dad."

"And you had to bake a new batch of brownies. Pretty sure that's when I decided to become a police officer. Dad gave me and Myra and Jean the pan of brownies you'd defiled."

"Including the center piece," he said. Then he half bent, not a bow, but leaning in like he was sharing a secret. "You're welcome."

I scoffed. "You did not do that so we girls could get a pan of brownies."

"Didn't I?"

I wouldn't put it past him. Crow always had some kind of scheme going. He was a trickster god, and even though he was on vacation, there was only so long he could go before he was up to his ass in trouble.

"You just wanted to mess with my dad. The brownies were a means to an end."

"I was always surprised at what little thing finally got to him." He grinned, and lines spread away from the corners of his eyes.

He was trouble, but it was usually happy trouble.

"So what's up with the statue?" I asked.

"It was left on my doorstep."

"In a box?" Myra asked, coming up to us.

Ryder had taken his call back down the hall toward the storage room, ignoring us completely.

"No box. I was going to open the shop early. See if I could get some of those sweet tourist bucks. Talent show's day after tomorrow, you know."

"We know," we both said.

"This was propped next to my door."

"No box?" Myra asked again.

"Why are you so focused on a box?"

"Odin received a package he didn't order," Myra said.

"That's a crime?"

"It was a weapon," Myra said.

"Someone mailed a gun to Odin?" Crow's eyebrows went up. "To Odin?"

"It wasn't a gun," I said. "It was a spear."

"O-kay. Through the mail?"

"No," Myra said. "Dropped off beside his doorstep."

"What kind of spear?"

We didn't say anything.

"Just a random spear, though, right?

"Why?" I wouldn't put it past him to be a part of this. He might have found Odin's secret spear closet and picked the lock. He might have left the spear on the doorstep just to brag about what he could do when Odin wasn't looking.

But Crow was watching me, his expression calculating as if he were working through possibilities. I'd seen his scheming face all my life. I'd seen his lying face too. But this was his god face—or as close to it as I saw in Ordinary.

"It was magic," he said. "He wouldn't care if someone sent him a random spear. He'd use it as a prop for one of his carvings. Bear with a Spear. Dog with a Spear. Spear with a Spear.

"It was Gungnir, wasn't it?" He wiped his hand over his mouth. "Hells. Grungnir?"

I nodded. "It was."

"Who the fuck got into Odin's realm? How did they even break into his realm? And who smuggled it into Ordinary without *you* noticing?"

"We don't know," I said. "But I don't feel weapons— magical or otherwise—when they're brought here. I only notice gods."

"Did Odin say when it was stolen?"

"Just that it was delivered."

"This is…Breaking into a god realm. Holy shit, how could…" His voice trailed off, and he stared into the distance for a second.

"You have some ideas on that?" I asked. "How it could have been done? Who could have done it?"

"First," he stuck up a finger. "I would check that he didn't send it to himself."

"Why would he—"

"Shush-sha. He's a drama queen, that's why."

"He's not as bad as—"

"He is. All gods are. Trust me on that, cookie."

"You did not just call me cookie."

"Pumpkin? Sweetie? Cupcake?"

"Wanna try that again?"

"Trust me that gods are drama queens who always make every little thing about themselves, Chief Reed."

I just shook my head. "I kind of want to go back to the statue you were so worried about so I can get rid of you."

"No. Come on, Delaney, I'm just giving you a hard time. Things have been so boring. The busted penguin is the most excitement I've had all week."

"Did you break it?"

"You learn quick, don't you? But no. I found it knocked over on my doorstep. Probably just kids screwing around."

"Where do you keep it normally?"

"In the flower pot out front. The penguin was busted, a couple flowers were picked, dirt thrown around. I'd say a dog had been digging in the dirt, but it's a pretty tall pot. A dog couldn't reach it."

"What about that thing about you being hunted?" Myra asked.

He shrugged. "You weren't taking the penguin seriously, so I lied."

I pinched the bridge of my nose. "Go away now."

"But I was helping. Before you forced me to admit I was lying about being hunted, and confess I think the penguin is just some kids goofing off, and call you every delicious pastry on the shelf, which is a compliment when you think about how much I love pastry, I was helping."

"Do you want to file a report about the statue?"

"I do not," he said.

"Good. Go away.'"

"C'mon, Nancy Drew. Let me help you solve the mystery of the stolen spear."

"No."

"He's a god. It's a god item."

"No."

"I'm a god. I like stealing god items."

I gave him a hard look.

"Well, not lately."

"That doesn't mean you get to play detective."

"Consultant. I'm not going to tromp around dark alleys and chew on old cigar butts."

"That's not what a detective does," I said.

"Which is why I'm not going to do it. I'll consult."

"Okay," Myra said.

"What?" I turned on her. "What did you just say?"

"I think we need a consultant."

Ryder's voice rang out from the back. "Cheddar? What do you think this is, a retirement party?"

"We're a little short-handed," she went on. "And

Crow knows how things can be stolen from gods because he's stolen things from gods."

"Allegedly," he said. "Crow has allegedly stolen things from gods."

"You literally just confessed to it a minute ago," she said. "There are dozens of stories about you stealing from gods. It's kind of your thing."

"Talk about typecasting. I steal from other people, too, you know."

"Not helping," I said.

Myra pulled her phone out of her pocket, and it rang. "What's up?" she answered.

"Look, Crow," I said. "If you're bored, Bertie could use some help."

"Working for Bertie isn't what I'd call fun."

"Solving crimes isn't fun either. It's work."

"We gotta go," Myra said, striding back to her desk to grab a small backpack.

"What's wrong?" I asked.

"There's been another mailing."

"Who?" I dug my keys out of my pocket and headed toward the door.

"Zeus." She was across the floor, right behind me.

Ryder spun from the hallway, his whole body zeroing in on me even though he still had his phone to his ear.

"Gotta call," I said. "Zeus. Myra and I got it. Hold down the fort."

He nodded and made his way between desks to the front counter.

Crow had jogged around us, and held the door open. When I strode through it, he jogged after me.

"You're not coming."

"I'm coming."

Myra opened the cruiser door and ducked inside. I slid behind the wheel of my Jeep.

Crow popped the passenger door and got in beside me.

"This isn't a game, Crow. You stay behind."

"Do you know what Zeus's weapon is, Delaney? The one he locked away before coming to Ordinary?"

"Lightning bolt," I said.

"Lightning bolt," he agreed. "Zeus's weapon is a lightning bolt. So let's get there before the fire department arrives."

Since I was losing time as it was, I threw on the lights and hauled out of the parking lot.

CHAPTER SIX

WE FOUND Zeus lording over his garden, a magnificent landscaped area with topiary and fountains and sparkly lights. Zeus had a trim build, copper-bronze skin, and dark hair. Even in this nice weather, he wore a three-piece suit that was tailored to enhance the width of his shoulders and narrow waist. Sitting there with a martini sweating in one hand, he fit the Hollywood, rich playboy stereotype to a tee.

The luxurious garden around him only added to that image.

Jean was perched on the edge of one of the thick, pillowy outdoor couches scattered around a centerpiece that was both a fire pit and a water feature. As soon as she saw us, she stood.

"You got here fast. Hey, Crow."

Crow gave her a little wave.

"Zeus," I said. "Where's the weapon?"

"Exactly where I left it. What is Crow doing here?

"He's acting as a consultant."

He puffed up his chest.

"On a trial basis."

His chest deflated.

Zeus's eyes cut to him, weighing Crow's worth. From the look on his face, Crow came up short. But he nodded. "Of course you would be a part of this, Trickster. How much a part is what interests me."

Crow bit off a smile. It was hard and bright. "Something you want to say? Something you want to accuse me of?"

The air crackled with tension and the ear-popping pressure of gods not using their power, but using their godly presence to push at reality a little.

"No fighting," I said. "Save it for outside Ordinary, boys. Crow's with us on this part of the investigation. End of story."

"I see," Zeus said. "Well, then. Would anyone care for refreshments? I have tea, coffee, drinks?"

"Nothing for me," I said.

Myra shook her head, and Jean held up an ice-cold bottle of imported CC Lemonade.

"What kind of beers ya got?" Crow asked."

"All of them." Zeus waved long fingers toward the outdoor kitchen.

Crow strolled that way, stopping only long enough to pluck a flower from a bush and tuck it behind his ear.

The corner of Zeus's eye twitched, but he otherwise acted as if Crow wasn't even there.

"The weapon?" I asked.

"I left it where I found it," he said.

"I thought you both might want to see where it was delivered," Jean said. "So I didn't move it either."

"Good," I said. "Did you take care of the car from this morning?"

"Yep. Frigg put it up in the garage beside her shop. Whenever we want to go look at it, it's ready for us."

"Good, thanks."

"Car?" Zeus asked.

"It fell from the sky," I said. "Down the beach a way toward 50th. Did you see it?"

"I did not. Do you think it has something to do with my weapon being stolen?"

"We don't know yet. We do want you to come see the vehicle just in case it is familiar to you."

"Later." He stood. It always surprised me that, close up, he shed the god-like bearing and was, to all appearances, a regular sort of man, albeit a beautiful and powerful one.

Every god went about hiding their godness in different ways. Odin's barely contained wild nature tucked beneath his gruff disposition, Crow's chuckling confidence hidden in his sense of humor, and Zeus, well, Zeus looked like he thought he owned the universe. But importantly, he looked like a *man* who thought he owned the universe.

"I found it twenty minutes ago," he explained as he led us through a maze of topiary that would have made the Red Queen happy and Alice very curious. "I was taking my drink out to the balcony to enjoy the fresh air in privacy."

I couldn't help but look around us. "We're not in the fresh air? This isn't private?"

He made a soft humming noise. "No, this is my parterre. Many people have been here. My balcony is a...for me."

He took a left through a hedge that was a clever blend of braided tree branches and masonry work which created an archway only visible if you came at it from the right angle.

Well, it was definitely private.

"Step through carefully," he warned.

I did, and so did Myra and Jean behind me, though Jean just grinned at me when I shot her a look.

I didn't see Crow. I hoped he wasn't casing the joint.

The arch led to a balcony.

If the parterre had been extravagant and cultured, this was something else entirely. The balcony was an arched platform situated at the top of the cliff side, looking down upon beach and the ocean beyond.

Oh, the railing was polished to a dull glow that gave the little space a bit of shine, but this was clearly a place to watch over the quiet stretch of beach with nothing more interesting to see than an occasional seal or the low, slow processions of pelicans pumping their way southward above the tattered waves.

A set of stairs spiraled down a central column attached to the side of the balcony. The steps ended at big rocks and tangled whitened driftwood that had been rolled against the base of the cliff like dice tossed by winter's stormy hands.

Myra walked to the railing and studied the beach below.

I studied the balcony and the god who owned it. The god looked unflappable. He even gave a small toast with his glass before taking a drink. But his eyes were judging me, watching me. Watching what I thought of this space.

There was only one chair made of the same wood as the railing, bent into the perfect shape to lean back and rock in, or maybe lean back another way and sleep in. On that chair was a thick wool Pendleton blanket, striped in the red, green, yellow, and black of the Glacier National Park pattern, and two pillows.

A table took up the corner, a little cooler at its feet, three thick hardback mystery books on top.

This small space, no more than eight by eight said more about the god in front of me than all the lush extravagance we'd left behind. I wondered if he came out here barefoot. I wondered if he came out here to stare at the stars at night.

I wondered if this was the reason he stayed in Ordinary, if this tiny space was what he craved when he was out amongst the cosmic and unfathomable. If this simplicity was balm to his soul.

"I like it," I said.

"Thank you." He pointed his glass at the package resting at the very top of the stairs. "I didn't open it."

Myra crouched next to it without touching it.

"You found it and then immediately called Jean?" I asked.

"Yes."

"Why didn't you open it?"

"I am very aware of what it contains. I thought an officer of the law should see it. Record the event."

Myra took a couple photos, stepped back, and took a few more.

"I got some shots of it too," Jean said.

Myra nodded but finished with the set she wanted to get. It never hurt to get as many angles on a problem as possible.

Perspective, different ways of looking at things, different ways of coming at a problem were the best skills a detective could have.

"What's the chance of you opening it so we can see what's inside without something exploding?" I asked.

He tipped his head to one side. "It's…contained. If I open the package Ordinary won't cease to exist."

That sounded like he was being a little overly dramatic, but I knew he wasn't. God weapons were pure, blazing vessels for their power. If Zeus wanted to vaporize a beach town out of existence, he could.

Although Ordinary would be a tough nut to crack. It had been built by all the gods joining powers to create the space and the laws and the rules of it. One god alone could not bring it down. Not even Zeus.

"All right," I said. "Let's see what's inside."

He set his martini on the little table, then bent and lifted the package. I knew, even before he opened it, that it was exactly what he said it was. There was something about his demeanor, about the shift in his body language that screamed, *god god god power*.

He calmly propped the box on the railing and

produced a very slick little retractable razor blade. His day job here in Ordinary was buying, importing, and selling fine furnishings, so he knew his way around a box.

The cardboard top rocked back on its hinge and suddenly there was more light here, blue and burning.

Jean was at his elbow, excitement turning her face ten years younger, and even Myra was breathing a little faster as she peered at the contents.

It wasn't every day, really, *any* day that we got a good close look at a god weapon.

"Delaney?" He shifted the package so I could see the interior from where I stood.

And oh, the magnificent fury of it. Even as my mind tried to shove it into something human, something *this world*, something *earthly*, it was none of those things.

A lightning bolt, but none like this world had seen.

It glowed like a chunk of ice, glacial blue, cold and burning. Deep iron fissures cracked through it, throwing off red and violet sparks. All of it was liquid as water, but burning, burning, burning with white-cold electricity.

It would fit in my hand—it fit in the box which was maybe two feet long. But my brain rejected that. Somehow, just like Odin's spear, this weapon did not follow the rules of space. I knew if Zeus pulled it out of that box it would be as wide as the sky, it would stretch the heavens.

"Is that it?" I asked. "Is it your weapon?"

"Yes."

"And where did you last see it?"

"Where I left it before coming back to Ordinary after Crow lost our powers to that demigod and forced us all to leave."

Grudge much?

"No," Crow said, emerging from the hidden arch. "I think you're remembering that wrong. I'm sure it was Poseidon getting murdered that made us all leave town." He didn't step onto the balcony, but remained there, on the path, just on the edge of this private place.

Zeus did not invite him farther, and he didn't ask to be invited.

"Peaceful," Crow noted, his gaze taking in the place.

"It is," Zeus said.

"Nice view."

Zeus looked out over the waves, and I wondered if he saw more than any of us mortals could. I wondered if he saw across universes.

"It is." His words were softer. Not awe, not reverence, but something like relief.

Crow didn't say anything else, but when I glanced at him he just gave me a small inscrutable smile.

Gods. They might be drama queens but they were also a relatively small group of beings. And I knew that no matter how long I lived and no matter how many times I contained each god power to allow it—through me—into Ordinary so that it could be put down into rest, I would never understand what it was to be a god.

"Big bolt you got there," Crow noted. "Though not the biggest I've seen."

Zeus's jaw locked, and when he turned, there was nothing wistful about him. He just looked like a rich, annoyed, businessman. A businessman with a god weapon.

"So the lightning bolt was left in your god realm?" I asked.

"Yes. Which is heavily guarded and locked while I am gone."

"The realm is locked or the weapon is locked?" Myra asked.

"Both," he said. "This isn't something anyone could access."

"Locks are made to be picked," Crow noted.

"So you have always said," Zeus agreed.

"Has this happened before?" I asked.

He paused, thinking. He cast a quick glance at Crow, as if asking something. But whatever that question was it didn't appear Crow had an answer.

"No one has ever stolen my lightning bolt and then mailed it to me ground shipping."

"I don't think it's ground," Jean said. "There aren't even any stamps on it, or addresses."

He gave her a quick wink. "Just a turn of phrase."

She nodded. "The point I'm making is not only did someone know where to find the weapon, and how to access it, they knew how to handle it. I'm guessing not everyone can touch that without…. What did you say it would do?"

"Vaporize."

She nodded. "Vaporizing. And whoever handled it also knew to leave it here in your private space. Not say, at your front door, or in the garden."

"Parterre," he corrected.

"Right," she said. "Fancy garden."

"Who can do that?" Myra asked. "Or let's start here: Is it something a human could do?"

I could tell Crow was suddenly very interested in Zeus' answer and had a moment to worry that Zeus wouldn't want to answer.

"With the favor of another god," he said slowly, "with the right spells," his eyes flicked to Crow again, who was holding very, very still, "or armor. With some combination of assistance and magic of their own, there is a very—an extremely—small possibility a mortal could have done this."

"Okay," Myra said in her calm way that also said *thank you for being honest.* "How about supernatural beings? Are there any who might be capable of pulling this off?"

He shook his head. "You're asking me to weigh and measure thousands of different sorts of living beings with millions of combinations of abilities. So in general, those who are either more powerful or, alternatively, more resistant to power might have an edge. It is still an extremely small possibility."

I knew where Myra was going with this. I knew what her next question would be and I braced for it.

"How about gods?" she asked. "Could a god do this?"

He scowled at Crow. "Perhaps."

"And demons? Are they capable of finding the weapon, stealing it, and delivering it to you?"

The scowl deepened. "I would like to think not. But no matter how carefully any of us lock away our weapons, the very act of setting our powers down and living in Ordinary can create complications."

"What kind of complications?" she asked.

"Each god and goddess bears their power differently. But setting it down does create possible vulnerabilities."

"Like the fact that you becoming almost mortal while you're here," I said.

He nodded. "It is possible I underestimated the vulnerabilities of my realm. No living creature should be able to breach my protections."

Crow didn't say anything. Not a jibe, not a tease. It was a rather amazing display of self-control I wasn't used to him possessing.

"But there are things in this universe even a god cannot control," Zeus said.

"Is there an impression left on it?" Crow asked.

"What does that mean?" I asked.

Crow, still standing there in the shadows of branches and leaves, shrugged. "Sometimes gods leave behind... well, not fingerprints, but power prints. One power brushing another can leave behind a scent, or taste, or impression of that power."

We all turned our attention to Zeus. He still hadn't taken the lightning bolt out of the box, but his hand was near it, close enough I could see the radiance flaring toward his fingers, as if it were asking to be picked up, as if inviting him to battle.

His gaze was in some middle distance, cast north over the sea. The wind lifted, warm from the sun-heated sand, then cold and damp from the ocean spray. It tasted of sunlight, and salt, and the promise of summer.

"Magic," he said. "Though I cannot discern what."

Which was fair. He couldn't use his power, not here in Ordinary. Asking him to do godly stuff—any godly stuff—was pushing that boundary pretty hard.

If a god used their power in Ordinary, they were required to pick their power back up and leave town for a year. So any god who enjoyed their vacation, or say, buying, importing, and selling furnishings in a quiet little beach town while they lorded over their very private slice of sand from both a fancy garden and also a humble wooden deck, would be wise not to so much as touch their power while here.

Maybe that was all it was. A test. A dare. Maybe whoever was behind the thefts and mailings was just trying to tempt the gods into picking up their power and leaving town.

Who would want Ordinary godless? A chill ran down my spine at that question. I could think of a few people. Mithra, the god of contracts didn't like that he couldn't rule Ordinary. He'd been fostering a grudge against my family for generations.

Demons were taking more notice of our town. Particularly the King of the Underworld who, if the demons who had escaped to and now lived in Ordinary were to be believed, might be very unhappy with our little sanctuary.

Monster hunters. That was more of a stretch, but the Department of Paranormal Protection had recruited Ryder to search Ordinary for signs of supernatural beings to hunt and study.

Ordinary was stuffed with all sorts of magical

beings: vampires, werewolves, shifters, bigfoots, and more.

There were books out there too. Ancient, magical, powerful things. Someone could have found an old journal, a magic book, an ancient tablet that contained a spell to steal god weapons, although I didn't know what kind of magic would be strong enough to break the locks on a god's realm.

"Okay," I said. "We need to deal with the weapon. How would you like us to handle this?" I asked him.

"I could send it to a safer location," he suggested. "Better locks."

"You'd have to use your god power to do that."

He held his breath a moment, then nodded, just the slightest dip of his chin.

"Then you'd have to leave town for a year, which you don't really want to do." It was a guess. But the balcony, comfy pillows and blanket, the stack of books all showed he wasn't planning to leave Ordinary any time soon.

"True."

"Would you entrust it to us?"

"Who is 'us'?" His gaze ticked over to Crow again. Crow just lifted his bottle of beer and took a drink.

"The Reed family. Well, Myra specifically. She can keep it with the other powerful items in the Reed library."

"Which I have no access to," he said.

"Right," Myra said. "No one has access to it except me. You can enter if I enter with you. But if you picked up your god power, you could draw the weapon to you in a snap."

"Clever. Under lock and key no one can access except a Reed."

"It's the best solution, I think," Myra said. "Store it with me, or leave town with your power to put it somewhere safe."

"And hunt the thief down," he said.

"That's within your godly rights of course."

He looked at the caught lightning, then back at the stack of books by his chair.

He slowly closed the lid of the box, pressing until the light was snuffed out, and nothing but a box remained. "I'll accompany you to the library."

CHAPTER SEVEN

"So the way I see it," Crow said, as he forked coleslaw into his mouth. "You're the weak link in the chain."

"Excuse me?" We were outside, eating at a picnic table that could seat six in front of Chris Lagon's Jump Off Jack brewery. A steady stream of people were getting curbside pickup, and a few were making themselves comfortable with indoor dining.

The weather was so nice, the patio area in the back that overlooked the bay, and the picnic tables right here out front by the parking lot were catching the most dining interest.

Myra had left for the library with Zeus to store the weapon, and Jean told me she'd relieve Ryder at the station, since he had to go check a job site for a build he had coming up in a couple months.

We were going to meet up later this evening to show Zeus the car, see if he knew anything about it or could get any impressions off it. Jean had also extended the invitation to Odin. Crow, of course, had invited himself along.

We didn't know how the car fit in with the stolen weapons, or if the two cases were even related. I hoped the gods might have some sort of idea about that.

Crow had offered to buy lunch, so I was halfway through a bowl of chowder, homemade garlic knots, and having my character insulted.

"You're the stress point in the whole," he wiggled his fork, "god power vulnerability situation."

We were keeping our voices down, but the nearest diner wasn't in earshot anyway.

"Someone is projecting." I bit a garlic knot, and immediately took another bite. That was one damn fine knot, the garlic set off with something peppery, and a hint of rosemary.

"Oh my gods," I mumbled. "Have you tried these?"

"Not yet." He reached for the pile on my plate. I smacked his hand.

"I don't share my knots with mean people."

He shook his hand and laughed. "Do you want to know why I think you're to blame?"

"Not really, since I am not to blame."

"You store the god powers."

"I don't store them. You know that. A god or goddess stores the powers. I just act as a bridge for the powers to go from god to storage."

"That's where the weakness is introduced. You are not a god, so when the god powers are in your hands, they're in a limbo. During that limbo, someone must be gathering information. Enough to find a way to hack into the god realms."

He moved on to his fries, pouring about a metric ton of malt vinegar over them, then shaking salt on top.

"Add more salt. If you die of a stroke, I'll find somebody nice to be the next Raven god."

He chortled and added a little more salt. "So cruel." He shoved a fry in his face and made a big show of chewing and rolling his eyes in ecstasy.

"Gross. So this brilliant theory of yours is that someone what? Hacked my brain? Installed malware in my bridging power? Now they're accessing information when I bridge power, is that it? The whole idea? That's your explanation for weapons getting stolen?"

"You sound upset. Are you upset? You know you shouldn't make that face, it wrinkles you all up." He pointed to his own forehead and eyes and mouth. "Think of the wedding photos."

"That is a terrible theory."

"No, there have been scientific studies. Your face can literally freeze that way."

"For one thing, I haven't bridged god power for months. The last person was Ganesha, and he hasn't had a weapon shipped to his doorstep."

"Not yet."

"Two, if something or someone could actually use the god-given, god-protected bridging power to access god realms, it would have happened years ago. Centuries ago. There is nothing different or special about Ordinary and its citizens today that wasn't in place fifty or a hundred years ago."

"Just because someone hasn't thought of a crime doesn't mean it hasn't always been possible to do the crime. You're forgetting Mithra has your man bound to him. Ryder Bailey being the Warden of the town, under Mithra's order is something very different than what was here fifty or a hundred years ago. Mithra does not like you, Delaney."

I took a drink of my iced tea with extra lemon and thought it over. Mithra forcing Ryder to sign the contract that locked them together was a problem. So far, Mithra hadn't been able to use Ryder to do anything to undermine my or my sister's abilities to look after the town, but it wasn't for lack of trying.

And if we were married...well, Mithra had made it clear he would use that bond between us, that signed contract, to his advantage. The way the god saw it, once we were married, he would have influence over Ordinary. He could rule it.

Something I would never let happen. My family had been tapped generations ago to uphold the laws the gods had all agreed upon for Ordinary. I was not going to abandon that duty just because one god got uppity about things.

"Maybe," I said. Crow gave a little toast with a fry. "But this doesn't really fit Mithra's style, does it? Stealing god weapons? And they're not like a good pair of battle boots, or a lucky dirk, or a sturdy staff.

"These are the big weapons. Weapons that identify gods. Stories are written about these. Legends. So, either someone is aiming big, or doesn't know that gods have more weapons than the myths and legends say they have."

"Now you're narrowing it down. It's someone who knows everything about gods, or someone who knows nothing about gods."

I picked up a garlic knot and threw it at his face. He caught it and popped it in his mouth. "Damn, those are good. What do I have to say to make you throw another one at me?"

"Crow."

"Delaney."

"This isn't a game."

"Of course not."

"It's not funny."

"Absolutely right."

"It's my job. Finding out why weapons are showing up on doorsteps is my job. And it's important."

"I can tell. You haven't even had time to pick out your wedding cheese."

I pelted his head with another garlic knot. This one left a satisfying shiny buttered spot just above his left eye.

He was laughing too hard to make any of his injured cries believable, then he was chewing the garlic knot.

"I didn't ask for your help," I reminded him, finishing off the chowder.

"No, Myra did. I don't know about you, but that's a woman who follows her instinct, and backs it up with well-thought-out logic."

He wasn't wrong. Out of us three sisters, she was the most serious. The most focused on solving the problems at hand without letting her emotions get in the way.

Which was why it was so wonderful and strange to see her fall in love with Bathin, a demon, who had possessed my soul for just over a year before we got things sorted out and he was able to stay here in Ordinary.

After signing the demon contract of course.

"You're thinking about Bathin, aren't you?" Crow propped his elbow on the table and rested his chin in his hand. "How he and Myra are together and how you trust her, and almost completely trust him, but there's this tiny sliver of distrust because he's a demon and demons are so new to Ordinary.

"You're thinking that if he breaks her heart you will tear him apart, and probably feel guilty and never forgive yourself for letting her risk herself over him.

"You're thinking that you're proud of her for risking her heart all the same, because she doesn't take wild chances like that, not the way Jean does with gleeful abandon, not the way you do with heart-felt need and desire."

"I'm thinking my uncle isn't a very good mind reader," I said, but without any heat, because he was right. On all of that.

"And you're thinking about change. Your sisters. The new people on the force. The wedding. Your life is changing Delaney Reed. And these are some of the big changes that send you down new paths. Out there into the wild unknown. Could be nothing but happy and flowers at the end, you know. Could be danger at every turn."

"I don't know what you're talking about."

He smiled, his cheeks curving up to make his eyes into crescents. "You know exactly what I'm talking about. I can see it in you, Boo-boo. You're afraid of what's coming. And it isn't power or gods or demons that scare you. It's big life changes. It's letting go of something to grab hold of something new."

"Here's what I'm thinking," I said. "You just happened to show up when the first weapon was delivered. You've inserted yourself into the investigation and are trying very hard to take my attention away from the fact that you and Zeus had a little silent discussion back on his balcony."

"I have no idea what you're talking about. Are you going to finish those garlic knots?"

"So here's an idea." I spread my hand over the knots, blocking his grab. "I'm going to give you a chance to practice telling the truth.

"Why are you so interested in this, Crow? No bullshit. If it really is a threat, some kind of blackmail or break in security, I need to know everything you know about it."

"Practice? I'm always truthful. A book with my pages spread wide."

"Talk."

He pressed his fingertips to his lips, then sat back and wiped his mouth with a napkin.

He was my almost-uncle, the man, well, god, I'd known all my life, but he was more too. He was something I hadn't seen very often. He was serious.

"There's something about this whole thing that bothers me."

I held back on the snide commentary, because I didn't want him to clam up. I didn't want him to go back to throwing shit, just joking around. I needed him serious. I needed that clever trickster mind of his to shove things together and break them apart into smaller, stranger pieces.

I needed him on my side of this fight. Because I knew my town. Things didn't happen for no reason, especially not god things.

"I can't quite put my thumb on it, which is why I haven't said anything." He crossed his arms, like he was about to tell me something he didn't think I would believe.

"I'm sitting right here," I said. "Anything will help."

"Demons. I've been around them through the, well, through a lot of years. I can respect their strengths. The ability to lure someone by promising their desire, feeding off high emotions, off what some people would say are sins. I can get behind that kind of thinking. Especially when they deliver. You want to be rich? You'll put kings to shame. Beautiful? You'll be on the cover of every magazine in the world. Wanna play that guitar? We got your back, Johnny.

"But they make you pay, don't they? Offer you everything and make you pay twice as much as that. It's a con. It's a big trick. Sleight of hand. They're showing you which cup the prize is under. And yet… and yet…people trade, people sign on the line, people get what they want, and in the end, they lose everything.

"You gotta admit that's a hell of a trick to pull off.

Trade your soul, sign in blood, you'll be ecstatic, until you aren't."

"So you respect demons?" I asked.

"I respect how they play the game. How they hook the trick. As one craftsman to another." He nodded.

"I know how to spot a demon and their work. From a mile off. From a world away. This weapon thing, it has something to do with demons. I don't have proof. But I know it. Something about this is tangled up with demons."

"Do you think Bathin and Xtelle are involved? Or Avnas?" I understood why he hadn't said anything yet. Because he was right. I did worry about Myra falling in love with Bathin. I worried about Jean too, as she was the one currently keeping an eye on Bathin's mother Xtelle who preferred the form of a pink unicorn, but had settled on being an annoying pony while inside Ordinary's borders.

Xtelle had broken the contract with the King of the Underworld and was no longer the Queen of the Underworld. She could be trying to start a fight with her ex and wanting to use Ordinary as the battleground, or worse, as the prize.

"I don't know," Crow said, and it might have been the most honest thing I had ever heard out of him. "I don't think...I don't think a demon could pull this off on their own. But stealing those weapons is something big. The *why* of this is just as interesting to me as is the *who* of it.

"Someone is moving the game pieces on the board,

and I don't like it. And not because I'm not the one pulling the strings. Well, not only because of that."

"Do you think Zeus would have told you if he thought a demon had stolen the bolt?"

Crow shrugged. "We get along well enough in general. I think he would have said something if he'd sensed a demon's involvement. I don't know why he would keep that a secret."

"He said he sensed magic. Demon magic?"

Crow shook his head. "He would have specified. It's distinct."

"Anything else?" I asked.

He dropped his hands to the edge of the table, and messed with the grain in the wood. "What kind of magic can break into a god's realm undetected?" he asked.

"I don't know."

He nodded. "Neither do I."

I pushed the plate over to him. There was only one knot left, but I wasn't hungry anymore.

If demons were behind the stolen weapons, if they had gotten their hands on a new kind of magic that even the gods couldn't protect against, it didn't bode well.

"Thanks, Crow. I'll call you in if I need anything." I gathered up my bowl and cup and stood.

He shoved the last knot in his mouth and slugged down the last of his root beer. "Where we going next?"

"*We* aren't going anywhere. *I'm* going to talk to some demons."

"You aren't getting rid of me that easily. I'm the one with the demon bullshit meter."

"I can meter their bullshit just fine."

"Sure. So I'll come along to observe. As a concerned citizen. And a consultant on the case, appointed by your sister."

"Not listening." I dumped the paper bowl and tray liner in the trash on my way to the Jeep.

I unlocked the Jeep and swung behind the wheel as quickly as I could, hoping I could lock it before he wiggled his way in. But he was in his seat and buckled before I even finished opening my door.

"No fair using powers." I glared at him.

"Not even the power of my amazing athleticism? Working out every morning is really starting to pay off. You and I should go running together some time."

"You don't run in the morning. I know. I see you up on your porch eating Lucky Charms and watching cartoons."

"Of course I'm eating my Charms. They're lucky aren't they?"

I buckled my seatbelt and started the engine. There was no shaking him when he was like this. Though I hated to admit it, I did want a second witness there when I grilled Myra's boyfriend within an inch of his life.

CHAPTER EIGHT

IT DIDN'T TAKE LONG to get to Bathin's place because in a town as small as ours, it didn't take long to get anywhere.

When he'd first come to town, Bathin had spent his nights in one of the stones in Ordinary that he, because of his power, could access.

But after some time, he'd stopped hiding out in those stones. A few months ago, he'd found a rental house. He paid for it by taking care of the house and yard while the owners were away (they'd been away for over a decade) and covered his other expenses with the money he brought home from his work with the veterinarian and animal shelter.

Three cats lazed out in the sunlight under the big rhodie bushes that hedged one side of the tiny, cedar shake cottage that had weathered down to a soft, dove gray.

"You don't need to come in," I said.

Crow just rolled his eyes and pushed open the Jeep door.

I sighed, shut the door, and followed after him.

By the time I reached the little covered porch, he was knocking on the door.

There was the sound of footsteps, heavy footsteps, and then the door opened.

Bathin filled the doorway, and I do mean filled.

All demons could choose their appearance. It was part of what made deal-making work so well for them. They could appear just as ugly or attractive as the job required. Bathin had gone all-in on attractive. He was built like a stack of bricks, muscles on top of muscles, a rugged, but damn fine-looking face, sun-baked skin, dark wavy hair, and eyes that could set panties on fire.

My sister's panties, not mine.

His shoulders were too wide for the narrow doorway. He tipped them down slightly and angled his body toward us.

"Can we come in?"

"No." He tucked his phone into the front pocket of his short-sleeved, forest green button-down shirt. The color made his eyes pop, and the short sleeves showed off his huge forearms and the swell of his biceps.

"I'm fostering a couple cats, and they aren't comfortable with people yet."

"We aren't really *people*," Crow said.

"Neither am I, Crow. What do you need, Delaney? Everything all right? It's my mother isn't it? She told you?"

"Told me what?"

Little kitten *meow*s called out from deeper in the house. He stepped out, letting the screen door close behind him.

"Sounds like a lot of cats," Crow observed.

"It's eight. It's not a lot until you have over a dozen."

Crow made a show of counting while pointing at the half dozen cats in the yard. "Sorry to break it to ya, buddy…"

"Mother received a message from the courts."

"What court?" I asked.

"Hell. The kingdom she once ruled."

"Okay, what was the message, and how was it delivered?"

"It was left on her doorstep."

"Let me guess," Crow said. "In a box. With nothing but a circle and a red feather stamped on it."

It was a subtle shift. A hardening of Bathin's stance, his muscles, and then it was gone, washed away like water over stone. In place of that sudden dangerousness, was an affable smile. As if he and Crow had been buddy-buddy for years.

"That's right," Bathin said. "In a box, just like you guessed, with a feather, just like you guessed. You want to tell me how you know that, Trickster god, when she hasn't told anyone but me?"

"She doesn't have a front door," I said. "She's a pony. She's supposed to be in Hogan's yard eating grass."

"She took over the spare room."

Of course she had. "It was left at his front door?"

He shook his head. One of the kittens decided to

Mission Impossible the screen door, and made a jump for it. The kitten stuck on the screen like a furry dart that slowly inched downward.

"She was very specific about it being in front of her door, not Hogan's front door," Bathin said. "Hogan has assured me there are boundaries he was more than capable of enforcing. He mentioned his gnome army."

I huffed a laugh. "Yeah, he sort of has an in with them. Do you know what the message was?"

"It was a ring."

"How is that a message?"

"It was the ring she wore when she led the hoards into the Bothersome Battle against Sticksquim the Screamed."

I frowned.

"You never read about that battle? Well, she also wore the ring into the Conflict of Consequence with Boraka the Bad."

"Who names your wars?" Crow asked. "You need to fire them."

"Is the ring a weapon?" I asked.

"Why?"

"We're following up on two other packages that have been left at people's doorsteps. Both reported this morning. Did Xtelle receive her package this morning?"

"According to the call I got from her screaming about it? Yes."

"She has a phone?"

He cast his eyes heavenward, which was pretty funny considering he was a demon and even less likely to receive relief from those quarters. "She has a phone."

A second kitten attacked the screen, this one finding less purchase. It burped out little mews all the way back down to the ground.

"What kind of weapons have been delivered?" Bathin asked. "I'm assuming none of them are as mundane as guns or switchblades."

"You assume correctly," I said. "What does your mother's ring do?"

"It makes her invincible. Might stop time."

"For real?"

He shrugged his shoulders. "That's what she's always said. I was there with her in the Skippy Skirmish against Thatbottom the Thick. Some of the things she did there, I still can't explain."

"Really," Crow said. "Fire your marketing department. They're making all your fights sound like they took place on a kindergarten playground."

"Is the ring famous?" I asked. "She's well known to use it in battle?"

"Among her enemies, she is."

"And her allies?"

"Not sure she has those anymore. But yes, demons know of it. I'd guess other beings do too. Or at least those who occasionally crack open a book and read up on this stuff."

"Hey, I read."

He gave me a small smile. "Not according to your sister you don't. You just ask her about the important stuff."

"That's because she's the keeper of the library. It's her job. You can stop grinning at me now. Did she tell you to try and get a rise out of me about this?" I knew I was starting to blush, could feel the prickly heat on my cheeks.

I'd been slacking a little on keeping up on my ancient lore refreshers. Myra had inherited the library instead of me. I was so glad it was in her capable hands, I'd stepped away from the studies we'd all been doing pretty much since we could read.

Dad had never forced it on us, but books were important, and all three of us Reed sisters were voracious readers at heart.

"You are so easy sometimes, Delaney," Bathin said. I was reminded that he had been in possession of my soul for a long time. Long enough to know how to push my buttons. "Feeling a little guilty your studies have slacked off now that you've gotten yourself a fiancé?"

"Good-bye, Bathin. I'm going to go talk to your mother now." I turned.

"Spending too much time in the bedroom instead of the classroom?" he called out.

"Call me if you hear of any other weapons being delivered."

"Checking him out instead of checking books out?"

I was at the Jeep, one hand on the door. "Save it for the talent show," I yelled back.

I got in the Jeep and Crow swung into the passenger side. Bathin gave us a wave before very carefully opening the screen door, dislodging kittens who fell like fat, fuzzy snowballs.

He bent and gently gathered them into his arms,

cradling four of them close to his chest before stepping into the house and closing the door.

"He's good with them," Crow noted.

"The kittens?"

"Insults." Crow threw me a look. "Yes, the kittens. I didn't know."

"You? One of the snoopiest gods in town, didn't know Bathin had a thing for cats?"

"I'm not snoopy, I'm attentive. I've seen him at the clinic and the adoption place, but in those spaces there is an expectation for him to behave a certain way. There isn't that same expectation here."

"Is it hard to believe he likes cats?"

"Been around demons for a long time, remember?"

"Yep. You remind me daily. Even twice daily."

"Demons don't like kittens."

"Agreed. But Bathin had Dad's soul for a long time. Then mine. He's not just a demon anymore. Or, maybe he is just a demon, but one who has continued to learn and grow. One who has learned there are more important things than torturing humans.

"Plus," I said, "he's in love. There's a chance he might screw it up with Myra. But that's how it goes, right? Life? You just jump in and give it your best shot with the people you love, and make the most of it you can."

He wasn't smiling, not really, but there was a softness to his face as he glanced over at me.

"You might want to apply that to a certain reluctant bride I know."

"Every word. I regret every word I just said."

"Might want to tell her she can just jump in and it's going to all work out. Messy, maybe, but weddings and marriages and *life*," he said with a little extra emphasis, "tend to work out."

"I'm officially declaring this," I waved a hand between us, "a relationship advice free zone. Good?"

He mimed zipping his lips and throwing the key away.

For a very short minute, he was silent. Then he started humming *Going to the Chapel* by the Dixie Cups.

I drove faster.

CHAPTER NINE

"DELANEY, CROW! WHAT BRINGS YOU BY?" Hogan's smile contrasted beautifully with his dark skin and startlingly blue eyes. If he weren't half Jinn I'd think his magical power was always being in a good mood.

He'd pulled back his beaded braids, and wore a black apron over jeans and T-shirt.

The smell of butter, baked bread, and dill wafted out of his house.

Or maybe I'd think his baking was his magic power. He was the owner of the Puffin Muffin, an amazing bakery that was just starting to catch full-time customers from towns on either side of us. Hogan had bought a delivery van and hired a delivery driver named Bob. So far, Bob was busy fulfilling orders every day of the week.

"Is Jean okay?" he asked, his smile dimming.

"She's good," I assured him quickly. "We're here to talk to Xtelle. I didn't see her in the side yard."

"Sure," he said. "Come on in. Hey, Crow. You still

up for a game this weekend?" He held the door open while we walked past him.

"Hell, yes," he said. "But Rossi might be hosting. I'll let you know."

"Sure. Yeah. All good, man."

The living room furniture was mismatched and homey. A pair of Jean's favorite Cthulhu slippers were on the floor, and her Venture Bros. lap blanket swagged the couch. A few other items that belonged to her: the eye of Sauron mug, a pair of wadded General Servius socks were scattered here and there.

I knew if I went to her little apartment, I'd find Hogan's stuff mixed in with hers too.

"She's in the back. Can I get you anything? Coffee? I have a couple experimental rolls if you're up for it."

"Experimental as in..." Crow mimed smoking a joint.

Hogan laughed. "No, man. I'm trying some new flavors of bread."

"What are you going for?" Crow followed him into the kitchen.

"Dill, bacon, but also peanut butter, and maple. Think breakfast, but with pickles on the plate…"

I left them to it and walked down the hallway, past a half bath, a spare room that had been turned into a computer and gaming room, a linen closet and then, to the guest room.

The door was decorated with sparkly red tulle, creating a stage framing a photo of Xtelle in pony form. She was standing on the beach in a very regal pose, one hoof raised, her head tipped down, her short pony neck curved as her ridiculously long, silvery mane blew in the wind behind her.

Just below the picture was a little shelf and a tip jar.

There were two dollars in it. I figured she'd put them in there herself.

I knocked on the door.

"I told you I hate maple syrup," Xtelle said.

"It's Delaney. Can I come in?"

There was a thump and then a lot of scrabbling behind the door. I thought I heard a window open and then more scrabbling—moving books? Furniture? Finally hooves clacked across hardwood to the door.

She opened it, and there was a chain on her side. She stuck her eye in the crack and blinked at me. "What do you want?"

I smelled chocolate on her breath and a faint hint of cigarette smoke.

"I heard about the delivery you got today," I said. "I need to ask you a few questions."

The eye narrowed, then she shut the door. The chain slid and clicked against the wall.

I waited for the door to open. Nothing.

"Xtelle?"

"Come in," she sang out.

I opened the door.

Hogan was a nice guy who obviously wanted Xtelle to make herself comfortable in the guest room. The demon queen had done exactly that.

The queen-size bed was shoved to one side of the room, mirrors covered three of the four walls. Everything in the room was red, pink, or sparkling silver. It was positively funhouse chic.

I felt like I'd fallen into a cheap punch bowl spiked with bootleg gin.

"Delaney. Why are you bothering me? I haven't done anything wrong."

She rested in the middle of her red fur quilt, a pile of satin and velvet pillows stacked behind her so she could lounge with all four legs tucked up under her.

She was in unicorn form, and the clash between the pink of her body and the diamond bright horn in the room gave me an instant headache.

The mirrors weren't helping with that.

Which was absolutely her intention. She might look like a cute little unicorn, but she was a demon queen through and through.

"You had a package left at your door this morning."

She reached over to the box of chocolates on the night stand and popped one into her mouth. Horse hooves, well, unicorn hooves shouldn't work like that but Xtelle was a demon. She could make her hooves do whatever she wanted.

"Did you see who brought it in?" I asked.

"No."

"Did someone knock?"

"No."

"How did you know it was delivered?"

"I could feel it. Don't make that face. I felt it. I felt what was in the box."

"This is my normal face. I'm not making any faces."

"You poor thing."

"What was in the box?"

She squinted at me. "Bathin told you already, didn't he?"

"I spoke with him. I want to hear it from you."

"This isn't my fault," she groused.

"Okay."

"I'm following all the stupid rules of stupid Ordinary stupid Oregon."

"Okay."

"It's not even supposed to be here. I didn't bring it here."

"You're going to drive the long way around to the answer, aren't you?"

"I know I'm supposed to bow to your authority and toe the line. Well, hoof the line. I know I have to be a good pony."

"You're not a pony."

"*Thank* you!" she said. "I am a beautiful, sweet unicorn." She tossed her mane and a thousand Xtelles in the mirrors did the same. "Isn't beautiful more important than good? Isn't sweet better than well-behaved?"

"Succinct is better than dramatic. Straightforward is more important than looks. Direct will work."

"Sweet and beautiful and carefree and…and innocent!" She lowered her head and coyly fluttered her eyelashes. "Such a pretty unicorn deserves a present."

"I will present you with a jail cell."

"You wouldn't!"

"I would. No mirrors allowed."

She gasped. "Monster."

"The box. The delivery. The contents." I made a keep it rolling motion with my finger.

"It's a trinket. Just some old junk."

"Show me."

"The box?"

"Everything. The trinket, the box, everything."

"I burned it."

"Then show me the ashes."

She rolled her big horsey eyes. "Fine. Fine! I've done everything you've asked and still, not a single thank you. I don't know why you haven't been replaced with a much nicer, taller, and better-looking chief of police by now."

She hopped off the fur cover and trotted across the room, trailing the scent of burned strawberries behind her. She made a quick right, then trotted down the hall to the back door, which she opened with a hoof. "There," she minced to one side, not stepping out. "Happy?" She minced the other way.

The door opened onto the patio. I hadn't been back here since Hogan had taken over the place, but what I remembered from the past owner was a blank concrete slab, a few rusted patio chairs, and a broken barbeque.

Hogan had swept that all away. Now a cobbled patio, with a pergola above it, looked out upon the long backyard.

Fairy lights twinkled up there in the vines that grew across the wooden roofing, and instead of rusted chairs, there were two small couches with bright, weather-proof upholstery, a baby-blue table in the center, and two wooden rocking chairs in red and yellow. The barbeque had been replaced with a shiny new one.

Also there were gnomes.

An awful lot of gnomes.

Like, more gnomes than I'd seen in one place in my life.

They were statues at the moment, but I knew under certain circumstances they would come to life. Last time had been on Halloween. Luckily, Hogan had figured out how to not only talk gnomish—a knack I'd never developed—he had also become their guardian.

Of course Headless Abner was a big part of that. His head was right there on a pedestal near the corner of the patio where he could keep an eye on the yard and all his fellow gnomes.

"Where are the ashes?" I asked.

"Out there." Xtelle waved a hoof toward the grill but still didn't step through the door.

"How about you come out here and show me?"

"How about you find it. You're a detective." Her gaze darted back and forth around the patio, as if the gnomes were going to come to unlife at any moment.

I smiled. "Sure are lots of gnomes out today."

"Yes." Her eyes flicked faster, as if she expected each statue to move a little while she wasn't watching. "I suppose. Yes."

"I bet more keep showing up every day now that Hogan is in charge of them."

"They do?"

"Yep. Last time I was back here there were maybe

two, three gnomes. Now it's, what? A couple dozen? Three dozen?"

"They just keep coming!" she wailed.

"Well, now that word has gotten out on G-Nom radio, I expect even more of them will be arriving."

"Those pointy-hatted abominations!"

"Every abomination has a place in Ordinary as long as they follow the rules. The gnomes won't hurt you. Well," I said glibly, "they aren't supposed to."

"But I'm so beautiful!"

"That doesn't… Wait." I pivoted and stared at a blue-capped gnome with a wheelbarrow full of flowers.

Xtelle backed farther into the house, her head squishing into her neck so she had chins. It was a strange look on a pink unicorn.

"What?" she said. "What did it do?"

"I just thought maybe… No, I'm sure it's fine."

"Stop it. Do something to stop it! You're supposed to save me."

I lifted the barbecue grill's lid. It was spotless inside. "Is this where you burned everything?"

"Of course not. Over there." She waved her nose in larger swings.

I walked to the edge of the patio. A charred section of grass spread out in a three-foot circle.

"You burned Hogan's lawn?"

"That patch of crab grass and dandelions? I should have fanned the flames."

I bent and poked at the ashes and char. "This is all that was left of the box?"

"I'm going to say, yes?"

I strolled over to the door and opened it. Xtelle trotted backward, her eyes wide.

"There's no burned trinket out there. I know you received a ring. Tell me what the ring does."

"It makes me invincible in battle."

"Is that the truth or is that what you tell people?"

"I'm alive, aren't I?"

"You didn't answer the question."

She tossed her mane. "It protects me."

"You use it for defense only?"

"Of course not. It can cause great destruction. The best defense is offensively smashing your opponent in the face before the battle even begins."

"Sounds useful. Why didn't you bring it with you when you came to Ordinary?"

"I assumed it was not allowed to bring that kind of power here. Was I wrong?"

"No. You were right. But now I need to see it."

"It's mine."

"I understand that. Let's see it."

She sashayed all the way back to the bedroom, and hopped up on the bed again. "I'll show you, if you answer my questions."

"Pass. Show me the ring."

She blew air out through her pony lips, making them flap. "Fine." She turned over her hoof. There in the center of her hoof was a ring made of metal that glowed red, as if it were made of pure fire.

Power radiated from it, and in the back of my mind, I heard a song. The shriek of agony, the terrifying echo of battle horns. Mountains cleaving in two roaring in a crushing, burying doom.

Demon ring. Demon power. Demon song.

"Okay," I said. "This needs to be stored somewhere safe. Myra can put it in the vault."

"Vault?" She narrowed her eyes. "Where is this vault? It contains valuable items doesn't it? I will of course need to inspect the vault to make sure my valuables will be safe. You do have a record of giving all sorts of undesirables access to this town, Delaney."

Like demons, I thought to myself.

"No. You give me the ring, I give it to Myra, it goes in the vault."

"Well, that's just not going to happen. For very practical reasons."

"So you can practically plan how you're going to break into the vault?"

"Only a demon can touch the ring. If any other creature touches it, it will instantly destroy them. Splatter like a roasted tomato." She showed a lot of teeth in her smile, and it was not pretty on a unicorn.

"All right," I said thinking quickly. I pulled my phone out of my pocket and dialed.

"Miss me already?" Bathin asked in lieu of answering the phone like a normal person.

"Not even a little bit," I said. "I need you to meet me at your mother's place."

"Hell?"

I choked back a laugh. "Her place here. Hogan's house."

"Ah. What'd she do now?"

"I'll fill you in when you get here."

"Are you all right?"

"I'm fine. But I need your help with the ring."

"Sounds interesting. Be there in five."

"Why would you think my son can make me do what you want me to do?"

"Okay, I'm going to go over this again. You know my job is to take care of Ordinary and all those who call it home."

"Boring."

"That means you too, Xtelle. You call Ordinary home. Which means I'm looking out for you too."

The look on her face didn't fit the shape of the pink unicorn she was wearing. It was suspicious, yes, but also…considering. As if she were weighing more than just my words. As if she were weighing the fortitude of my morals. My soul.

Who knew? Maybe she was. She was a demon after all.

"I am the only one who looks after myself," she said with no trace of histrionics at all. The statement was more than just the facts. It was the core of her, the core of how she'd lived her life all these years. It was the core of how she expected to live her life in Ordinary.

"As long as you live here, I look after you too. And so do my sisters. That's how it is."

For a moment, for the short silence that followed, I thought maybe I'd gotten through to her. Thought she was starting to understand what it meant to be a part of this town. What it meant to have other people willing to do good for one another because it was the right thing to do no matter where any of us had come from.

I thought for half a second, that the glimmer in her eyes was realization. If she could understand I was here to help her live a good life, that I would stand with her, and stand up for her, maybe it would be the first step on the path to learning how she could do the same for her fellow Ordinarians.

Then a knock on the door brought Hogan and Crow laughing out of the kitchen, and whatever glimmer I'd seen in her eyes was gone.

CHAPTER TEN

"BATHIN," Hogan said from the living room. "Come on in. Want some bread?"

"You do," Crow said. "You want the one with pickles."

"Delaney called me over," Bathin said, "but I could eat. Is Delaney out back?"

"Bedroom, I think," Hogan said. "I'll get you a slice."

Bathin's heavy footsteps grew louder down the hall, and then he was in the bedroom doorway, squinting against the drunken punch color scheme.

"Delaney," he said, his voice a deep baritone. "Mother." Little more venom in that word.

"Now you visit me?" she said. "All this time I've been here, alone, and you couldn't even stop eating those cats to come see your own mother?"

"I saw you yesterday," he said to his mother, then to me: "I don't eat the cats."

I knew that. Myra had shown me several pictures of

him lounging on the couch at her place, looking comfortable among the doilies and lace of her decor, his legs kicked out. There'd be a cat sleeping in his lap, one snuggled under his arm, and one across his shoulders, head tucked in under his ear.

Bathin always looked relaxed and happy, and I liked seeing him that way.

Especially since I knew how much my sister loved him.

"I need you to take your mother's ring."

Xtelle made a sound like an angry goose.

Bathin was very still for a moment. Then a small smile curved the corner of his lips. "Do you, now?"

"No!" Xtelle said. "I forbid it."

"You can't keep a weapon that powerful with you while you're in Ordinary," I repeated. "There's simply no need for it. And if it were stolen, or fell into the wrong hands, we would have all kinds of problems to deal with."

"Who would steal it from me? They'd disintegrate the moment they touched it."

"One, people disintegrating would also be a problem. Two, there are magic users in town. Vampires, and other creatures who are not quite alive, might be able to handle a demon ring just fine. Does the power of the ring only work for you?"

Narrow eyes again as she worked through which would get her what she wanted: a lie or the truth.

"Yes," she said slowly. "As far as I am aware, I am the only demon who can access the power in the ring."

I shot a look at Bathin.

He nodded. "It tracks. Demons are pretty good about locking that kind of thing down."

I raised an eyebrow.

"She wouldn't allow the power in the ring to be used against her. None of the other weapons she's forged can be used by anyone except who she intends to use them," he continued.

"She made this?"

"Of course I made it," Xtelle scoffed. "Do you think I would trust anyone else to create a weapon that my life might depend upon?"

Distrusting everyone must be exhausting. No wonder she wanted to live in Ordinary.

"Okay," I said. "If anyone other than a demon touches the ring, it will harm them?"

"Yes, and no," Bathin said, just as Xtelle said, "Yes!"

She glared at Bathin. "Don't you dare tell the truth."

He chuckled. "I am so enjoying this. At first, I didn't want you here. But now? Moments like this. A true pleasure."

She hissed at him in what I assumed was Demon and he only laughed more. "As if you could, you Old Scratch."

"Scratch! Scratch? I'll show you…"

"Nope." I took two steps so I was between them, facing Xtelle. "I know you don't want to give up the ring. I understand. No, don't look at me like that, I do. But this is a god-level weapon. Anything that powerful has to be secured while inside Ordinary. So either you send it out of Ordinary, back to where it came from, or we secure it while it's here.

"This isn't because you aren't the rightful owner. This is the rule, the law built into Ordinary all those years ago when the town was made by the gods. No god-level weapon is allowed to remain in Ordinary in the hands of its owner. Understood? That level of destruction is too great a risk for everyone inside Ordinary. Even the gods have to put down their god power to be here."

I didn't go into the rest of it. Didn't really think she would understand that, when the gods vacationed here, they were vulnerable in a way they were nowhere else in the universes. They were mortal—or as close as they could be. They could be killed. Even with very human, non-god weapons.

If the gods had been allowed to keep their god weapons while in Ordinary, more than one brawl between the deities over the years would have ended in deaths.

The gods had known that when they created the place. They'd all agreed to the weapon rules.

"The ring isn't a god weapon," I said. "But you told me how powerful it is, and I believe you. So we need to keep it safe. If I can't touch it, and you won't allow it to be locked away, then you have two options.

"One, take it out of Ordinary, back to where it came from."

She seemed to pale a little, though it was hard to tell under all that pink hair.

"Or give it to someone who can touch it, but whom the weapon will not work for. That means another demon."

She opened her mouth.

"Not Avnas," I said. "He hasn't been in Ordinary long enough for me to trust him with that responsibility."

"But my son has?" She trilled a little laugh. "Oh, Delaney, how foolish are you? I left this with my other son."

Bathin grunted. "Goap?"

"He obviously couldn't hold on to it, and he's a demon. Bathin will do no better."

I spread my hands. "Those are your choices."

I expected arguing, tears, threats. Instead she hopped down off the bed and stomped over to Bathin. "Take the stupid ring." She held out her hoof, the ring blazing red, orange, blue. "When you lose it, don't come crying to me."

Bathin calmly plucked the ring out of her hoof. No hesitation. I had to give it to the guy. He was awfully confident his mother wasn't lying about the ring harming him. But then, he'd known her for centuries and could probably spot her lies from miles away.

The moment his fingers touched the ring, the moment it was lifted from her hoof, the flames extinguished and the ring turned into a flat silver band, scuffed and hammered.

It looked like a cheap ring that had been left in the middle of the freeway for a couple years.

"What do you want me to do with it?" he asked me.

"Keep it safe. Keep it away from people. It disintegrates...."

"Not while I'm wearing it."

Xtelle sniffed and looked away.

"So it's unarmed?"

He nodded. "My demon nature cancels it out. Mother wouldn't want any demon to have this little bit of her power—"

"I like *some* demons," she interrupted. "At least your brother writes me."

"—so unless she has a spell on it that triggers its powers when it's under an actual attack…"

Xtelle sniffed again.

"…in my hands, it's nothing but a crude lump of metal."

"You're a crude lump of metal," Xtelle muttered.

"What was that?" Bathin leaned toward her, cupping his ear.

"This is dumb," she said. "You're both dumb. Go away." She swished her tail and tossed her head making her mane float and flow.

"You wanted me to stop by. To visit, remember?" Bathin pressed. "Don't you want me to stay awhile?" He made a big show of shoving her ring onto his pinky and her eyes got wide. Then they started to twitch.

"You're a monster," she hissed.

"Yes," he said with a satisfied smirk. "I am."

"Okay, so that's all good," I said, trying to take control of the situation before I had a domestic on my hands. "Thank you for cooperating, Xtelle. If you decide to leave Ordinary, Bathin will return the ring to you, no questions asked. Won't you, Bathin?"

"I might ask a couple questions."

"Blackmail me, you mean," she said.

He hummed like he was thinking right along those same lines.

"No blackmail. Xtelle, if you decide to leave, just come to me. I'll make sure you have all of your possessions to take with you."

Bathin didn't acknowledge me, but he did straighten up out of the slightly aggressive stance he'd fallen into.

"Fine," she said.

"Fine," Bathin echoed.

Dear gods, save me from demon family dynamics.

"Okay. We're done here. If something else is delivered to you, any other weapon, anything from an anonymous sender, I want you to call me or the police department immediately, and please don't burn the box."

Bathin snorted. Xtelle just lifted her chin and nose in the air. "You may leave me now."

I didn't have to be asked twice. I left her bedroom, Bathin following. A second later she slammed her bedroom door. Six times.

I exhaled and scrubbed at the headache building behind my right eye. "Your mother."

"Why do you think I left centuries ago?"

"Hey, still up for the bread?" Hogan asked. He and Crow were crowded up on the couch peering at a board game spread out on the little table.

"Give me a second," Bathin said.

"We could use a third player," Crow said. "I mean, unless you need me for the rest of the day, Delaney?"

"Nope, no," I said. "I do not need you at all. Today. Or ever." I grinned at him and he made kissy faces at me. Then I was out the door before he could change his mind, but not before Hogan pressed a thick chunk of bread in my hand.

Bathin stepped out onto the porch with me.

"You sure you're going to be okay with that ring?" I asked before I took a big bite of the bread. I moaned a little, it was that good.

Bathin just shook his head at me.

"Wait until you try it," I mumbled around another big bite.

"The ring isn't going to be a problem. You can touch it, I promise you won't go up in smoke." He held his hand out, palm up, and I decided someone should make sure it was safe.

I swallowed and then brushed my hand on my jeans. "Not that I don't trust you," I said.

"Of course not," he agreed.

I poked at the scratched silver band with the tip of my finger.

Nothing. No zing, no zip. Not even a single spark or note of magic.

"That's pretty remarkable," I said.

"She does good work. I hate to admit it," he said, "but she knows her stuff. Are you sure you don't want to lock it up?"

"I do want to lock it up. But we've had to put some powerful weapons in the vault today. I don't know how a demon weapon would interact being near them."

"Powerful weapons?"

"God weapons."

Bathin's eyebrows went up. "You didn't say that before. Who brought their weapons to town?"

"Not the gods. The weapons were dropped off on their doorsteps. Just like Xtelle's ring."

We'd started walking toward our cars. Parked next to my Jeep was the slick '68 Corvette Bathin had somehow gotten his hands on. Cherry red and hot as sin, it was flashy, pretentious, and frankly, suited him.

"Correct weapon to the correct god?" he asked.

"Yes."

"And these weren't previously in Ordinary?"

"Nope. Just like your mother's ring wasn't here. The rules don't allow the gods to bring their weapons here. Hell, the rules force the gods to put down their power, so why would they be able to keep weapons that are directly connected to that power? This is supposed to be a vacation town, not a battlefield."

"Which gods?"

"Why?" I leaned on the door to the Jeep, and stuck my hands in my pockets.

We'd been connected to each other in a strange manner not so long ago. I'd agreed to give him my soul for him releasing my father's trapped soul. I still believed it had been a good decision, even though Jean and Myra had been horrified and furious about it.

They'd forced me to agree that I wouldn't make deals with demons, or any other creature, god, or human that involved anything precious and rare without first consulting them.

They called it the Don't Do Anything Dumb Without Talking To Us First, Delaney rule.

DEVON MONK

When he'd had my soul, Bathin had gotten a good feel for how humanity ticked.

In return I'd gotten a feel for how demon-kind ticked.

Which meant I knew he was putting pieces of a puzzle together right now, something about the god powers, something about the ring, and something more.

"The gods don't leave their weapons lying around where anyone or anything can pluck them up." He rested against his vehicle, rocking it under his weight, his thumbs tucked in his belt loops.

"True."

"Most gods lock those weapons away."

"Also true."

"Stealing a weapon like that is…" He shook his head.

"Impossible?"

"Yes. Even touching a weapon like that is problematic."

"Why do you say so?"

"God power, by its very nature, is something most living beings can't really handle. Certainly not in large doses or for any duration. A god weapon laid bare is even more destructive than this." He shifted his fist so the silver ring glinted dully. "How were they delivered?"

"Cardboard boxes, no postal markings, two red ink stamps."

"What were the ink stamps?"

"A red feather and a circle with a line through it."

A robin called out, its liquid song reminding me of spring rain and mossy creeks sparkling like diamonds.

"Alchemy? The circle with a line is salt. Represents the body. Red feather...could be flight? Fire? Blood, of course, or transformation?"

"Does that add up to something to you? Point to anything?"

"Not really."

"Talk to Myra about it. She's doing research. Do you know any demons who would try this?"

"To move a god weapon against the god's will, without the god knowing would take massive power, or incredible subtlety."

"So you don't think a demon is behind this?"

"Oh, I think if a demon wanted to transport a god weapon, they'd find some way to do it. But to show up in town and deliver the weapons without you knowing we had another demon in Ordinary? Much less likely."

"Do you think your mother or uncle did this?"

He didn't immediately answer. I wondered how many past actions he was running through his head. How many other betrayals and double crosses and schemes and deals he had seen his mother and uncle Avnas make over the years.

"It would have to be royalty. Demon royalty. The level of magic demon royalty can wield is far beyond a more common demon. My mother is...was," he corrected himself, "the queen of hell. And my uncle the king's knight. They might have the power to slip into a god realm."

"But?"

"It's a hell of a risk." His cool gaze met mine. "Stealing god weapons and leaving them on their

123

doorstep is either a power move to show the gods they are not as mighty as they think they are, or someone's trying to stir up suspicion and hatred. Make them angry enough to leave town."

"Or someone wants to arm them," I said, throwing out the third, less likely option.

"Against what? Against who?"

"I have no damn idea," I said. "If you think of anything that would help us figure this out, I want to hear it."

"All right," he said. "Myra said a car fell out of the sky. Have you figured out what's behind that yet?"

"We're working on it."

"And we're saying?"

"Microburst. Happens every once in a while around here. Oregon and its crazy weather."

"Good to know." He pushed away from his car and took a couple steps toward the house. "Oh. Ryder said he was looking for a venue."

"For?" I opened my car door. The faint scent of coffee and the shampoo and soap Ryder used, wafted out of the Jeep.

"Your wedding."

"Right. Yep. Wedding." Even I heard the crackle in my voice.

"Delaney."

"No."

"You're not having second thoughts are you?"

"Of course not."

"It's just one vow," he said. "Then eternal bliss. You aren't getting cold feet about a tiny little vow are you?"

"No vow is little," I groused.

He grinned and waggled his eyebrows. "Marriage is a beautiful joining of lives."

"Marriage is a changing of lives."

"Of course it is. It's love," he said. "Marriage should be the easiest thing in the world. Everyone does it. Why even normal people do it. And if normal people can do it, then surely you can too, right?"

I scowled. His laugh was, warm, teasing. But I was still annoyed.

"Go eat a cat, Bathin."

"You have your dress, right? And the flowers picked out? Have you written your vows or are you going traditional? My goodness, who is going to officiate this momentous day? I bet every god in town wants in on that action."

I swung into my Jeep, and then very slowly, and very maturely flipped him the bird.

He laughed harder, waved, and turned back to the house.

I sat there, his words looping through my mind. Life changing. Vows. Promises that would transform everything about us.

Promises we would have to perform in front of people. Maybe most of the town. It was easy. Something normal people did all the time. Just a normal event that any normal person could pull off. My palms started sweating and my stomach flipped.

"Oh, gods." I rested my head on the steering wheel. "I am so screwed."

CHAPTER ELEVEN

"No," Ryder said. We were sitting on the tailgate of his truck in Frigg's parking lot, watching the cars go by. The sun coasted down the sky's curve toward the horizon, all the light deeper gold now, the shadows brushed in purple. I'd spent several hours at the station trying to track down anything I could find on the falling car and had come up empty handed.

"It would be easy," I said. "And fast. We wouldn't have to make so many choices and spend so much money and deal with so much…" I waved my hands around, "cheese."

His arms were braced on either side of his thighs, and he leaned forward just a bit, fingers curled over the edge of the tailgate. I snuck a peek at his profile to see if he was wavering.

He was not wavering. But gods, even in profile with the sun limning his strong, straight nose, the stubble of his jaw, the curve of his lips, even angry, or maybe just frustrated, he was beautiful.

"We're not eloping," he said. "It's not in me, Delaney. I need a ceremony, an event. Even if it's a small one." He glanced my way and saw something in my expression. His hand came up and fingertips smelling slightly of dust and wood shavings traced my cheek, then tucked a stray bit of hair behind my ears.

"I know you're stressed about it. Worried," he said gently. "But I got this. Trust me. All you'll have to do is show up and remember to say 'I do.' You trust me, don't you?"

"I do."

He grinned. "See? Just like that. You already have your lines memorized."

"You don't think we're going a little fast?"

"Fast? You know when I first fell in love with you? Do you know, Delaney?"

"When you found out what an amazing cook I am?"

"You are a terrible cook."

I squawked and pushed his shoulder. "I'm learning. I'm getting better. I did eggs."

"You destroyed those eggs. Incinerated them."

I laughed. "Nothing caught on fire. I'll take it as a win."

"This," he waved a finger between us, "has been my forever. I've loved you since I first had an idea of what that might mean. This isn't fast for me. Is it too fast for you?"

"It's just a lot of change. Feels like…I don't think it's too fast. No, I don't think so."

He was frowning now and opened his mouth to say

something, but I hopped down from the tailgate, my shoes crunching on the loose gravel and concrete.

"There's Zeus," I said. "We can table this for later, right? Tonight after work?"

"Sure," he said, although it was a little tense. "We can table it."

He pushed off the back of the truck and started toward the two vehicles that had just rolled into the lot.

Okay, that could have gone better. But how did I tell him I was hesitant to commit to a date, a venue, even a guest list because I was afraid if we got married, we would change? That *I* would change, and then everything we had together would be gone?

Loving Ryder was easy. There were days when I wanted to do nothing but laze in his arms and watch stupid reality shows with him.

There were moments—him racing Spud down the beach, faking a fall and laughing as Spud tried to rescue him, or him so focused on a new building design that he'd stuck one pencil between his teeth, one behind each ear, and had another in his hand—that I wanted to tell him I loved him. There were moments—dawn's light through our bedroom window coating him in the softest blue, his eyes when he first opened them gone silver-jade —that I kissed him trying to tell him everything written inside my heart.

All the words for him. Always for him.

Maybe my holding on to the dream of a happily ever after was getting in the way of the actual reality of our fairy tale ending.

"Hey-a Delaney." Jean waved at me. She had driven

in behind Zeus, and parked her truck facing the street. Hogan stepped out of the passenger side and held his hand up in a wave too.

I waved back at both of them.

Ryder greeted Hogan, then they made room for Zeus, who had exited his car to join their conversation.

Jean ambled my way. "Are you still fighting with Ryder?"

"Still?"

"It's always something with you two."

I ignored that. "Did you tell Odin to meet us here?"

"Yup. But you know how he is." She shrugged.

Yeah, I knew. Odin usually operated on his own timetable. Maybe he'd be here this evening, maybe he'd show up a week from now, covered in wood chips and moss.

Hogan, Ryder, and Zeus strolled toward us, talking about something that involved 'clean lines' and 'excellent use of negative space.' It was either artwork Zeus had bought for his store, a new architectural project Ryder was bidding on, or Hogan's delivery van.

Odin rolled up in his junker car, which was in serious need of a new muffler, and gunned it over the driveway lip and into the parking lot.

Zeus, who had been smiling, stiffened. He scowled at Odin's car, then scowled even harder when Odin, every inch of him looking wild and thorny, stepped up out of the rust bucket.

"I'm here," Odin announced. He scowled at Zeus. "Peacock."

"Old stump."

"Snuff pincher"

"Rock licker."

"Where's my check?"

"Where's the *elegant refined* statue of a seahorse I ordered?"

"I delivered it last Tuesday."

"That was a seahorse?" Zeus brushed invisible lint from his cuffs. "I thought it was a large burned piece of macaroni and threw it in the bin."

Odin curled his huge hand into a fist, his knuckles cracking. "It's been a few years since I've punched you in the face."

"No," I said. I stepped between the two gods and faced Odin just as Ryder turned to put himself in front of Zeus. "This fight is going to be taken care of through business channels. I'll assign you two an arbitrator if you can't come to an agreement that doesn't involve broken bones."

Odin stopped glaring at Zeus over my shoulder long enough to look down at me.

"I mean it." I put my hands on my hip.

"You always do." He sniffed, then nodded. "We'll renegotiate cost and delivery."

"Zeus?" I said without looking back. "Agreed?"

He hesitated a moment. Then: "Agreed," he said. "Now where is the vehicle?"

"This way." Ryder led him toward the detached garage to one side of Frigg's shop.

"You're trouble." I poked Odin in the chest. "I don't need more trouble."

"Tell Zeus to pay me before he throws my work in the trash."

"You two bicker like old hens," I said.

He grinned and stepped around me. "Jean, Hogan. Have you found out who broke into my realm and stole my spear yet?"

"We're working on it," I said.

"Well, I'm not." Hogan leaned forward to offer Odin his hand.

Odin gave it a hearty shake. "You don't know anything about it, do you? No one came wishing to you?"

"No. The few people who know what I can do aren't stupid enough to steal from the gods. If anyone had asked, I would have told them no, then told Jean about it."

"I thought as much," Odin propped his wide, calloused hands on his hips. "What about you?"

He had his one eye turned on the shop behind us. I glanced over.

Frigg stood in front of the door, a huge travel mug of coffee in one hand. She was built like a volleyball player, tall and lean. Her golden hair was pulled back from her face with a clip, leaving the majority of it to fall free.

She looked like summer sunshine, gold and gleaming. Her eyes sparkled.

"Well, I work here," she said. "What's this about weapons and wishes?"

"Someone left my spear on my doorstep."

Frigg froze for a second before the easy smile returned. "That's not allowed."

"No," I said. "It's not."

"Does our falling car have something to do with it?"

I shrugged. "Could. It falls out of the sky, then just hours later, weapons start showing up on doorsteps."

"Weapons. Interesting," Frigg sipped coffee. "I suppose this is where I tell you I got a package in my mailbox. Let me get it." She disappeared back inside the shop and came out with a padded mailing envelope.

"It showed up this afternoon." She brought out a now familiar cardboard box and lifted from it a beautifully crafted wooden stick with metal inlay. She held it out so I could better see it.

The staff was about three feet long and tapered to a blunt end. Clusters of mistletoe leaves and berries were carved at the top, creating a leafy crown. Sunlight ran like amber pitch down the staff, catching rainbow prisms from symbols of sheep, grasses, water, clouds. Threads of copper, silver and gold looped through it all, like spun silk.

I could see the power in it, hear it. The call of battle was there, voices rising in shouts of victory, but there were other songs: weeping, celebration. The wind and water, the hushing murmur of love, all blending with the shift and clack of twine between wood, fate spinning universes into thread.

"This is one of my distaffs," she said.

"Mistletoe," Odin added quietly. "But how?"

Her gaze flicked to him, and something passed between them.

Many legends said they were husband and wife. In Ordinary, it was clear they were fond of each other and shared a long, long history. But as far as I knew, they weren't living as a married couple.

Maybe that was part of their vacation. Maybe being married that long meant they wanted a break from it. Wanted some time alone.

I thought about Ryder, and all the years he had been away from Ordinary. I couldn't imagine ever wanting to take a break from him. Couldn't imagine ever wanting to be alone.

It wasn't my job to keep track of Frigg and Odin's private life. From all I knew—and from that look they were sharing—they were seeing each other quietly on the side.

"I would love an answer to that," Frigg said, and it took me a minute to remember I was supposed to be paying attention to the mistletoe distaff she was holding.

"Is it a weapon?" I asked.

Odin chuckled. "Is it a weapon."

"It is," Frigg said simply.

"Okay," I said. "I didn't know that."

"That's the thing," she said, walking toward me. "Almost no one knows of its existence. Those who do assume it is a part of my weaving, a part of fate and future and knowing."

"Knowledge can be a weapon," Jean said.

"True," Frigg agreed, "but this kills."

It glinted again, catching a harder edge of sunlight.

"We'll need to lock it up," I said. "Put it in the vault with the other god weapons."

She nodded. "I'd wondered what I was going to do with it. It's against the laws for me to carry it here."

"Myra put the other weapons in the vault," I explained.

"Which vault?"

"The one in the library," Myra said striding up the sidewalk. She must have parked on the street. Right place, right time.

"We get another delivery?" she asked.

Frigg held up the distaff. "Do you want me to go with you?"

"Yeah, I'll need you there."

"Can I see the box?" I pulled latex gloves out of my pocket and worked my hands into them.

Frigg handed it to me. Just like the others, there was no name or address written upon it. But on the back, there was a circle with a line dissecting it, and a single red feather.

"I'd like to keep this. See if I can get prints off of it," I said.

"Knock yourself out," she said.

"I don't suppose you saw who dropped this off today?"

She shook her head, gold catching in her hair. "No. I've been out on calls this morning, and had to pick up supplies this afternoon. I shut the shop down and forwarded calls to my cell."

"No one was here to see it get dropped off?"

"No one."

"Any cameras?" Jean asked.

"Who's going to break into a tow truck shop?" Frigg grinned. "A hubcap burglar?"

"No cameras," I said.

"No cameras," she agreed.

The garage door opened and Ryder and Zeus walked our way. "Looks like it's your turn," I told Odin.

"Finally," he grumped.

Frigg just rolled her eyes and started toward Myra. "Wanna get this stashed before the night falls?"

"Sooner is better than later."

"Big plans for tonight?"

They strolled toward the cruiser, Myra's voice drifting back to me. "Just dinner. With Bathin."

Frigg chuckled. "Which one of you is cooking?"

I didn't hear Myra's answer, but a moment later, Frigg laughed louder, and then they were out of sight.

Ryder and Zeus were closer now. "Anything?" I asked Ryder. He shook his head.

"Thank you for coming, Zeus," I said. He just nodded, and he and Ryder continued their quiet conversation as they walked to his car

"Are you coming, Delaney?" Odin threw over his shoulder as he stomped off to the garage.

I tapped Jean's arm. "Get some photos of the mailbox, the door…"

"…box, the parking lot. I got this. Go."

I caught up with Odin just as he stopped on the threshold of the big open garage doorway.

"This it?" He jabbed a blunt finger toward the car.

"That's it. Fell out of the sky this morning over by

the 50th street access. Jean was there, so was Myra. They both saw it land."

He grunted then walked into the garage, the light was lower here even though the overhead lights up in the metal rafters were blazing.

I parked myself on a 55-gallon barrel of rusted parts and watched.

Odin was quiet, except for his big boots clomping across the concrete. He circled the car once then stopped by the driver's side, bent, and looked into the interior.

"Any problems with me opening it?"

"Go ahead."

I knew Hatter and Shoe had already been by to dust for prints and look for forensic evidence. They'd found bupkis.

He opened the door and crouched. Balancing on the balls of his feet, he looked across the seats.

"You find anything in here?"

"No. Well, if a crab counts, yes."

He leaned back and sort of twisted to see me. "A crab?"

"Yeah, one of those little ones. It came out from under the seat and then made a run for it."

"And nothing else was in here?"

"Nothing but a little crab claw it had been chewing on."

He stood, shut the door and walked over to me. "Let's see it."

"The crab claw?"

"It's what you found in the car. The only thing you

found. I want to see it."

"It isn't here. It's at the station in evidence."

"Crab claw."

"With a bite out of it."

Odin frowned, his one eye narrowing as if the crab claw was important. I let him think it through. He was a god known for his wisdom. Maybe he would come up with something, some way that a crab and an old chewed up crab claw would explain the car. And if not the car, the weapons.

But all he said was, "Huh."

"So much for wisdom," I muttered.

"I heard that," Odin said, straightening. "I'm on vacation. I don't have to be wise. And I don't have to solve crimes. That's what you're here for."

"Thanks a lot."

"I heard how long it took Ryder to talk you into a vacation. You love your job. Maybe too much. More than getting married, anyway."

"I guarantee I am not loving it right now."

"Then do something about it," he challenged.

I didn't know if he meant my job or getting married. Maybe both. And what was I supposed to do with that?

Jean strolled into the garage. "Got all the pictures. You need me for anything else?"

"I don't think so. Wait, maybe. You didn't happen to bring the crab claw did you?"

"It's still in lock up. You want me to go get it?" Jean asked.

Hogan stepped into the space. His head snapped up,

his nostrils flared and he waved his hand in front of his face.

"What are you doing?" Jean asked him.

Hogan pinched his nose. "It stinks in here. You don't smell that?"

All of us sniffed.

"No?" Jean said. "Smell what?"

He pulled the collar of his T-shirt up to cover his nose in a makeshift mask and mumbled something.

"What?" she chuckled, leaning closer. "You are such a weirdo. School?"

He plucked at the fabric. "No. Smells like ghoul."

CHAPTER TWELVE

I shook my head. "It smells like ghoul? What does ghoul smell like?"

"Rotted flesh and melted vinyl," Hogan said. "You really don't smell that?"

I tried again, but the only thing I smelled was musty concrete, motor oil, and the salty green of the coastal wind.

I glanced at Odin. "Don't look at me," he complained. "I'm not half Jinn. I don't smell the undead."

"Are you sure it's a ghoul?" I asked Hogan.

He nodded. "I met one once. Before I moved here. Same smell. Exactly."

"What do we know about ghouls?" I said, wishing Myra and her encyclopedic knowledge of all things magical were here.

"They stink." Jean flashed me a grin. I rolled my eyes.

"They eat flesh?" I said, sorting through the differences between ghouls, undead, and zombies.

"Lure people into graveyards," Odin added. "Nibble on the living or the dead, and walk out looking like whoever they ate."

I swallowed back a little bit of revulsion.

"Gross," Jean said. "If you can smell one, does that mean one of us is a ghoul?"

Hogan blinked. "Uh...maybe?"

Jean waggled her eyebrows. "You're gonna have to sniff us to make sure."

"We are all who we say we are," Odin grumbled. "This is a waste of time, and I have things to do."

"No," I said. "You stay. We all stay. Let's all take a step backward so we don't muddy up each other's scents.

Odin muttered something that sounded like "bullshit" but stepped back with Jean and me. Hogan sniffed Jean first, pulling his T-shirt down away from his nose and nuzzling her neck.

She giggled, her face stained pink. "Stop it. I hate that. Anything?" she asked, holding perfectly still.

"You smell amazing," he said. "I love that perfume. I also love that you're ticklish right here." He sniffed again, and she leaned back.

"I am not."

He moved in for another sniff. She tucked her chin down to stop him and pushed his shoulder. She was smiling wide. "Go smell my sister."

"Now who's the weirdo?" he asked. He turned to me and came in close, his body carefully not touching mine, his face lowering toward my neck.

"You smell like you. Did you change your shampoo?"

"Got lazy. I'm using Ryder's."

"Smells nice on you."

"I like it."

Odin grumbled something under his breath, and we all turned to face him.

"I'm not a ghoul," he said.

"That's pretty much what a ghoul would say," Jean noted.

Odin glared at her then crooked his finger at Hogan. "Get it done with."

Hogan stepped over to him, squared off, and took a big sniff.

"You smell like Doritos."

"I was hungry. I had a snack."

"You also smell like wood shavings and moss and motor oil."

"Unlike some other people around here, I work for a living," he griped.

"You don't smell ghoul on any of us?" I double checked. "Where is the smell the strongest?"

Hogan lifted his chin, sniffed again then winced. "It's the car."

We all turned to stare at the car.

"The car's a ghoul?" Jean asked with a mix of excitement and horror.

"That's mechanical," Odin said. "Ghouls are the unliving."

"But they take on the shape of stuff they eat," Jean said. "What if it ate a carburetor and turned into the car?"

"I just told you it ate flesh," Odin said.

"Living flesh?" I asked.

Odin opened his mouth, then scratched at his beard. "Mostly, yes, but not always. I've known ghouls who got a strand of hair and could take on the form of the person it came from. Same with fingernail clippings, spit, tears. Really anything that carries DNA."

That wasn't good. That wasn't good at all.

"So if we have a ghoul," I said.

"We do," Hogan said through his T-shirt.

"It's been in this car, or around this car. It can take on the shape of anyone in town."

It all clicked in my head, like a stack of thick dominos toppling.

"The crab claw." I turned to Jean. "It ate the crab."

"The ghoul is the crab?"

"Maybe. Probably. It was chewing on that crab claw. I think the ghoul turned into a crab and scuttled to safety right in front of our noses."

"Well, hell," Jean said.

Odin clapped, and the sound ricocheted like thunder in the metal building. "I'll leave you two capable Reeds to it. Find my thief. I'd very much like to meet them."

The way he said 'meet them' sounded more like 'punch them in the face repeatedly.'

"We'll keep you in the loop."

He walked out of the building.

"I'll wait for you out there," Hogan told Jean, and followed Odin into the fresh air.

"Want me to call Myra and tell her about the ghoul situation?" Jean asked.

"I'll tell her." I walked around the car, looking in the windows. "Pop the trunk, will you?"

Jean reached under the dash to pull the trunk release lever. I pulled up the trunk lid and stared into the empty cavity. Nothing in there except clean black carpet. Not even a spare tire or jack.

"It's normal, you know," she said.

"What's normal?" I tipped my head side to side to relieve the tension in my neck.

"Ryder getting cold feet about the wedding."

I sighed and wondered if I came back in another life, if could request a sister who didn't stick her nose in my love life.

"Ryder's not getting cold feet about the wedding."

She turned and thumped against the car, her arms crossed over her chest. "Well, I know it can't be you," she said. "You're not actually screwing up your wedding to the man you love. That's not what you're doing, Delaney? Right?"

I flipped back the corners of the carpet, then folded it in half toward the middle. Nothing but metal. I flipped that back down and folded the carpet the other way.

"It's not that I don't…" I leaned into the trunk. Something was caught in the back corner. Just a small brown strip of…cardboard?

"Because I have not waited practically my whole life for the two of you to finally get married just to have you chicken out…"

I ignored her and carefully tugged on the cardboard. It came loose in one piece. I turned it to the other side.

Half of a red ink circle was stamped on it.

"Jean."

"…like I'm expecting a niece or nephew one of these days, but at least do yourself a favor…"

"Jean," I said a little louder.

"…he's been waiting a long time for you too, you know…"

"Jean."

"What?"

I straightened and held up the cardboard scrap. "Does this remind you of anything?"

"The delivery boxes?"

"Ding ding ding."

"We already looked through the car. *I* looked through it," she said. "How did I miss it?"

"It was wadded up pretty small and shoved in the corner. It looked like a clump of sand."

"Damn it," she said. "Sorry about that."

"Okay, so what do we have? The car fell out of the sky, and it contained the god weapons and the ghoul? Which we all missed, even though you and Myra were both watching the car?"

"We were thinking the ghoul turned into a crab that almost got eaten by seagulls this morning," she said. "How did it turn into something that could carry the weapons away?"

"Did you keep your eye on the car while you waited for Frigg to tow it?"

"Yes. I might have missed the cardboard, but it's pretty hard to overlook an entire car."

"Was it ever out of everyone's sight?"

Jean nodded. "When it was stored in the garage, I suppose, before Hatter and Shoe got here. So now are we thinking the ghoul was the crab, and after it hid from the seagulls, it snuck back into the car?"

"Maybe," I said.

"It snuck back into the car and rode here to the garage, then got out and somehow pulled the weapons out of the trunk—which was empty when I looked at it on the beach, by the way—and with all those weapons in its tiny claws, it skittered around town dropping off packages like a jolly ol' Santa Claus."

I sighed. "It sounds outrageous."

She shrugged. "It sounds like Ordinary. Maybe it happened that way, maybe there's more we don't know. So what do you want me to do next, boss?"

"Take this into evidence." I pulled a bag out of my pocket and dropped the cardboard into it. "See if Jules or one of the other witches has some time to do a scrying on it tomorrow. Then we'll run it through the labs."

"Got it." She plucked the bag out of my fingers and started off. "Promise me you're not going to screw up the wedding of your dreams."

"Can I not hear about the wedding for ten frickin' minutes? You do know there are other more important things happening around here."

I slammed the trunk and there was this moment of

silence, like someone had punched all the air out of the world.

Jean cleared her throat and raised her voice. "Oh, hey, Ryder. Um…yeah. That was. All on me. I was just giving her a hard time, you know. And now I'm gonna go get this to evidence because police work is so important and I am so police-working right now."

I closed my eyes and groaned.

Jean disappeared into the sunlight and Ryder stepped into the open bay, his thumbs tucked in his back pockets. He looked like everything I'd ever wanted in my world. Strength, patience, humor, love.

He looked like summer when the days drifted golden and endless. He looked like the boy I'd crushed on so hard, I thought my heart would break, and the man I'd fallen for so hard, it knocked the stars out of my sky.

"Hey," I said, and it came out soft, barely enough to move the dust in the air. A fox sparrow called out its sweet trilling chorus, once, twice. In the distance, an answer echoed.

Ryder watched me. I wondered if he was doing as much mental gymnastics as I was—a whole dang Olympic floor routine, twists, saltos, hard landings.

"Did you get a break in the case?" he asked.

Triple flip sailing right over what he'd heard me say.

I started toward him, and he waited there for me.

For a moment I wondered how long he would wait. If I asked for an extension on the wedding date, would he be okay with that? Autumn? Winter? Next summer?

But Jean's words came back to me, distant as the fox

sparrow echo. "*He's been waiting a long time for you too, you know.*"

I walked a little faster, wanting to erase this space between us. Wanting to level out my flips and spins so I was on the same trajectory as him. So we were flying across that mat, step-in-step, launching and landing at the same place at the same time.

"The wedding is important to me," I said, and even as the words came out of my mouth, I knew that was the wrong thing, the wrong move.

He looked over my shoulder like the garage walls were the most interesting thing in the world.

"Okay," he said.

"What I said, what you heard. Jean was poking and poking."

"Okay."

"Everyone has been asking," I said. "And I'm all...I don't even know what I am, but then it just feels like a lot and then there's Jean: poke, poke, poke."

"Okay."

"I wanted her to drop it because this is ours, this is between us and we're the only ones who get to decide what we are and what we want and..."

His hands stretched out, caught both my wrists and closed around them. The heat of his palms was a pressure, a brand, grounding me.

"Okay," he said again. This time I nodded. "Breathe."

I did that too, until I could hear the world around me again, the soft hum of traffic, the squawk of jays, the sweet distant sparrows.

"Little worked up, aren't you?" he asked.

"I don't think…" then, at his look, "I guess."

"But I'm dealing with the event, right? All the details and decisions?"

"Right. But I should…"

"I don't need you to. Whatever you're thinking, I got it. All of it."

He was smiling, yes. But the tightness at the corners of his eyes told another story.

"I hate this." The words were out of my mouth before I could stop them. I watched as they hit, the slow-motion flicker of confusion, then realization, and then anger that spread across his face.

His whole body leaned back from me. "Okay."

It was hard. Flat. A bad landing. The kind of landing that broke an ankle.

"I hate that it's so…we aren't doing this together. Aren't on the same page."

He took a couple steps backward, and did a fair job of patching the smile back on his face. "Well, when you decide what page you think we should be on, will you tell me, Delaney? Instead of going around to everyone else complaining about how much you hate that I'm going forward with our plans. *Our* plans."

"Don't," I said, my face hot, my heart pounding hard.

"Don't what? Ask you to be honest and tell me what you really feel?"

"And what do you think I really feel?" My voice shook. With anger, yes. And with pain. "How can you know? You just tell me not to worry. To just…do nothing. But that's not right."

He wiped one hand over his mouth, then scratched at the back of his neck. "Look," he said, his eyes coming to my face, then sliding sideways before flicking back again. "Look," he repeated to the ground. "I know it's… stressful. And right now…maybe we should…let's just let it go for a while."

"Okay," I said, swallowing. "Thank you. We can push it out a bit. Maybe winter. Or next year. Do a summer wedding but give us enough time…"

The look on his face told me I'd blown it. Botched the landing. It wasn't just a broken ankle, it was a snapped spine. A busted neck.

He wasn't talking about letting it go that long. He had just meant a day or two. A week or two. Just until we cooled down.

"Ryder—"

"I'm hungry," he said, his voice not quite steady, but getting there. "Are you hungry?"

I was. But I was also very aware he was changing the subject. Trying to stay out of a fight. And maybe that was good. Maybe that was the right way to deal with this. But I couldn't leave this here. Couldn't remain in the hurt we'd caused.

"It's not the wedding," I said.

"I'm thinking tacos."

"It's not *just* the wedding." I was striding along with him now, out of the garage, the wind gone cooler with the setting sun, heat and dust still drifting up from the gravel around us.

"Or we have chicken in the fridge. Grill it? We might have mushrooms."

"I feel shitty that I'm not doing more for it. It's like I'm not even a part of it."

"Then do more!" he snapped. "Be a part of it. Make a decision. Pick a color. But if you say you're going to do it, do it."

"This is what I'm talking about. Everything is so serious. You have seventeen notebooks on flowers. Just on flowers!"

He spun and glared at me over the open back of his truck. "Now I'm the bad guy because I was trying to do my research?"

"Do I need to mention the cheese? The award-winning cheese that isn't good enough for you? Or how about the twenty-four venues we've looked at that all had something wrong with them?"

"Mold is a health hazard. So is a leak in the roof. But if you want to get married on a leaky houseboat crawling with black death, then by all means, bring the hip waders!"

"Maybe I want to wear hip waders! Maybe that would be fun! Maybe it would be spontaneous. Hip waders for everyone."

He tipped his head skyward, and I watched his Adam's apple bob as he swallowed down a scream. "Do you want to wear hip waders?" he asked the sky.

"No," I said. "That wasn't the point I was trying to make. I got a little off track."

"So what is the point?" He tipped his chin down again, gave me a carefully neutral look. He was trying to listen. I knew he was. This was my chance to sort through the jumble of feelings and make everything better. Make everything right.

"I don't…I don't know."

"Hello there?" a voice called out. "Hello? Might I ask you a question?"

Ryder frowned, and I'm sure my expression mirrored his.

Than, the god of Death, stood on the sidewalk, one hand lifted shoulder high like he was in class and uncertain if he should draw attention to himself.

"A question?" he repeated.

Ryder looked back at me. "See you at home."

"I have to stop by Myra's to tell her about the ghoul stuff."

"What ghoul stuff?"

I nodded toward the garage. "Hogan smelled a ghoul on or in the car. Ghouls can eat flesh and take on the appearance of the thing they ate."

"That's disturbing."

"Fingernails and hair works, too, I guess. So we might have a ghoul in town. Who might look like anyone. Except me. You know I'm me."

"I do," he said, "because no one drives me batty like you." He must have heard how that sounded, and pulled up a smile, soft and genuine. "I'll throw kebabs on the grill."

"That sounds amazing. Need me to bring anything?" This was good. This was a way back to the neutral zone, toward solid non-yelling ground. I was breathing a little fast, my pulse thrumming in my ears.

"Beer. Any kind you choose is fine. It doesn't have to be…special."

"Right. Yeah. Yes."

Ryder swung up into the truck. My heart hammered away in my chest, still running through the routine, bruised, aching, but stretching for that final flip. I raised my hand in a wave.

Ryder didn't look back.

CHAPTER THIRTEEN

THAN WAITED ON THE SIDEWALK, his hands crossed in front of himself. The eye-watering short-sleeved, button-down shirt he wore was smothered in fluorescent flamingos bent into alphabet shapes. He had on a pair of knee-length chino shorts, white tube socks, and sandals.

I'd never seen his knees before. Or his shins. All together it was a little shocking to see him looking so vacation-y.

"You're really getting the hang of it here, aren't you?" I said.

"Why do you say so?"

I waved at the shirt, the shorts, the sandals. "You look like a proper tourist. I thought you were taking a walk for a couple days to clear your mind."

His eyes widened, and he glanced over my shoulder. "Well, I was? But you can see I am not?"

"I can see that. Did you need something?"

He pressed his thin lips together and gave me a conspiratorial nod. "Will you give me directions?"

"To where?"

"I believe it is a residence?"

"Uh-huh."

He leaned in slightly and lowered his voice even more. "Do you know where the demon lives?"

"Three choices in town. But I thought you knew where they live."

"I am...uh...unfamiliar with their current whereabouts?"

My phone buzzed. I pulled it out of my pocket and checked the screen. Myra. "Hold on. What's up?" I said to the phone.

"I just thought I should call you. Are you all right?"

"Other than sticking my foot in my mouth and almost cancelling my own wedding? I don't even own a pair of hip waders. What was I thinking? Yeah, I'm doing really great."

"Oh-kay," she said, dragging the word out. "Do we need to talk?"

I scowled. I knew what 'talk' would involve. Myra lecturing me on being my most honest self, and not sabotaging a good thing before I'd even gotten a chance to enjoy it, and to face my own crap and deal with it so I could be happy instead of grumpy and therefore more apt not to make everyone work overtime at the station.

"No, we don't need to talk. Ryder and I need to talk —hold on." I lowered the phone. "Where are you going?"

Than was several yards down the sidewalk,

wandering off like he had forgotten we were in mid-conversation. At my shout, he peered back over his shoulder. He looked a little guilty.

"Didn't you want an address?"

"Yes, but I have suddenly remembered I have... another...appointment?"

"Okay?" I said. He was acting a little strange—well, stranger—so I told Myra to hold on a second longer and jogged down to him.

"Are you sure you're okay?" I asked.

"Yes?" He waved a hand down his body, at the shirt, at the shorts, at his shins, his socks and sandals. "I need a walk to...clear my mind?"

I chuckled. "I have no idea why you're asking me. You're the one out here walking."

"Isn't that the truth?" he said. "Perhaps I will see you later?" He stretched those long legs of his and got moving.

I stared at him for a second. Something about that exchange had felt off. Awkward. But then, Than was always an unusual conversationalist. Still, he'd been a little twitchy. Or at least twitchier than I'd seen him.

He wasn't the sort of person that I'd ever say was overly emotional. Droll and unimpressed seemed to be his default.

But there was always something right behind that slightly bored mask. He had a crackling curiosity for all manner of things, a sense of humor he couldn't quite squelch with feigned disinterest.

He was kind, which was sort of a surprise, given his god power. He'd always been warm to me.

That conversation had just been awkward with none of that warm stuff. The kind stuff.

I wondered if a ghoul could take on the shape of a god.

We were both walking in opposite directions, but just in case, I turned and sniffed the air. I didn't smell anything ghoul-ish. All I smelled was dry concrete, exhaust, and cooked garlic from someone's kitchen.

"…going to hang up if you don't talk to me," Myra's voice came from my phone.

"Sorry," I said, heading back to my Jeep, but throwing one last look Than's way. He paused at the corner, looked both ways twice, then continued down the road. "I'm back. What were you saying?"

"Have you even set a date?"

I stepped up into my Jeep. "Technically?"

"Actually."

"Yes. We have a general time nailed down."

"A day?"

"Well, not that nailed down."

"A month? Tell me you landed on a month that works for both of you."

"So have you seen Than lately?"

"You haven't chosen a month? What's wrong with August? Or September when it's a little cooler?"

"Last I heard he was going on a long walk, right? Did he come back? I mean, I know he wasn't leaving Ordinary's boundaries because he'd have to pick up his power, but is he back from that?"

"We're going to ignore the wedding conversation? We know that won't make it go away."

"Is this the royal 'we'?"

"Dear lords, okay. Fine. Last I heard he was going for a walk a couple days ago, so yeah, he should be back around today or tomorrow."

"Okay, well, I think he is. I just talked to him."

"I thought I heard his voice in the background," she said. "And now you need to tell me why you were asking me where he was when you were looking at him."

I switched my phone to speaker and started the Jeep. "Odin and Zeus didn't see anything strange with the car. But I found some cardboard stuck in the trunk."

"That's good. That's something. Was it like the packages?"

"It had red ink on it. Also, we might have a ghoul in town. Hogan walked into the garage and smelled ghoul."

There was a pause, a stretch of silence as I flicked on my indicator and pulled out into traffic.

"A ghoul," she finally said.

"Whose ghoul?" Bathin's voice rumbled in the background.

"Nobody's," Myra answered. "What does ghoul smell like?"

"Rotted flesh and melted vinyl, according to Hogan. How about I stop by and fill you in on it?"

"No."

"No?"

"You only want to come by because you're avoiding something—and I'm going to guess it's dinner with your very patient, if slightly cheese-obsessed, fiancé."

I groaned. "But I have more stuff to tell you about the case."

"He'll figure out the cheese, Delaney."

"But then it will be flowers, and not just flowers, but award-winning flowers. He'll probably have them flown in from some exclusive hothouse in Antarctica, because only tropical frozen Baby's Breath will do."

"He'll figure out the flowers too."

"It was the crab," I said.

"Ryder wants crab? Well, at least that can be sourced locally."

"No. The ghoul was the crab."

"In the car? Are you sure?"

"No, but the chewed up crab claw we found could mean the ghoul saw you and Jean coming, found something to eat and boom. Crab escape."

"Crab escape," she repeated. "So you want me to put out an APB on a crab?"

"I'm guessing it switched forms pretty quickly after getting harangued by seagulls."

"And now it could be anything. Including seagulls."

I made a quick decision and headed toward the Puffin Muffin. Apology dessert might be a good move tonight.

"Yeah," I replied, "anything living."

"But how does that work with mass? I mean if a ghoul is of a certain size can it become something much smaller in mass, and also expand into something much larger? Are there rules for how it can take on likenesses? Does it have to change size in incremental amounts? Work its way up to a size or down to a size?"

"That sounds like something my brainy sister is going to figure out."

She huffed a little laugh. "Okay, yes. I'll check the lore. See what I can find about ghouls. If it was a ghoul in that car, then it wasn't breaking any of the god rules to get here. Other than falling out of the sky."

"Yeah, it doesn't have to put down powers or sign a contract to get into town. But still, if it didn't have anything to hide, it should have at least checked in with one of us and explained it wanted to live here."

"Maybe it's just visiting," she said.

"Maybe."

"Maybe it's just delivering a bunch of stolen god weapons, for reasons unknown."

"Yep. That's the maybe I'm stuck on too."

"I'll head out to the library tonight."

"Don't... No, don't let this ruin your evening. Unless you think there's a quick and easy way to spot a ghoul, then whatever you dig up can wait until morning."

She hesitated. "Are you sure?"

I turned into the Puffin Muffin's gravel parking lot, avoiding most of the potholes. "Do you think you need to go out there? Family gift-wise?"

"No."

"Then let's pick this up tomorrow."

"All right. Talk to Ryder."

"I plan to."

"Pick a date for the wedding at least."

"Yep."

"Delaney," she said, then the background noise

changed, and I thought she might have moved out of the room she'd been in with Bathin.

"Yeah?" I turned off the engine, and paused with one hand on the door.

"I know why Ryder's working so hard to make the wedding perfect."

"Yeah?" My heart was beating a little hard. This was part of what both baffled me and stressed me out: Why was he working on it as if it were some giant production? What kind of expectations did he have for this event?

"Because if he left it up to you, you'd overthink it and be flying to Antarctica to try and find flowers."

"Hilarious." I hung up on her laughter. Then, to absolutely no one: "I do not overthink things. Do I? No. Okay, maybe sometimes. Or maybe a lot of times. But only in certain circumstances. Which is normal, isn't it?"

I got out of the Jeep and strolled into the bakery. The place was mostly empty, which was a rarity for the shop, but we were rolling into dinner time and the bakery, which did the bulk of its business in the morning, would be closing soon.

Gale was working the counter and gave me a wide smile. "Hi, Delaney! What can I get you?" Gale was human and had been working at the bakery since she'd retired from teaching.

"I'm not going to ask what's good," I said, "because I know it's all good. So what's left?"

She leaned back and ducked a bit to scan the display case. "A few caramel snickerdoodle cookies, some of those mini fruit tarts, and three, no two kinds of brownies. We also have some refrigerated pie left. Um…I think a cheesecake, a key lime and a chocolate mocha silk."

"Better get me the pie. Let's do key lime."

"Special night?" she asked.

"Nope. This is an apology pie."

"Well, key lime is a good choice. Coffee to go?"

"I shouldn't."

"Aw, but apology, right?"

I laughed. "Yeah, why not? How about a nice dark roast. Make it two. And strong."

"Drop in a shot of espresso?

"Perfect."

"Let me just get that pie." She slipped through the door behind her.

I pulled out my phone and texted Ryder.

Bringing dessert

I pressed send, and stared at the screen, waiting for his answer.

Nothing.

Okay, either he was angry and ignoring me, or more likely, he was busy getting the grill ready for dinner and didn't have his phone on him.

But just in case it was the first thing, I sent another message.

Be home in 5

There was still no answer by the time Gale came back with the pie in the bright Puffin Muffin box.

"Two coffees, dark with espresso, yes?" she asked, even as she was pulling out cups and lids and prepping the machine.

"Yes." I thought about sending another message,

changed my mind and stuck the phone back in my pocket. I'd be home in five minutes, and whatever mood Ryder was in, I'd figure it out.

We'd talk. I'd tell him we should pick a date, for this year. September. I'd always liked September. It would be a good wedding date. A good anniversary date.

Just choosing the month settled something in me. I could imagine the fall colors, deep green fir trees, vine maples gone rust and gold. Maybe we'd hold it outdoors, even if it rained. I didn't think we had a place indoors large enough for everyone.

I could tell him all those things. Things I knew he'd already thought of. This could be the beginning of us being on the same page.

I'd admit I had invited all the gods to the wedding, and I was pretty sure I couldn't retract that. I'd admit I'd been pretty awful about the whole thing, had been over-thinking all of it and getting nowhere. I could step up. Do my part. Maybe mess with his orderly plans and add some fun to it.

"Need a carrier?"

"Sure," I said.

Gale placed everything on the counter. I handed over my card, and she rang me up.

"So have you decided on a wedding date yet?" she asked, as she punched buttons.

"Not yet. Why? Are you part of the betting pool?"

She laughed. "No, I just was hoping it was going to be soon. I got this cute dress I want to take out for a spin. If I'm invited to the reception, that is."

"You are. Of course you are. We're still working out all the details."

"Sure," she said. "Not a problem. This is going to be amazing. The wedding of the year."

I stepped aside as a young man walked in. "Please tell me you still have those caramel snickerdoodles."

"I still have a dozen," Gale said.

"Life saver." He dug out his wallet.

I waved over my shoulder and stepped outside.

Now all I had to do was stop at the store for beer, go home, offer up my apology pie, and tell Ryder I was ready, really ready to pick a date and get this wedding going.

CHAPTER FOURTEEN

I DIDN'T RECOGNIZE the green Mini Cooper parked in front of our house. Ryder's truck was in the drive. Light poured out through our living room windows, but that car...That car didn't look like any in Ordinary.

I got out of the Jeep and glanced at the California license plate, committing it to memory so I could run the tags if I needed to.

Even without a close look, I saw several hangers with dresses and maybe jackets hung in the back seat. Fingerprints scuffed the dust on the trunk, and road dirt flecked the wheel wells.

Someone had been on the road for a while. Maybe visiting, maybe moving.

I wondered who that somebody was.

I balanced the pie, coffee and beer, thinking it might be too much—too much like an overreaction, too much like an apology I'd overthought and I wasn't sure would be accepted—and walked up to the front door.

I tried the handle. It wasn't locked. I paused with the door half open.

I didn't smell the grill he said he'd have ready for dinner. I didn't hear the music Ryder usually played when he was home alone.

What I heard was a woman's laughter. A stranger's laughter.

Time stretched through a *tick, tick, tick*, and everything in me went numb.

Why was there a stranger in our home? Why was she laughing, and why was Ryder laughing along with her, their voices pitched low like they were sharing secrets?

Was she a friend? A customer?

From another state this late in the evening?

My heart thudded against my breastbone, hot and sick. It felt like —

—*jealousy*—

—something was wrong. Something was wrong about a strange woman from California being in my living room.

In *our* living room.

I was over-reacting. I was taking huge jumps to conclusions that I had absolutely no facts to back up. Maybe Myra was right about the overthinking thing.

I just needed to be calm. To use logic.

But then, so many things in Ordinary weren't logical. Following my instincts, following my gut, even overthinking things usually worked out for me.

All of those thoughts flashed by in seconds. Then I

unstuck myself, took a quick breath and called out as I walked through the doorway.

"Hey! I'm home. I brought pie." I strode into the foyer. Which led right to the kitchen and open living room.

The fire was going, even though it had been a warm day, but Spud and Dragon pig were not curled up as usual in front of it with their pile of toys. As a matter of fact, all the toys that got dragged daily into the room were missing.

What else was missing was my fiancé, but from the voices coming from beyond the sliding glass doors, I knew he was outside. Maybe starting the grill.

Maybe dishing food for the woman, who was saying, "RyRy—that's so great! Just so great!" in a we're-not-doing-anything-we-shouldn't-be-doing voice pitched loud enough I was pretty sure she, at least, had heard my entrance.

I stowed the pie in the fridge, put the beer in there too. I didn't know what to do with the coffee, so I just left one of the cups by the toaster, and took a couple big gulps out of the other one.

Whoever it was sounded like a friend, someone Ryder knew. She hadn't left a purse or a coat behind, there were no kicked off shoes in the entry, so she probably hadn't been here long and wasn't planning to stay.

Okay. A friend was good. I wanted to meet more of the friends he'd made when not living in Ordinary. The—

—*jealousy*—

—worry I'd felt when I'd first seen the car was gone

now, shoved aside so that there was only room for curiosity. Ryder rarely talked about his friends from college, from the years he'd spent working for the architecture company in Chicago.

The only people he'd mentioned more than once were his boss at the firm he worked at, and a classmate he tried to keep in touch with online.

Well, he'd had to talk a little about the DoPP monster hunters he'd gotten involved with, especially since one of them had come to town a year after he'd been here and stirred up trouble.

We were a town full of supernaturals. Gods too. We would be an absolute gold mine for a monster hunter.

Which was why we kept a low profile. Most people in Ordinary didn't know their neighbors were anything other than what they appeared to be and it was my job to keep it that way.

One more sip of coffee, relax the shoulders, smile, and off I went to the deck.

"Beautiful, but the winters are pretty rough," Ryder said.

"Oh, RyRy, you know I like it a little rough."

"Hi," I said, pushing the door wider and leaning there. "Are we grilling tonight?"

Ryder and the woman—the very lovely woman with wide eyes and tanned skin and golden hair twisted back so most of it cascaded down around her shoulders—glanced up at me.

She looked fresh and carefree, like she'd just come from the forest, or the beach; hemp bracelets on one wrist, the lightest blush nail polish and a couple silver

167

rings on her hands. I quickly cataloged the rest: flowing skirt and white tank—both designer—and perfume with notes of cocoa.

Okay, not the forest or the ocean. She looked like she'd just come out of a boutique that charged big bucks to make you look like a boho babe.

Interesting.

"Hey, Delaney," Ryder said, not moving from where he sat on our outdoor couch, which gave the best angle of the lake below. "Thought you were busy at Myra's."

"We wrapped it up pretty quick." I stepped onto the deck, glanced at the grill, which was not heating. "Do you want to introduce me?"

"Oh, sure. Say, Vivian, this is Delaney, my fiancé."

"What?" Vivian laughed and slapped Ryder on the arm playfully. She sat right next to him, cozied up as if there wasn't any space on the couch except pressed against his side, which was not true. We'd bought that couch and wanted it to last. Wrestling that huge beast of a thing through the door had been a pain.

I knew how big that couch was. It sat three with a dog. Three.

"You didn't even tell me you had a girlfriend," she cooed. "Naughty."

"Fiancé," I said, leaning forward to offer my hand. "Chief Delaney Reed."

For just a half second, her eyes sharpened, and her body language projected something dangerous, something ready to spring.

That second passed, then she tossed her hair back

and dropped her fingertips into my hand. They were cold and dry.

"I'm Vivian, well, I'll be Viv to you from now on because I am officially your best friend!" She stood, her fingers hooking and holding. Even though she didn't use me as leverage, I could feel the coiled strength in her.

Was she a supernatural? Some kind of monster in disguise?

Before I could finish that thought, she threw her arms around me and squeezed, once, twice, three times, each squeeze harder than the last. "I am so happy to meet the woman who makes my RyRy so happy."

I stood there like a plank, let her get the hug over with, and as soon as I was released, took another drink of coffee.

Human, I thought, from being that close to her. Annoying. Fake. Maybe hiding something. But human.

"Oh," she said, looking at my drink. "I would love a cup. It was such a drive. And traffic—I thought I'd never get out of LA. Tell me you have more?"

"Kitchen by the toaster."

She slapped one hand over her heart like I'd just handed her the Academy Award. "I'll just…" She puppy-dog begged with her hands, dipping them up and down to mimic a trot, and then turned and strolled into our house.

Once she was gone, I studied Ryder. He sprawled with one arm across the back of the couch, his long legs kicked out in front of him. Watching me, relaxed, like nothing was wrong. If I didn't know him as well as I did, I might believe it.

But his jaw was set and the one hand curled in a fist told me something was wrong.

"RyRy, huh?"

He sighed. "Apparently."

"That's super cute."

He raised an eyebrow.

"And you know Vivian from?"

"She's going to tell you she contracted for our company. Did all the decor for the condos we built."

"All right. What are you going to tell me?"

He opened his mouth, then his eyes went to her purse, which was a natural fiber macramé-type thing with wooden beads. He frowned.

"I'm going to tell you I love you," he got up off of the couch, "and I missed you." He was smiling and advancing on me, but the change of subject was a cover. "And I want to know what kind of pie you brought me as an apology."

"Who said I was apologizing?" Then he was right there in front of me, and all the clever things I'd been about to say dried up to dust. It was everything I could do not to just fall into his arms.

"I hate fighting with you," I said.

His hands landed heavy on my hips and he searched my face, maybe trying to decide if that was my apology. "Delaney." He leaned forward, his mouth right next to my ear, so close I could feel the stubble on his cheek. "She's a monster hunter."

And, yeah, maybe I was distracted by his touch, by his nearness, by the scent of his shampoo and deodorant that had become the scent of home to me. But it took me a second.

"Who?"

"Vivian. I worked with her at DoPP."

It hit all at once, hard as a slap. "We have a monster hunter in our house?"

"Shhh." He pulled me closer. "She left her purse and might be recording us."

I tucked my head into his shoulder and hoped that if I was being recorded, it was only audio. "We have a monster hunter in our town?"

"Yep. She said she's stopping by to catch up, like old times."

"Bullcrap," I said into the warm cotton of his shirt.

"I know. How do you want to deal with it?"

"She's not leaving?"

"I don't know."

"Well, I don't want her snooping around our house." I pulled back, and he nodded at my fake smile.

"Did you find the coffee?" I called out as I made a quick trip through the doors and living room.

Vivian was not in the kitchen.

"Vivian?" I started down the hall.

She was walking toward me, smiling and innocent like she hadn't been snooping.

"Did you get lost?" I asked nicely.

"What? Oh, no. Silly." She was close enough she tapped me on the arm, then kept her hand there. Holding me in place.

It was a subtle power move.

I didn't like it.

I didn't like her.

"I just had to use the little girl's room. Coffee's this way, right? By the toaster?"

I did some calculations for how long she'd been out of our sight. Two minutes. Maybe three. Long enough to do a quick look around of the bottom floor.

"Yep," I said, switching our hold so I had her arm and could move her more easily. "Right in here." I gave her a full-watt smile and started walking so she'd have to start moving.

"When did you meet Ryder?" she asked, pressing close to me all buddy-buddy like.

"I grew up here and he did too. So I've known him for a long time."

"Oh, that's so romantic. I don't know why he never mentioned you!" She laughed like we were both in on just the greatest joke.

I knew what she was doing. I knew her type. Had been around this chummy-with-claws kind of person more than once in my life.

"So how long are you staying?" I asked, moving in front of her to get the coffee and then handing it to her.

"Didn't Ryder tell you?"

I lifted my fingers to indicated that no, he hadn't.

"Well, he does like to keep secrets, doesn't he? I bet he never even mentioned me."

I bit the inside of my cheek to keep from telling her she could pack up her game board because I wasn't gonna play.

"Are you looking for a hotel for the night?" I opened

the fridge and pulled out cream and flavored creamer, putting them on the counter next to her.

She sipped the coffee and then frowned at the cup. "This is really good."

"We Pacific North Westerners know good flannel, good blue jeans, and good coffee."

She reached for the cream and poured a dollop. "I couldn't possibly bother you and Ryder to put me up on the couch for the night."

"No," I said, "you couldn't. But the Sand Garden should have a room open. Or if you'd rather a bed and breakfast we have one of those in town too."

"I wouldn't want to be in the way."

"Of what? Ordinary counts on touristry. We have plenty of local shops, a couple restaurants, a brew pub, and of course the beach, which is never crowded, and 100% public access."

She made a sound like she was impressed. Then glanced over her shoulder as if she were expecting Ryder to be standing there. "You're the police chief here, is that right?"

"Yes."

"I would love to do a ride along. See what small-town policing looks like these days. Maybe write up an article about how one little town in Oregon keeps the peace."

"Article? I thought you did interior design?"

She blinked, her expression freezing before her smile was back on. "Oh, I do. I'm sure Ryder told you I did the decor for all his most prestigious clients back in the day. But since then, I've spent some time in California, and decided my passion is writing. Not screenplays, which is what everyone always asks me down there. You know," she made a weird smiling grimace, "Hollywood. But I write feel-good, slice-of-life travel pieces. I like to make people happy. Totally a people pleaser, you know."

What I knew was she was spinning a line of horse hockey.

"Well, the Sand Garden has a great view of the beach. I'm sure they'd love to be mentioned in your slice-of-life."

"I'm not a hotel reviewer, Delaney. I'm a journalist."

What she was was a spy snooping around my town looking for monsters. I didn't like it. I didn't like her. And I didn't like her suddenly showing up when we had a ghoul on the loose, and stolen god weapons popping up on doorsteps.

I sniffed, trying to sense if there was anything ghoulish about her, but she smelled the same, the kitchen smelled the same, and all I wanted was for her to get a hotel room and leave my house.

"Just a teensy little ride along?" she asked. "Please, Delaney? Half a day? A few hours is all I'm asking. It would just mean everything to me."

Fact: I do not like being manipulated.

Fact: I do not like being manipulated by a stranger.

Fact: I do not like being manipulated by a stranger who was also hunting supernaturals in a town full of supernaturals who were my friends.

"Not going to happen. Even in a small town, police business can be dangerous. We don't let anyone ride along."

"Boo," she said, sticking out her lower lip before taking another sip of coffee. "Maybe Ryder will show me around instead."

I opened my mouth to tell her good luck with that, but the back room door smacked open and a set of paws and hooves hit the hallway running.

Spud was barking his *danger protect* bark, and I hurried into the hallway to head him off at the pass.

"Spud," I called. "Hey, Spuddo, it's okay."

I'd never heard him snarl like that as he tried to push his way into the kitchen. I caught his collar right before he skidded around the corner and pulled him back before he could reach Vivian.

He did not like her.

Good. Neither did I.

"That's enough," I said. "Settle down." I put one hand on his back haunches to get him to sit, but he resisted, sidestepping. He was big enough and strong enough, I had to tug on his collar to keep him from barreling forward.

I was so busy with the dog, I didn't even notice the dragon pig.

"Oh my god!" Vivian squealed. "Is that a pig? Delaney, do you own a pig? Of course you do—just look at you. Come here little fella. Hey, there cutie patootie. Here piggy piggy piggy."

Fortunately, I managed to get Spud to lay off his "attack" mode. Unfortunately, I had another terrifying situation on my hands.

This woman had just said: "here piggy piggy piggy" to a dragon. A dragon who could be a real grump sometimes. A dragon who could devour cars, houses, maybe even cities if it really got a good angry binge going.

A dragon who could swallow this woman down in one lazy chomp.

I was half-bent over Spud, hand still on his collar. Out of the corner of my eye, I saw Ryder moving this way fast. But my real attention was lasered in on the dragon pig.

It had been trotting along, maybe heading into the living room, maybe heading to the fire where it liked to bask at night, maybe heading toward its hoard of toys.

But as soon as it heard that "piggy piggy" it stopped in its tracks, one front leg still raised. Its little pink head swiveled. Its eyes narrowed and one ear flopped back as it glowered up at her.

"Oh, aren't you a darling?" Vivian bent over and stretched her fingers out toward the dragon pig.

The dragon pig rolled its eyes toward me. I shook my head and mouthed "don't," but right then, her fingers stretched out just that bit more and she booped it on the nose.

Booped the dragon pig.

The dragon pig unhinged its jaw. I faked a sideways stumble to get between it and her.

It growled, but I raised my voice to cover the noise. "Ryder! Can you take over Spud here, maybe put him outside, and I'll…um…handle the pig?"

He was there instantly, switching off to hold Spud's collar, and gently talking to the dog. I turned my back on Vivian keeping the dragon pig out of her line of sight. I bent and scooped up the dragon and pulled it against my chest.

Its eyes were burning red with blue centers. I'd never seen that much fire in them before. I mouthed, *monster hunter*. Then out loud, "Cool it, okay?"

The dragon pig growled again, but it was all vibration. No sound.

"That's good," I said. "You're good."

Ryder muscled Spud down the hall toward the spare room.

Vivian straightened. "What are you—can I hold it?" If she suspected the pig was anything other than a pig, she didn't show it.

"You don't want to hold it."

"But I do. I really do. Look at the sweet little piggy-poo face."

I felt the dragon pig tense in my arms, and I knew if I handed it over to that woman she would be burned to a crispy snack.

"It pees."

The dragon pig huffed a weird little *oink* that sounded like outrage.

"Oh, I'm sure it's fine."

"No, no," I pulled the pig back, tucking it into my side in a football hold. "Anyone who picks it up gets wet. Dripping."

"It's not peeing on you."

"That's because..." Warm liquid trickled down my shirt and pants.

Ew. I didn't even know the dragon knew how to pee.

It had never peed in all the time it had been with us. Which might be why it just kept on peeing. And peeing.

Gross.

"Oh, that's hilarious!" She clapped. "Where is my camera? I need a picture of this."

"Gotta clean it up!" I shouted.

I jogged down the hall to the bathroom, passing Ryder who was talking Spud into staying in the small spare room we used as an office. There was a bed in there for him and the dragon pig, several of their favorite toys, and a water dish.

"Stay here, boy. I'll get you dinner in a minute," Ryder said.

I pushed into the bathroom and plopped the pig down in the sink.

"Oh my gods. That was disgusting!"

The dragon pig growled and stomped its little piggy feet pacing a circle in the sink.

"You didn't have to pee on me," I hissed.

It stopped pacing and planted two front feet on the edge of the sink. Smoke curled up from its nostrils and it rumbled at me.

"Don't give me that look." I shucked off my shirt and got a washcloth wet from the tub spigot. "It was the first thing I could think of."

It snarled.

"No," I said. "Because you were already growling at her and pigs don't growl."

It grumped while I finished washing away dragon pee, which was colorless and smelled like burnt marshmallow.

Knuckles softly rapped on the door. "Got you a new shirt." Ryder opened the door and stood there, grinning.

I grabbed his wrist and pulled him into the bathroom. "Not that I'd ever say no to a quicky," he said, crowding all up in my space, "but we have company." He pressed the bright orange Henley into my hands, and stepped back.

"Hey, buddy," he said to dragon pig. "Nice work out there."

Its little curly tail wagged.

I shrugged into the shirt and rucked the sleeves up to my elbows. "She needs to get out of here," I whispered.

"Motel for the night. Sand Garden?"

"Yes. She wants to do a ride along."

"I can handle that."

"She is not riding along with you to spy on this town."

"You want her spying on the town on her own? Because that's what she'll do. She'll poke around until she finds something we can't explain. And then the entire DoPP will be down our throats."

I ran through options, trying to come up with other ways to deal with her. But his idea of basically letting her think she was seeing all of our town while actually being babysat by someone who could steer her away from the worst of it was the best chance we had of convincing her we were just a normal, boring, ordinary beach town.

"Fuck," I whispered.

"It will be okay."

"How long?"

"With her? Week, tops."

"Fuck."

"But hey, at least I won't be focusing on the wedding so much."

"Not funny."

He shrugged and from the purse of his lips and the twinkle in his eyes, I knew he thought he was hilarious.

"A little funny," he said.

"Are we sharing secrets?" Vivian called out. "I love secrets. Did Ryder tell you about that night we both flew into New Orleans and there weren't any rooms left? About how we ended up sleeping on the couch in suite of a very nice older couple who liked to swing?"

I raised an eyebrow. Ryder's face slashed red at the cheeks.

"It was a weird weekend," he muttered.

"You'll have to tell me sometime."

I turned to the dragon pig. "No more peeing to the rescue, got it?"

It squeaked.

I picked it up and put it on the floor, then opened the bathroom door. "Off to bed," I told it. I moved to follow, bur Ryder caught my hand, and pulled gently.

"Nothing happened between us. She not my type. I've never trusted her. She has too many secrets and hidden agendas."

"I know," I said. "We got this." I squeezed his hand, he squeezed back. Then I walked over to the spare room to make sure dragon pig was settled.

Dragon pig was in the middle of its little bed,

kicking toys across the room. Spud picked up the stuffed octopus and carried it over, wagging his tail.

The pig grumbled, but accepted the toy, then dropped down on the bed like an angry little pink rock. Spud curled up around it.

I shut the door.

"Are we doing something naughty?" Vivian strolled into the hallway, all loose and cat-like, her gaze sharp.

She was looking for something. She was looking to make trouble between Ryder and me, sure, though I didn't know what her angle was there. We were in love. We were living together. We were going to get married.

She was out of luck if she thought she could drive a wedge between us.

But it was clear she was still a hunter looking for living breathing beings who were not supposed to exist.

Hell, maybe she thought I was something supernatural. Being the Bridge for the god powers to be set down and stored was a power no other human had.

A chill washed down my spine as it suddenly occurred to me that I could be the something she wanted to tag and bag and throw into a governmental test lab.

Yeah, that wasn't going to happen.

"We were just talking over the motel options," I said. "Sand Garden is the best."

Ryder stepped out of the bathroom. "It will have a room open for sure. Need directions?"

She bit her bottom lip, then smiled. "In a town this small? I don't think I'll have any trouble finding it. But," she looked up through her eyelashes at him, "I still haven't had dinner. I wouldn't want Delaney to get jealous, me keeping you all to myself, but maybe you and I could get a bite to eat and catch up?"

Someone else might not have seen it, the slight tightening of Ryder's stance, the way he hitched one shoulder down just that smallest amount. But I'd been staring at Ryder for years.

When he was a boy, and the way he threw a rock in the water made me wonder how he could be so strong and amazing.

When he was a gangly teen, and his voice wobbled and his laugh deepened.

When he'd broadened, put on muscles and height and fallen into the easy manner that drew people to him like bees to nectar.

He didn't like this woman, and just like he'd told me, he didn't trust her.

"Or," I said, "you two could catch up tomorrow. You must be tired from your long drive."

She raised her eyebrows and gave me a look of mock-shock. "How do you know I had a long drive?"

"Your car has California plates."

"Maybe I've been in Oregon for a while."

"Have you?"

She laughed, and it sounded forced. "No, not really. I drove straight through, and I *am* awfully hungry. Are there any cute little diners you can take me to, RyRy? Please feed the little birdy?"

She reached over and held on to his forearm. Laying a claim on him. Exerting her control.

Ryder was a lot less subtle than I'd been. He picked

up her perfectly manicured hand and dropped it off his arm.

"Delaney and I had plans," he said.

"No, that's okay," I interrupted, because Ryder was right. She should not be left to wander around Ordinary alone. Not until I got the word out that there was a hunter in our midst. Ryder taking her to dinner was the best move. He'd keep an eye on her, and I could get the info spreading through town.

"I'm probably going to turn in early after I do a little paperwork anyway." I put my palm on the small of Ryder's back and gave him a little push toward her so he'd know I was on for his plan.

"You want me to bring you back something to eat?" he asked.

"Naw. I'll just make a sandwich."

"Or that pie," Vivian said. "Although how sad is it, you sitting here all alone eating an entire pie while I'm out on the town with your handsome boyfriend?"

"Fiancé," I corrected. "You two have fun." I gave her a big ol' smile which made her frown, so I kept smiling. "Don't eat anything I wouldn't eat."

Ryder tossed a bemused look my way, but got moving.

"Let's take two cars," he was saying as he ushered her out the door. "That way you can head straight to your motel after."

"Boo. What if little birdy wants a night cap?"

"Or worms for breakfast?" I muttered. Apparently, a little too loudly.

They both turned to me.

Vivian burst out laughing. "You want a little sleep over, RyRy?" she asked. "You could give me a nice juicy worm for breakfast."

Oh, for the love of gods. This woman.

Ryder did a top-notch job of not rolling his eyes.

"Or," Ryder said, "we could meet you for breakfast."

"Forget the worm comment," I mumbled.

"Of course," she said, her hand landing on Ryder's forearm again. "She is just adorably awkward, isn't she? I didn't know you had a thing for small town girls."

"Just the one," he said, his voice growly enough to make my stomach flip. "You better leave me some of that pie," he said to me.

"You mean the key lime I picked up from Hogan's? Your favorite pie? That pie?"

He groaned a little. "Yes. That pie."

"I'll do what I can, but I'm awfully hungry. I missed my chance at kebobs."

He stepped up to me and kissed me hard, then growled over my mouth. "You'll pay for this."

Then he was gone, shoulders square, easy-likeable-guy smile on his face, following Vivian out the door.

I stood there for a moment, my fingers pressed to my lips, savoring the heat of that kiss.

CHAPTER FIFTEEN

I OPENED the door for Spud and the dragon pig. "You can come on out. She's gone."

My phone buzzed and I was not surprised to see Myra's number.

"Hey," I said.

"So what's going on?" she asked distractedly. I heard a low voice in the background, and then something that sounded an awful lot like a kiss. At least my sister got to spend her evening with the man of her dreams.

"There's a monster hunter in town."

"What?" A shuffle of sounds came through the phone, then a soft *whump* of a pillow, and a deep chuckle. "Okay, you have my attention. Where are you? Are you okay?"

"I'm at home. I'm fine. Ryder's taking her out to dinner, then getting her settled in the Sand Garden for the night."

"Her? So our monster hunter is a woman? Is she a paranormal investigator? Ghost hunter?"

"She works for DoPP."

"Well, shit."

"Yeah."

"Why is she here now?"

"She used to work with Ryder. I came home, and she was out on the deck giggling and flirting with him."

"That bitch."

Gotta love sister loyalty.

"She's a piece of work. I wouldn't trust her near my silver."

"What does Ryder think is going on?"

"We didn't have much time to talk and didn't want to let her out in the town on her own. Since she," I pitched my voice into babytalk, "just wants to catch up with my RyRy."

"Gag."

"He took her to have dinner. I'm guessing the Blue Owl, but he didn't say."

"Okay, so which part of town do you want me to cover?"

"I'll call Bertie, and that should take care of half the town right there. But we'll need to make sure the gods, and all the anti-socials know to keep a low profile."

"I'll take south, put Jean on door-to-door east. Where do you want Hatter and Shoe?"

"Give them north. Kelby can door-to-door west. And I'll talk to Than. See if he wants to pitch in or lay low."

"Want my vote?" she asked.

"Lay low?"

"Subterranean."

"I'll see if I can convince him."

"Good. Okay, call if you need anything."

"Will do."

I needed to call Bertie and have her tap into her massive list of the supernaturals in town who she conscripted for community events. She kept email lists, social media profiles, and good old-fashioned phone trees memorized. Telling Bertie to find people was like asking a fish if it would enjoy a dip in the water.

So I cut a hunk of pie, then dialed our local Valkyrie.

———

BERTIE GOT the word out so fast, I wasn't sure any of the rest of us needed to go door-to-door. But the safety of the people in my town wasn't something I took lightly, so I was out doing my part of the knocking.

I drove up to Old Rossi's first, knowing he could spread the word to his clan of vampires faster than I'd be able to do it by checking in on each vampire one-at-a-time. I knocked on his door, and was surprised when Rossi himself opened it.

"Delaney. You're working late."

Rossi was rangy as a runner or yoga instructor. His dark hair had a streak of silver spreading back from his temple, which was new since he'd been almost killed by Lavius, an ancient evil who had been more-or-less his brother.

He wore a patch made of very soft, probably expensive, material over his left eye which he'd lost in that battle. His right eye was filled with a deep light that brightened the ice-blue of it. With the soft gray pants and loose, cream-colored tunic with embroidery on the cuffs, he looked like a rich retired hippie.

"Your voice sounds better," I noted.

He leaned his shoulder against the door jam, his glittering eye taking on the growing shadows behind me.

"Thank you. Is this a social visit? At this time of night? What would your fiancé say?"

"He'd say I work too many hours, but he knows this time it isn't my fault."

"Is it ever?" he asked, holding back a smile.

"Sometimes," I said, with a shrug. "But not tonight."

"Come on in."

He moved so I could step in, and shut the door behind me.

The living room was scattered with comfortable couches and chairs, rich patterned rugs, and art on the walls that didn't look fussy, but probably cost a couple arms and legs. Three of the Rossi clan were gathered on the couch and a chair, a table with a complicated looking board game set up between them.

Senta, who worked on our emergency response team, and Keenan who often pulled night shifts at the lumber yard, came into the room carrying sodas and bags of chips tucked under their arms.

The Rossis usually got their sustenance from the blood drive bags, but even vampires got the munchies.

"Chief." Senta tipped her chin at me, her silver-white hair swinging with the movement. Leon lifted a couple fingers and the others in the living room raised a hand my way without looking.

I waved back to the crew.

It was great to see his family here, relaxing and hanging out. It was even better to see that not one of them were hovering near him, snarling at anything that approached.

They'd nearly lost him. We'd all nearly lost him. But he'd finally turned the healing corner. He looked much more solid. Strong. The relief from every vampire in the room was palpable.

"Did you hear we have a monster hunter in town?" I asked.

"Yes."

"Bertie, right? She is *fast*."

"It's a requirement in her line of work."

I didn't know if he meant dragging dead heroes off the battleground or dragging volunteers into community events. Both worked.

"Vivian Dunn," he said. "Is she government?"

"That's her last name?"

"Bertie," he said.

"Okay, so that's her last name. Yeah, Vivian will tell you she handled interior design for that company Ryder worked for in Chicago, but now she's found journalism and wants to write about all the quirky little backwater towns she travels through. To make people happy."

"Which is utter yak shit. Do you know if she's looking for something in particular?"

"I don't know if she was tipped off, or if she just decided to roll through Ordinary because Ryder was here. She might have been sent to find out why he quit the DoPP. But why now? At the worst damn time, too."

"Well, not the worst," he said. "Unless Bertie's throwing a three-ring circus again?"

The vampires snorted.

"Oh, gods, no. Can you imagine?"

"I don't have to. I was there for the last one. Roselord the Ravishing." He made a loopy hand wave from forehead to waist amid several gagging sounds from the peanut gallery.

"Dare I guess what your act was?"

"Oh, I hope you dare."

"Striptease."

That got one bark of a laugh out of Senta. She gave me a thumbs-up while crunching through a chip.

"It could have been," he said, pitching his voice to the others in the room. "But no. I was a hypnotist."

"Holy crap, I bet you blew them away."

"I would have. If your grandmother hadn't stepped in. She drew the line at my suggestions that each person drop off a few bucks every month to the Rossi Family Farm."

"I forgot you were into farming back then. Why did you even get into farming?"

He grinned. "Life is change. I wanted to try something different."

"I am never shoveling cow shit again, Rossi," Leon said. "Or yak shit."

Rossi waggled his eyebrows, then whispered to me, "We'll see."

"No *we* will not see," Leon sang out. "If *you* want

cows, find some that shovel their own shit." Dice hit the table with a little more force, and I bit the inside of my lip to keep from laughing.

It was good to see Rossi giving them a hard time and them dishing it right back. If there was one thing I could count on from each and every supernatural in Ordinary, it was that they liked being here. They liked living a quiet, ordinary life and they didn't want that to change.

The other thing I could count on with my friends, who were more like family, really, was that they'd rise up to any challenger who came at this town and the people in it.

"Okay, so maybe it's not the worst possible time. Not circus time," I said, "but not great either. You heard about the god weapons?"

"Of course." Most of the Rossis held down full-time jobs. While not being blood related, they were all beneath the protection and laws of Old Rossi himself. They were close knit, and if I were honest, a little gossipy.

"And the ghoul?"

His relaxed posture changed instantly. He straightened and lifted his head, his nostrils flaring like he could smell danger in the air.

"Ghoul?"

"Yes. Hogan said he smelled one. Wait, let me back up. A car fell out of the sky this morning. Did you hear about that?"

"Landed on the beach off 50th. A muscle car. Was there anything in it? Were there injuries?"

"No injuries. We thought it was empty, but a crab crawled out of it."

"We have a crab ghoul on the loose?"

"No. Yes. Maybe."

"Well, that clears it up."

"We took the car to Frigg's so we could go over it. Odin and Zeus were there too, but only Hogan smelled ghoul on it."

"Ghouls don't have a smell."

"Hogan says they do, and he said they stink."

"That's…" Rossi stared off over my shoulder, and I wondered how much information he had stored away in that head of his. "It's possible. His father was a Jinn and his mother always seemed to have something…" He drifted off again, remembering people I'd never met.

I didn't even know Rossi knew them, since they hadn't come to live in Ordinary with Hogan, preferring warmer oceans. "Something *mmm* about her," he said.

"Is *mmm* magic?"

"I never found out. Are you sure Hogan wasn't the ghoul?"

"No, but Jean was there, and she would have known."

"Doom twinges?"

"Yeah."

"So you came here to tell me Hogan's going door-to-door to smell people?"

"Since it can take on the shape of any biological thing in town? No. He's going to let me know if he smells it, but Myra's looking into other ways we might be able to ferret it out."

"Do those ways involve vampires?"

"Not unless you know something about ghouls I should know."

"I've never met one I liked."

"Good to know. Made any enemies among them?"

"Briefly. Before I killed them."

I rubbed at the headache that been building behind my eyes all day. I wondered if I'd had any water today, or if it had been all coffee all the time.

From the slight ringing in my ears, I figured I'd gone full throttle on the java for a full twenty-four.

"How did you kill them?"

He smiled, and this time there was a little fang in it. "Any way that was available. They are not a fully living thing, which is why they prefer raw flesh."

"Gross," one of the players muttered.

"Says the man who mainlines sushi," Senta said.

"Fish aren't flesh. They're whatever delicious is."

I lifted my eyebrows, waiting for Rossi's real answer.

"Break a ghoul's neck," he said, "snap the spine. Smash enough of it, it can't maintain the shape it's stolen. There are other things: weapons, spells," he gave me a nod, "which are much less messy. And of course, much less satisfying."

"Good to know."

"Are you assuming it's still a crab? Because with all the marine life around here..."

"Crab sushi is also what delicious is," one of the other vamps allowed.

"...and other sushi afficionados," Rossi went on, "your ghoul problem might take care of itself."

"But why would it remain a crab? I think that was a disguise it used to sneak into Ordinary."

"And why is it sneaking into Ordinary?"

"That's always the question, isn't it? So many people who are used to hiding show up here and it's natural for them to think they are safer if they remain hidden. I'd think that was the case here, though dropping out of the sky in a car is the opposite of subtle."

"But?"

"But the stolen god weapons showed up at the same time. It might not be connected, or it might be we have a ghoul who somehow got into several god realms, nicked powerful weapons, and then left them on doorsteps."

"Never a dull moment around here, is there?"

"No. So keep your head down. Tell your people we need everyone to keep a low profile until we can get the hunter out of town."

"You know us. We are the shadow. We are the night."

More scoffing from the peanut gallery.

Rossi grinned. "Since you're here, I'd like to make an official request."

"Okay?"

"I prefer winter weddings."

"Nope."

"And not in a church—too stuffy, if you know what I mean."

"Not listening." I had the door open.

"Maybe serve those little shrimp cocktail things?"

"Or sushi," Leon called out.

"Gluten free, certainly," Rossi went on, "O positive preferred, so I hope you'll run a keto-friendly blood drive to stock up."

"Good bye, Rossi. I sure hope a ghoul doesn't eat you alive." I slammed the door on his cackling and stomped down the steps to my Jeep.

It was fully dark now, the air wet and salty and clean. I paused and took a deep breath, staring up at the sky where a scatter of stars glittered like ice in moonlight. The wind sifted through trees and brush, and I suddenly thought: this had been my home for all my life. These had been my stars, this had been my wind.

This would always be my home. I understood that when I took up being the Bridge for god powers. I knew I would live no other place than here and took solace in the security of it.

Ryder and I had managed to sneak off for a quick vacation a few months ago. It had been strange to leave this place for so long but after a day or so, it had been wonderful not to worry about everything in Ordinary. Not to worry about everyone.

I knew getting married wouldn't change how I looked after our town. But it would change something in me. I didn't know what that was, since I'd never been married, but that commitment, which I'd already given once when I committed my whole soul to this town, frightened me.

"You think it's safe to be out here all alone?"

I glanced down and searched for the owner of that familiar voice.

A shadow shifted near the dense line of Sitka spruce and stepped toward me.

"I'm not alone. There's a bunch of vampires who can hear us. You spying on me, Crow?"

"No, just following you around."

I grinned. "Need a lift?"

He stopped on the other side of the Jeep. "Telling the Rossis about the monster hunter or the ghoul?"

"Both."

"How'd they take it?"

"Didn't even look away from the game."

"They're watching a game?"

"Playing one. Complicated-looking board game with a bunch of pieces and dice."

"Those bastards," he said. "They're having a game night and didn't invite me? I love games!"

"You love cheating at games."

"Damn right I do, and I do not appreciate them taking that away from me." He started toward the house, and I was pretty sure he was just putting on a show, but in case he wasn't I grabbed his arm.

"Let them have a good time without you."

"They'd have a better time with me."

"I'd have a better time without you," I muttered.

"Oh, kitten. So catty." He grinned. "I heard the monster hunter knows Ryder."

"Yeah." I opened the Jeep. Crow walked around to the other side and got in the passenger seat.

"I also noticed them out having dinner together."

"Yeah."

"Wanna talk about it?"

"I don't. I want her gone. It bothers me that she's here right now. What is she hunting? Did it lead her here? Or did she just decide she wanted to find out why Ryder quit the monster-hunting business? Or is it something else?"

"Like maybe she's the ghoul."

"It's possible, but I don't think she is."

I started the Jeep and flicked on the headlights. "Home?" I asked him.

"I'd rather go with you. Share the good word about our monster hunter, ghoul thing."

"You really think she's the ghoul?"

"Do you?"

And it was weird, but I knew in my gut she wasn't. For one thing, the ghoul would have to have eaten a part of the real Vivian Dunn to take on the shape of her. And that would mean the real Vivian had been nearby. Or the ghoul had eaten her then driven her car here to get all handsy with Ryder, and…yeah. None of that fit together easily.

Answers to these sorts of problems were usually the most obvious.

"I'll send Hogan by to smell her," I said.

"Kinky."

"He can smell ghouls."

"Oh-kay," Crow said. "I didn't think they had a smell."

"It's a Jinn thing, as far as I know." I dialed Jean. She answered on the first ring.

"…my boss, so I'll be going now. Hey, Delaney, what do you need?"

"Where are you?" I asked, curious why she was trying to get out of a conversation.

"Banshees," she explained, as I heard the door to her truck open and shut. "Man, they can talk."

Crow grinned. "Did they corner you and show you pictures from their latest vacation?"

"Last *two* vacations. I never want to see another Areosmith cover band concert shot again. Hey, Crow, why are you with Delaney?"

He opened his mouth, but I spoke first. "Because he can't keep his nose out of our business."

"Hey," he said. "But also: True."

"I need you to have Hogan smell the monster hunter."

Jean coughed, then laughed. "Did you tell me to have my sweet hunk of a boyfriend go stalker sniff someone?"

"We need to know if she's a ghoul."

"*We need to know* is code for you're jealous of her spending time with Ryder, isn't it?"

"No."

Crow leaned over so his mouth was closer to my phone. "So jealous."

"I don't want to wake him up just because you're being dumb, Delaney."

I sighed. "I do want to know. I don't like her but I need to make sure she's not connected to the car or the ghoul. So far the only person in town who can even tell a ghoul is around is Hogan. I'm sorry to ask him to get up in the middle of his night, but she's staying at the Sand Garden.

"Okay," Jean said, easy and happy as always. "We're paying him to advise us, right?"

"You just want that new video card."

"Hey, a girl's gotta game, and if he had a little more cash, he and I could slay the dragon together. Virtually. The real life dragons in town don't need slaying."

"Yes, we'll pay him for his advisory time. Can he get out there tonight?"

"Sure. He might not be asleep yet. I'll pick him up and swing by."

"Thanks, Jean."

I ended the call and flicked on my indicator lights. The streets were empty, and I knew even the main drag through town wouldn't have all that many people on it. We had a bar and a brew pub and one diner that ran 24/7, but that was it. Even the tourists coming in to see the Ordinary Show Off event Saturday would be calling it a night, either walking the dark beach, or sitting out on balconies and decks enjoying the clean air, and the arc of stars thrown like loose change across the sky.

"Any more info about the door-drop of god weapons yet?" Crow asked as he fiddled with the heat.

"Why? Do you have something I need to know?"

"Oh, I have so many things, but you definitely do not need to know them," he chuckled.

"About the weapons."

He grinned, his smile bright in the darkness of the Jeep. Just like I'd thought, the main drag was nearly empty. I turned and started toward Ben and Jame's house. I knew we were getting close to the full moon, and would need to tell the werewolves to be extra careful with shifting and running in their wolf form.

I could just go to Granny Wolfe's house, the communal home of most of the werewolves in town and let her spread the word. But Jame and Ben's place was closer. Since Jame was a Wolfe and Ben was a Rossi, I figured they could relay the info to the rest of the Wolfes.

"I've been thinking," Crow said.

I waited. Crow was many things. A god. A trickster. A glass artist. My uncle, a friend—usually. But there were times when I was reminded that he was old. Very old.

This was one of those times.

He wasn't pulling on his god power, but he was settled. Centered. Right now, he was as close to godly as I'd seen him in a long while.

"How can a god's weapon be stolen? This may not surprise you, but it's a puzzle I've worked over for many, many centuries. Each god realm is guarded by the god's power, from the most minor god to the really big hitters.

"Possessions, knowledge, weapons are locked into those realms. They are an intricate *part* of those realms, and cannot be easily separated from them. I would have said they can't be taken without the god's permission."

"Would have?"

His finger lifted to the dash again, and this time he just dragged the tip of it across the leather, as if there were dust there and the trail he left behind held all the secrets of the world.

Air blew through the vents, stronger now that he'd

messed with it, and I smelled the heat, and the sweet green of plants and flowers, the hint of a nearby wood fire.

They were familiar smells. They were smells that riveted my life into place.

Crow's cologne mixed with it too, bergamot and cinnamon, and something that reminded me of copper and burning sand.

He took a small breath, then changed his mind and closed his mouth. He shook his head and chuckled softly. "I'm going to tell you something. It's not a secret but it happened so long ago, it might as well be. Forgotten days, those, but now...now I think it might matter."

I didn't dare say anything, not wanting to jostle him out of this mood. An honest Crow, a Crow who would share something he said wasn't a secret, but probably actually was, was a rarity.

So I waited, and hoped the fast beating of my heart didn't give me away.

"There are spells," he started, like he was picking his way through a language he'd never spoken. "God spells." He glanced at me, but I kept my eyes on the road. I nodded to let him know I was listening.

"I won't go into details of how they are made, but you should know they are rare. They take a sacrifice from the god. From the god's power. Many..." He paused. "There are some deities who refuse to even... explore them. The power a single god spell carries is..." He just huffed a small laugh and drew another line in the imaginary dust on the dash.

"It's almost unimaginable," he finally said. "So many

of the spells were experimental. Deities asking of their powers: *what if?* Some of those answers were horrifying. Some were... transcendently beautiful. Some were just very, very dangerous.

"Or tricky. Twisted reality, unraveled time, space hooked like lacework. It's...well, it's all very impressive."

He dropped his hand into his lap and rubbed his palms across his jeans.

"As I said, some gods pursued the spells, the *what if*s, and some, finding no use in their complexity, abandoned them altogether."

We were almost at Jame and Ben's place. I slowed a little, giving him time, not wanting him to stop telling me the point of the story.

"Someone, I don't even remember who." He narrowed his eyes, searching though memories. "Well, I'm sure I could find out, but it would take time. Someone decided the spells shouldn't be lost. That they might one day do great good. Or great destruction.

"God spells that powerful probably should have never been written down. God spells that powerful should have remained memories, no more than flashy little threads in the massive, chaotic power of any one deity.

"But others, well, the others liked the idea of preserving these co-experiments in power. And so we did." His hands were still now, each palm braced on his thighs as he looked straight ahead.

I thought he was still looking back through his memories, still seeing things that would probably melt my brain if I got a peek at them.

We were at Jame and Ben's place, and I parked alongside the curb and killed the engine. The heat lifted from the metal making the hood click and snap as if some creature with needle sharp claws padded across it.

"Where are they written?" I asked softly, not wanting to startle him out of this mood.

"It's a book. That seems like so little to describe it. The pages are Strange weave, the ink stolen blood. And each spell is cast into the book with a deity's intention.

"It is unfindable, unbreachable, unusable."

It sounded like prophecy. It sounded like a promise. It sounded like magic. God magic.

He finally turned to look at me again. "So of course someone found it, unlocked it."

"And used it?" I asked when he fell silent.

He frowned, and his eyes glowed a very soft yellow for a moment. "It was said, and this is rumor, that a page was torn from it. A single page. But no one knows how that could have happened."

"And if it happened? If a page were taken from the book? The spell book of the gods? What does that mean?"

"If it happened, then maybe...maybe I could believe there would be a spell that allowed entrance into any realm. Even a god's realm."

"Are you sure there was a spell like that in the book?"

"More so than most."

"Why?" I asked, my heart racing but this time out of more than excitement. This time out of fear too.

"Because I wrote it."

CHAPTER SIXTEEN

JAME AND BEN's porch light snapped on. They knew we were out here. They were probably curious as to why we were out here. But I wasn't ready to face them yet. I needed a better explanation from Crow.

"You made a cosmic lock-picking spell?"

He scowled. "No. It was a lot more than a lock-picking spell. What kind of god do you think I am?"

"One who wants to get into other people's things and steal them. By picking locks."

"You seem upset. Are you upset? Because the yelling says you are maybe a little upset." He held up his fingers, pointer and thumb held slightly apart to show how upset he thought I was.

"You gave someone a cosmic bump key set."

His smile was absolutely wicked. "Maybe. Maybe not. A god spell can't be used by just anyone."

"Can it be used by someone who wants to steal weapons, then sneak into Ordinary and deliver those weapons as a threat and show of power? Can that happen, Crow? You think someone used the spell to drop a car out of the sky? You think they used it to smuggle four weapons into my town without me knowing?"

"No," he said.

"No?"

He stuck a pinky in his ear and jiggled it.

Okay, maybe I was being a little loud. But someone had broken into my town and I didn't even know they'd gotten in. I hadn't felt the spell, the interloper, or the god weapons.

Holy shit, I felt exposed. I wanted to call in the National Guard and make them patrol our streets. But the National Guard couldn't do that because they thought our tiny town planted along a curve of Oregon coast was nothing more than a place to buy bad driftwood statues and seagulls made out of seashells.

"Loud. But descriptive," he said. "Settle down, Booboo. Uncle Crow won't let something sneak around your town doing the dirty."

"Something—"

He mimicked turning a knob down. I assumed it was a volume knob.

"Something," I said in a much more normal tone, "already *is* sneaking around doing the dirty."

"I know. But we have more to go on now."

"A missing page of a spell book? How's that going to help us? And why didn't you tell me this before?"

"I wasn't as sure. And mind you, I'm still not one hundred percent on this."

"Something happened to convince you, didn't it?"

"You are such a good detective. So smart. Fast to catch on. Good morals too, if the tiniest bit too strict for my tastes. Have I told you how proud of you I am?"

"Crow." It was a warning.

He laughed. "Yes, something happened."

"I'm all ears."

He pulled a string at his neck, drawing a necklace out from beneath his shirt. The medallion was either a stone or a shell with a heart of fire, I couldn't tell because there was so much power rolling off of it.

"What is it?" I asked, already knowing.

"My god weapon."

"On your doorstep? In a box?"

"Stamped with a red feather and circle with line. Yes."

"Well, shit," I said.

"Yep. I know all the other gods say nothing could have possibly broken into their realms, but I know...I can feel the tracing of the magic."

"And?"

"It's a demon. One of the royals."

The knock on my window startled me so hard I jumped. I was not proud of the squeak that came out of my mouth. Crow, the big jerk, was laughing so hard, he'd gone a little wheezy.

Jame Wolfe bent so he could better see inside the Jeep, though I knew werewolves had great eyesight. The moon had risen from behind the hills and while it was not full yet, I was pretty sure from the flash of light deep in Jame's eyes that it would be full tomorrow.

I rolled down the window. "Yes?"

"You want to finish this inside so we can hear all of it, or do you want to stay out here in the cold?"

"I was just coming by to give you a message," I said.

"There's a stolen page from a stolen book that allowed a demon to sneak into Ordinary and drop off god weapons?"

I opened my mouth to say yes, but then it struck me. "It can't be a demon. We set up triggers and warnings after Xtelle snuck in. If a demon—a new demon—tried to get into Ordinary, I'd know. We'd know."

"True." Jame folded his arms over his chest and glanced back at the house over the top of the car. I knew Ben had to be in the house listening to all this.

"Ben okay?" I asked.

"He was in the bath, and we both got tired of you yelling so I came out to see if you wanted to come in. He's getting dressed."

"No," I said again going back to the original reason for my visit. "There's a monster hunter in town named Vivian Dunn. She knows Ryder, and I don't like her. We're going to get her out of town as soon as possible."

"All right. We'll continue behaving as normal people just like we always do," he said.

"Even with the moon."

"How many years have you lived here?"

"All of them," I said.

"How many people have reported seeing a werewolf?"

"Three."

"Other werewolves making prank calls doesn't count."

I smiled at him. "Okay, then zero. Spread the word?"

"Can do."

"Oh, and there's a ghoul on the loose."

He ticked his tongue and exhaled. "A monster hunter, a demon, and a ghoul?"

"No, I think it's just a monster hunter and a ghoul."

"It was a demon," Crow said. "I felt traces of demon."

"I believe you," I said, "but I would know if a new demon came into Ordinary."

Crow hesitated, testing the truth of that. "All right. But a demon was involved in breaking into my realm."

"Realm?" Jame asked. "Are you calling your shop your realm now, Crow?"

"God realm," Crow said.

Jame grunted. "That is supposed to be impossible, isn't it?"

"Yep."

"So just a regular Thursday night, Chief?" Jame asked me.

"Hunters and thieves and ghouls? Yep. Pretty much a normal Thursday night."

He placed his palm on the roof and patted it twice. "Let me know if I can help."

"Do you know what a ghoul smells like?" I asked.

"Ghouls don't have a scent," he said.

"Would you be able to recognize a non-scented ghoul?"

"I would notice if someone didn't smell the way I expect them to. Like a few years ago when one of the

Persons decided to try to pose as Senta on April Fools. He didn't smell right, and I caught on before he had a chance to pull off his joke."

The Persons were a very nice, quiet family of shapeshifters who had at least a half dozen favorite appearances they wore at their leisure.

"So keep your nose sharp," I said. "And please ask all the Wolfes to let me know if someone doesn't smell right. Call immediately, but do not try to capture the ghoul. We don't know what powers it might have."

"We will totally not restrain the ghoul."

"Why does it sound like you're saying the exact opposite of that?"

"Because you know we would never citizen's arrest a ghoul that's trying to hurt anyone in our territory."

"Still sounding like you're going to jump all over the chance for arresting it."

"Nope. Totally don't have handcuffs with quieting spells for supernaturals. Totally won't use them."

I shook my head. "I'm serious, Jame. Call us. Call the station. Let the professionals deal with the ghoul."

"You got it, Delaney. You can count on us Wolfes to do exactly what you say." He grinned, and it smoothed all the stern lines of him. That smile was all wolf and no sheep's clothing.

"Good, because I will hold you to that," I said. "'Night, Jame. Say hi to Ben for me. Don't touch the ghoul."

He tapped the roof again, and I rolled up the window. "Why do I think all the werewolves in town are going to hunt for the ghoul?"

"Because you know them," Crow said. "They aren't going to let you throw yourself in the way of danger again."

"That's literally half of my job. A moon-drunk pack of werewolves playing detective isn't going to help."

Crow made a little sound. "It will be interesting, that's for sure. What's next?"

"I need to talk to some of our more secluded people. Bigfoot, for one. He should be awake now."

"I haven't seen him for a while. How's it going with his Heart?"

I smiled. A bigfoots' courtship was odd but sweet and involved lots of stolen light bulbs and group singing in the woods.

"Great, as far as I can tell. They've been keeping to themselves. No more stolen street lights, so I'm taking it as a win. You need to give me your weapon."

Crow went very, very still. His voice, however, was the same as always. A little mocking, a lot fond. "Why would I do that Boo-boo? You aren't made to carry god weapons."

"Rude. I can handle god power. That's literally the other half of my job."

He rolled his eyes. "That's a lie. Yes, you can carry our power, for a short amount of time. But Delaney," now his serious voice, "this is a weapon. My weapon. It isn't made for a mortal to carry."

"Something carried it out of your realm."

"A demon," he said. "Or something demon supported. And I hope whatever touched this suffered damage."

I rubbed a knuckle at the corner of one eye. "All right. New plan. I'll go see Bigfoot. You meet Myra and lock that up with the other god weapons."

"I can't tell you how much I don't want to do that."

"Good. Don't tell me."

"There…" he paused, and I could tell he changed his angle of attack. "You've heard, over the years, that there is a war coming to Ordinary, haven't you?"

A chill traced down my back and arms. "Yes. Several people have said it was coming. Rossi, Odin, Bathin's brother Goap. I thought the war was Lavius."

"That was…yeah, that was *a* war. A really old battle finally coming to an end between that vampire and Death. But I don't think that's *the* war we've all known was brewing."

"What do you know about it?"

Crow stretched his finger toward the dashboard again, but didn't touch it, didn't wipe away imaginary dust. "The future is…*can be* so many things. The power to see the one actual true outcome of all the colliding possibilities is rare."

"There are people in town who can see the future. Yancy at the Community College," I said.

"They see a likely future, but even that isn't set in stone," Crow said. "Every word we say, every thought we think, certainly every action we take and inaction we allow, changes the world.

"Changes all the worlds." He gave me a small, wry smile. "So knowing what war is coming, who is bringing it, why, and when it will happen is not a sure thing."

"Must be sure enough that lots of people have been talking about it," I said.

"True, but on some levels, all of those visions, all of those guesses are just that: guesses."

"So is this you giving me your best guess?"

The smile again. "One of them."

"Lay it on me."

"I think the weapons were stolen by a demon. I think they might have been stolen from that demon by something not human."

"Because a human can't carry a god weapon?"

"Not for the length of time it would take to package them all up and drop them off on doorsteps."

"Yours was in a cardboard box too. Was it torn?"

He tipped his head, studying me with a side eye just like an actual crow. "Yes. There was a little rip at the circle part. Why?"

"We found a scrap of cardboard with ink in the trunk of the car."

"Huh. The car that smelled like ghoul."

"All right. So you think a demon stole the weapons," I said.

"A royal demon."

"And there are what? Hundreds of minor royals in the demon realms?"

"Give or take."

"But you only noticed a demon using the spell you wrote when your weapon was delivered."

He hummed. "I sensed something. A pull of a string. But the spell is old, Delaney. I haven't thought of it in centuries. When bound into the book, it should only be able to be used by two who are neither of life nor death, who are heart-fettered, soul-bound, voice and hand."

I didn't know what most of that meant. "So a demon can't be those things? Heart-fettered?"

"Maybe, but those rules only applied when the spell was in the book. Once stolen, the rules of who could use the spell are gone. I don't know what beings can use it, hadn't ever planned for it to be stolen. There are things, futures, even gods can't predict."

"I'll remind you of that the next time you tell me what lottery numbers to play."

He chuckled. "Fair."

"Your theory is that a demon was able to use your spell, then pass the weapons off to someone or something, maybe the ghoul? Do you think a ghoul can handle the packages?"

"Since it's mostly not alive. It's possible."

"But why give a god his or her own weapon? What's the point?"

"To show what was done when they weren't looking. To prove them vulnerable. Maybe..." he paused. "Maybe to make them angry enough they will take up their powers and leave Ordinary to search for the thief."

"Again," I said, "if I were the thief, I wouldn't want a bunch of angry gods looking for me."

"But if you were a demon, would you like angry gods gone away from Ordinary? Would you like Ordinary without god protection?"

"Gods in Ordinary can't use their powers while they're here."

"Oh, we can. We just have to leave afterward."

"Splitting hairs there, Crow."

"If Ordinary were attacked, every god would rise. Split hairs or no."

"If something attacked Ordinary, we wouldn't need the gods to save us."

"It would depend on what that thing was," he said, "and what weapons it had at its disposal."

"And that brings me back to the same question. What war is coming? Is it a demon thing? A god thing? A human thing?"

He gave a short shake of his head. "I don't know."

I blew out a breath. "Okay. I'll tell everyone this info. You need to take your weapon over to Myra and get it stowed in the vault."

"Or, and go with me here, I could keep my weapon."

"None of the other gods kept their weapons."

"But I'm your favorite."

"And if you want to remain my favorite, heck, if you want to stay in Ordinary, you better take your weapon to the vault."

I was already dialing Myra's number when my phone rang.

"You're getting really freaky with that," I told her.

"Thanks. What's up?"

"I need you to take another weapon to the vault."

"Damn it. Okay. Which god?"

"Crow."

"Tell me he hasn't been hiding the weapon all day."

I glanced over at him.

"I'm offended." He pressed fingers to his chest.

"When was it delivered?" I asked.

"About an hour ago. If you want the box, it's at my place."

"We want the box. See you at the Crow's Nest, Myra."

"I'm already on my way."

"Of course you are."

I ended the call.

"You still going out to find Bigfoot?" Crow asked.

"Yep. I'm like the postal service. Neither ghoul nor demon nor stolen page of a god spell book, will keep me from finishing my rounds."

CHAPTER SEVENTEEN

I HAD to pick up dragon pig for part of my rounds because I'd never been very good with the languages of some of our most reclusive citizens. Still, I was pleasantly surprised when dragon pig acted as interpreter when we came across the family of Vodianoi. The human-ish, frog-like, fish-scaled water folk were delighted dragon pig knew their language. So delighted, they dragged a nice, tasty anchor up from the rocks as a thank-you snack.

Finishing my rounds took until one o'clock in the morning. Even though Ordinary was small, we had hills and forests and miles of beach and cliffs. Lots of supernatural citizens lived in those places, sometimes not leaving their homes for years.

Ryder hadn't texted the whole time that I had been out. I was worried about that, but tried not to let it distract me. Ryder was doing the very important job of keeping an eye on the monster hunter. I hoped he was squeezing her for all the information he could get.

I yawned my way into our house, dropping my keys in the dish and pulling the band out of my hair. Spud looked up from the fireplace bed, spotted dragon pig and bounded over, whining and wagging and happy. Dragon pig grunted, then allowed Spud to lick its snout.

I opened the door and let Spud out to do his late night business. I wondered if I'd eaten dinner, remembered it had been pie, and decided I was too tired to eat something more nutritious.

Spud scratched on the door, and I let him back in. He and dragon pig sprinted to the fireplace, burrowing into the huge pile of toys, until the dragon pig came out perched on top of the mountain, with Spud and the toys spread out below. Spud licked his paws a couple times, then his eyes closed and he was snoring.

The dragon pig watched me as I headed toward the stairs to my room. "You're good," I said. The dragon pig grunted. "Yes, I'm good, too. See you in the morning."

I didn't even have the energy for a shower, so I stripped, pulled on one of Ryder's T-shirts, and crawled under the covers. I checked my phone one more time for a message from him, but the only text was from Jean telling me Hogan had taken a sniff around the motel and hadn't smelled ghoul.

I sent her a thumb's up emoji, dropped the phone on the night stand, then stole Ryder's pillow. It still smelled of his shampoo. I hugged it to me, inhaling his scent, then fell asleep.

THE DOOR OPENED QUIETLY, so I knew that wasn't what woke me. It might have been the very soft grumble from the dragon pig, more of a greeting than a warning. Or maybe it was just that I knew those footsteps, the tread of those boots, the *thunk* of keys landing next to mine on the little shelf in the hall.

Maybe it was because my heart was tied to that man. When he was near, I could feel him, the shape of him, from his breath, his steps, his movements through our house. His palm on the back of the chair he always touched when looking in the living room at the dragon pig and Spud. The drag of his fingers along the wall as he climbed the stairs.

I breathed in, breathed out, everything settling in me.

Knowing he was here. Safe. Mine.

I waited with my eyes closed as he bumped into the dresser, then shucked out of his boots, his pants, his shirt.

He grunted softly as he stretched his shoulders and back. Then the covers lifted and a soft sound of laughter came out of him.

I didn't open my eyes, and didn't let go of the pillow I had totally stolen, wondering what he was going to do about it.

He lowered himself into bed, and pulled the covers over both of us. I felt his fingers grip the pillow. I held on as he tugged. Just when I thought he was going to give up, his grip already slacking, I loosened my arms and rolled over.

He shuffled the pillow into place under his head,

then pressed up behind me, his arm wrapping warm and heavy over my waist. He smelled of the diner: apple pie, bacon, and butter. He smelled like a strange perfume, and I knew it must be Vivian's. Knew she had touched him, hugged him, or hell, knowing her, sprayed him with it. It was weird to smell someone else on him.

I wanted to ask him how it had gone with the monster hunter, but three breaths later, I felt his whole body relax, his arm go heavy, and I knew he was asleep. Answers would just have to wait until morning.

HE WAS out of bed before me. It was barely light outside, the birds still running through their warm-up songs for the day. I smelled coffee, heard Spud's leash jangle, then the door opened and shut. Only a few seconds later, I heard the door open and close again.

Ryder must have forgotten something.

I pulled the pillow over my head, wondering if I could catch fifteen more minutes of sleep, but my mind was already chugging.

We needed to find the thief demon who had broken into the god realms. We needed to find the ghoul wandering through town and find out what part it had played in all this. We needed to get rid of the monster hunter before half of Ordinary got up on stage to show off their talents, some of which would undoubtedly be magically enhanced.

There would be no more sleep for me this morning. Darn it.

I shoved the pillow off my head, opened my eyes, and screamed.

There was a pink unicorn nose stuck in my face.

"Your man be cheatin'." Xtelle's breath stank of burned strawberries. "I saw him. Out all night with some floozy while you were working."

I shoved at her face. "How did you get in my bedroom?"

"Through the front door. How else do you think I'd get in your room?"

"You're a demon," I said. "Maybe you have demon ways."

"Oh, that's what you think I'd break Ordinary's stupid rules for? To smell your morning breath, which is hideous in case you wondered. I have followed all of your rules."

"Says the demon standing in my room in the shape of a pink unicorn."

"Well excuse me for expressing myself. I'm so sorry I can't be as plain and boring as the rest of you."

I pushed off the covers and sat.

There was a small, very muscular black bull with very long, sharp horns in front of my dresser.

"Avnas," I said to the newest demon in town.

He had been the king of hell's right hand man, his councilor. He'd given all that up to come here. Even though it had been a rocky start, he'd signed the contract and agreed to follow Ordinary's laws because he was in love with the queen of hell. Well, now the ex-queen. Xtelle.

And while I'd never quite understand why he had

also taken the shape of a compact farm animal, he had been one of the people telling me there was a war coming.

The war he thought involved the King of the Underworld.

"Delaney," Avnas said, inclining his head a bit. "Your man was, indeed, out at all hours of the night with another woman."

"I know." I stood, and walked past them both to the door. "How do you know?"

"We followed them."

I groaned and pressed my palm over my eyes. "Why would you do that?"

"Your heart is broken," Xtelle said, with a little too much glee. "I can see it. I know human hearts inside and out."

"After devouring so many of them you are, of course, an expert, my Queen," Avnas said.

"My heart is not broken. Out."

Xtelle narrowed her sparkling eyes. "Did you just order me? The queen?"

"You are trespassing in my home. Go away."

"Oh," Xtelle said dragging the word on and on. "He's bugged the house, hasn't he? I see."

"No," I said. "There's nothing to see. Go away."

"You can't say anything because he might overhear you."

"He hasn't bugged the house."

"Just stare at me stupidly if what I'm saying is true."

I scowled at her.

"Yes. That's the face. Your man is stepping out on

you, but before we murder the woman right in the eye, we'll need to discover her weaknesses."

"Xtelle." I stabbed a finger toward the open door. "Out. Leave Ryder alone."

"I will leave him alone right in the gut," she said, winking so much, it looked like she'd lost a contact.

"No doing anything to his gut. Leave Ryder and Vivian alone."

"Vivian. The little hussy."

I stared at the ceiling, but there wasn't a god up there who was going to help me with an annoying demon unicorn. "Vivian isn't a hussy. She's a monster hunter. You need to stay away from her, and stay in pony form. No more pink unicorn while she's in town."

Xtelle lifted her nose again, staring down it at me. "Vivian Dunn is a monster hunter?"

"You know her last name?"

Xtelle shrugged, which looked a little weird on a unicorn. "She's mortal. It's easy for my kind to know names. Ryder is cheating on you with a monster hunter?"

"Ryder is not cheating on me."

She *tsked*, and Avnas shook his big bull head, horns almost knocking a brush, some socks, and a glass of water off my dresser.

"You are in denial," Xtelle said. "That's very common. Don't be ashamed of yourself."

"I'm not in denial."

"Which is what someone in denial would say."

"I am not ashamed of myself. Ryder isn't cheating."

"How would you know? Are you spying on him?"

"Of course I'm not spying on him!"

"Good. Because I am."

Avnas cleared his throat.

"Fine. *We* are," Xtelle corrected.

"No."

"We'll keep a low profile. You have to admit it is a genius idea. Who would expect a unicorn—"

"You're a demon, not a unicorn, and you can't be a unicorn while she's in town."

"—a *beautiful unicorn*—"

"Pony."

She sighed loudly. "Fine. A beautiful pony. Who would expect a magnificent pony and muscular black bull to be spies? It's the perfect disguise within a disguise within a disguise." She frowned and muttered, counting backward. "Within a disguise."

"No spying. Do not follow Ryder. Do not follow Vivian. Do not spy. At all."

"Oh, thank the Grim! We're moving on to revenge already. Would you like to hire a hitman? I know several good hitmen."

Avnas rolled his hoof and somehow made it sound like he was cracking his knuckles.

"No hitmen, or hitdemons, or hitbulls. No revenge. Give me your word, Xtelle," I said. "You will not spy on Ryder or Vivian, together or apart, and you will not touch, harm, speak, or engage with either of them."

She blinked a couple times. "You are getting better at defining a promise," she said grudgingly.

"Thank you. No deflection. Promise."

"I give you my promise."

"You too, Avnas."

"You have my word."

"Good. Now, do you also know there's a ghoul in town?"

They both straightened, then looked at each other, then looked back at me. Yeah, that wasn't suspicious. Crow said a royal demon was involved. Xtelle was the ex-queen. Avnas the king's brother.

"How would you know there's a ghoul in town?" Xtelle asked.

"Hogan can tell."

"Really. The half Jinn. That's unexpected. Ghouls and Jinn aren't often found in each other's company."

"What else do you know about ghouls?"

"I know they're very nice people who don't get all judgey about demons hiring hitmen."

"Do you know any ghouls personally?"

"Of course," she said. "They are…friends?" she threw a look at Avnas who tipped his horns, considering that.

"Neighbors," he provided.

"Yes. A better term. Ghouls are neighbors to demonkind. We wave across the rivers of blood, share our torture recipes, but it's not like we go to every beheading and flay-cation together."

"Can you find the ghoul?"

They both shook their heads.

"I thought you were neighborly: beheadings, blood rivers, whatever a flay-cation is."

"Just because we're demons doesn't mean we know every ghoul," Xtelle griped. "Ghouls can hide from anyone, including demons. Since we haven't seen it, I can only assume it doesn't want to be found. You won't find it until it is ready to show itself."

"All right. So talk to me about god spells."

Silence stretched out for a full minute. It felt a little like a game of chicken, and I waited it out.

Xtelle was the first to break. "God spells are rare, to say the least."

"They are."

"There's a book. You must know about it. A book of god spells?"

"I know about it."

"A demon once had possession of it."

"When?"

"Many ages ago."

"And now?"

"As far as I know…" She looked at Anvas. He nodded. "As far as I know, the book is not in a demon's hands now. But it has been lost and found and lost and found many times."

"What about a page torn out of the book?"

Silence again. This time it was Avans who spoke. "I've seen it. The page that was torn out of the book of god spells."

"You have?" Xtelle sounded surprised.

He nodded. "I had been sent on a quest by the king to find it. I was not the only one looking for the lost page."

"Where is it?" I asked.

"I do not know. Not now. There was a creature, a Strange who had possession of it. I glimpsed it only briefly before the Strange nearly killed me and disappeared in a flash of dragonfly wings.

"It was said a demon by the name of Glorex the Greedy found it once. But Glorex is dead. The king put a bounty on the page. If any demon finds it, they are to bargain, kill, destroy for it. They are to give it to him."

Chills rolled down my spine. It was too damn early in the morning to suddenly realize the King of the Underworld might have access to every god's realm just because my almost-uncle Crow decided to doodle in the margins of the universe.

"Have they?" I asked. "Has a demon handed that page over to the King?"

"Not that I am aware," he said. But there was something about the way he said it. As if he had more information and didn't want to share it.

"There's more," I said.

He shook his head, bull nostrils flaring. "There is rumor. There is always rumor. What I've told you is all I know. All the *facts* I know."

"Did either of you use it to break into the gods' realms?" I asked.

"You're accusing *us*?" Xtelle demanded. "Us?"

"We *are* very powerful, my Queen," Avnas said.

"So powerful we are the first suspects in the crime of the ages," she agreed. "How dare you, Delaney Reed."

I just planted my hands on my hips, and got ready to wait out her tirade.

"How *dare* you be so...so *sweet*."

It was my turn to be shocked into silence. Finally, I managed: "Sweet?"

"We're *suspects*, Avnas. God thieves." She fluttered her eyelashes, and Avnas puffed up his chest.

"As well we should be," he agreed. "You do fine work, Delaney Reed."

"For a human," Xtelle said.

"For a human," he repeated.

"But you know we have been in Ordinary for months," Xtelle said. "With all the alarms you have on this place, you would know if we left."

That was true.

"Are you saying you didn't do it?" I asked.

Xtelle shook out her mane. "Yes. Unfortunately, we did not commit this crime. Vacationing here has obviously made us soft."

"You are as rugged as granite, my Queen," Avnas said. "As unforgiving as an inferno."

"You flatter me." She cocked her hips and swished her tail. "Don't stop."

"You know what?" I said. "I haven't had breakfast yet. Get out of my house."

"But you think someone used the god spells to break into the gods' realms and steal the gods' weapons."

"It's a theory."

"How does my stolen ring fit into your theory?"

"We're working on it."

"We could gather information for you," Avnas said. "Ask around about the whereabouts of the page of spells."

"Why would we do that?" Xtelle asked.

Avnas was still looking at me, so I pointed at Xtelle. "What she said."

He shifted his broad shoulders and turned in the limited space to face her. It was good he had decided to take on the form of a very small, very compact bull, otherwise he wouldn't fit in here at all.

"It would be a way to pass the time. A lark. A balm against the boredom of this dull little meaningless plot of humanity. No offense," he threw my way.

"None taken." Because this wasn't a bad idea. Gathering information from demons would keep Xtelle out of my hair. It might even keep her out of trouble. Maybe. Possibly. Hopefully for at least a few hours.

"You still need to follow the laws of Ordinary," I reminded them. "No beheading someone to use their spinal column for a demon-y fiber optics network."

"You have no idea how demon spells work," Xtelle scoffed. "It takes a least a dozen spinal columns for even a bar of connection, and that's bound to short out from all the goodie-good built into this place. We'd have to go miles outside town to pick up any kind of a signal at all."

I was suddenly glad that I knew nothing about demon spells.

"If," I said, "you can find any information on who might be in possession of the spell page, or where it was last seen, I would be very grateful."

"And you would owe us," Xtelle pressed. "A favor for a favor."

I knew that was the way demons worked. Everything in a demon's life was transactional. But that wasn't how things worked here.

"Information is usually a free exchange," I said. "But if you can get me a solid lead on who has the page of spells, or if you can tell me where the page of spells can be found, I will offer you a finder's fee."

"A bounty," she breathed. "Treasure? Rare items? Jewels?"

"A coupon for the Blue Owl."

"A *coupon*?"

I kept my face blank. "Two dinners for the price of one. No free dessert."

"A two-for?"

"But since you're a pony, you can't actually eat there. Maybe if you ask nicely, Jean will bring you takeout."

"That's not actually incentive, Delaney."

"Well, if the information is good enough, I might consider an upgrade. Free sugar cubes and carrots for a month."

She narrowed her eyes and flicked her tail. "You're enjoying this."

"Me?"

"You're enjoying having the upper hand over me."

That was not true at all. "I'm joking with you, Xtelle. Poking fun. It's something humans do. And while I know demons don't actually have a sense of humor…"

She made a growly sound that did not fit a pony at all.

"…I don't want an upper hand over anyone. We're all citizens. We're all doing our jobs. I'm doing mine, too, trying to keep us all safe. If you have any info that would help, I'll do what I can to see you get some kind of reward."

"Why should I trust you to do that?"

"Because it's part of living in and building a

community. We do our best to live up to the jobs we're responsible for. I don't have any say over the funds in town. I will see if there is some kind of reward if you can help us keep everyone in town safe.

"By getting information on the page of spells, not by following Ryder and the monster hunter around," I amended.

"I see," she said like she didn't believe a word of it. "Well, if we find any information, we'll bring it to you."

"Good enough. Now get out of my house, I need to take a shower."

She huffed, Avnas rolled his eyes. They both tromped out of the room, though not before Xtelle "accidentally" punched a trinket box off my dresser.

I followed them down the stairs, shut and locked the door behind them, and turned to assess the house.

Dragon pig was ruling over the top of his toy hoard, his eyes glinting with fire, smoke curling out of his nostrils.

"Spud still out with Ryder?" I asked.

He grumbled, and I knew it was a yes. I was getting pretty good at talking dragon pig.

I wandered into the kitchen and found a note by the full coffee pot.

MEETING VIVIAN FOR BREAKFAST. Am showing her "around" town. Plan to make it so boring she packs and leaves. Call if you need anything. Love you. —R

· · ·

I SMILED as Xtelle's words came back to me. "My man is not stepping out on me," I said, as I tucked the note into a drawer and poured a huge travel mug of coffee. "He's stepping up to protect Ordinary."

I took one heavenly gulp of coffee before jogging back upstairs to shower and change. While I knew I could count on Ryder to do his part, I needed to do mine. Which meant checking in with our local Valkyrie.

CHAPTER EIGHTEEN

BERTIE SHOULDN'T BE hard to track down. With the talent show being put on tomorrow, I knew she'd be at the stage, making sure every detail was attended to.

I finished off my coffee on the way to Dinghy Street. Myra left me a message that Crow's amulet was stored away. Hatter and Shoe checked in to say they'd contacted all the citizens on their list, and Kelby asked me when Ryan and Than were going to be pulling shifts again.

I told her I'd get back to her on Ryder.

As for Than, it was time for his walkabout to be over. I needed all hands on deck in order to cover everything that was happening. That meant the god of death had to come back and pull his weight as one of our Reserve Officers.

Dinghy Street was busy with people coming and going. Pickup trucks and vans lined either side of the road, and a variety of supplies and building materials were being ported from the vehicles to the Grand Old Ordinary Show Off stage.

And it was grand. Just two days ago, this had been nothing but a dead end with a weedy piece of dirt behind it, and behind that, the chalk line snap of the Pacific edging the sky.

Now it looked like the Hollywood Bowl made out of a patchwork quilt of wood. The stage sat beneath an arched ceiling that stretched back like the inside of a cornucopia. Different shades and types of wood created each of those inner arcs, all sanded and polished to a rich glow.

Lights hadn't been strung yet, nor curtains hung, but if the gorgeous green and purple and gold that I caught hints of among the supplies counted for anything, it was going to be a fabulous stage.

Much too pretty for even the best armpit farter.

The audience area was being prepared too. Since it was an outdoor event, there were places for blankets and chairs right up against the stage, and on the hilly rises on either side, which were two vacant grassy lots.

I knew Bertie would provide benches and chairs in neat rows for those who didn't like sitting on the ground.

Another small structure was being built to the left of the stage. That would be for the contestants who were waiting their turn.

But even in a crowd of people—construction workers, designers, volunteers in purple and gold and green T-shirts with O, Show Off printed across the back and front—Bertie sparkled like a jewel.

She wore a hot pink pantsuit, complemented by an

orange and purple scarf, and so many bangles on her wrists I was surprised she could lift her hands to point at people, or check things off the clipboard she had tucked under her arm.

I parked my Jeep at the far end of the block and got out. The air was fresh and breezy and full of voices, laughter, and construction tools really going at it.

It was just cool enough, I was glad I'd thrown on my windbreaker.

Bertie's voice carried over all the rest of the noise. "No, I want the aisles wider. You are placing wheelchair access to the outside, correct? If not, I could assign you to something with fewer moving parts. How do you feel about sweeping the sidewalks?"

Tark, the man in front of her and currently the target of her scorn, was part troll. He just rolled his eyes at her. "How many years, Bertie? How many years have I done this?" He hefted six folding chairs in each hand.

"Correctly or without complaining?"

"Both."

"Zero."

He chuckled and puckered an air kiss her way. "You know you love me."

"I do nothing of the kind."

"That's all right," he said, already backing away with the chairs and a big old grin. "I love you enough to make up for it."

And then I saw something I'd never see in my life. Bertie blushed.

She actually bit her bottom lip and her whole face

went an adorable shade of pink, totally clashing with her pantsuit.

What in the hell? Bertie never clashed. Never.

Did she have a crush on Tark? Were they dating? With some effort, I pulled my gaze away from Bertie and stared after Tark.

He'd turned his back and was lumbering toward the stage, carrying those chairs like they were feathers. Half troll meant he was short—the top of his thick, black curls put him a few inches under five feet. It also gave him massive shoulders, a barrel body, and legs like steam train pistons.

He was funny, a little grumpy, and a total power-house. I could appreciate all those things about him.

When I turned back to Bertie, it looked like she was appreciating all those things about him too.

Don't tease the Valkyrie, Delaney. No teasing, my sense of self-preservation warned.

"Looks like somebody's got a boyfriend," I sing-songed. What could I say? My sense of self-preservation wasn't worth missing out on this chance.

All the heat in Bertie's face washed away, and when she turned to me, she was ice cold, one eyebrow raised. "Delaney Reed. It's so lovely to see you. I have sidewalks that need to be swept."

"I'd love to help out—no, don't give me that look, I really would—but I have to put out other fires today. Thank you for getting the word out last night."

She glanced at her clipboard, then glared at the team of women sorting through drapery, as if that look alone could make them work faster. "I assume you reached the others who shy from modern technology?"

"We did."

"And the other issue?" She checked something off her list, then tapped the pen, looking at me expectantly.

I lowered my voice. "We still don't know where or who the ghoul is. We're working on it. Might have a lead on the god weapon thing. Have you heard of the spell book of the gods?"

"That was lost years ago."

"And found and lost again. I know. There's a missing page."

"I…" She narrowed her eyes, as if she were trying to decide if I was lying.

"That's what Crow told me. He said his spell was on that page."

She pursed her lips like she'd just chewed through the center of a rotten lemon. "Of course it was *his* spell."

"You don't know anything about the page, do you?"

She gave a short shake of her head.

"Crow thinks a person or demon used it to break into the gods' realms."

"While I rarely care to agree with gods, and that god in particular, it would explain how the seemingly impossible has been made possible."

"If you could keep your eye out for any sign of it, that would be really helpful."

She nodded. "Yes, yes. If I see it, I'll contact you. The ghoul is not what I was asking about."

I rolled the current mess of problems through my mind and came up blank.

"Have you spoken with Ryder?" she asked.

Oh. Yikes. "Um…I haven't had a chance. The, um, Vivian Dunn came into town. He's been with her."

"All this time?"

"Mostly?"

She sighed. "Delaney, it isn't as if I ask you to do much…"

"Every festival, every fundraiser, every clean-up crew," I counted on raised fingers. She ignored me just like she always did and kept talking.

"…but I am low on performers this year and his participation is vital."

"…crowd control, lost and found, that rhubarb judging…"

"If this is any indication of the level of dedication you and others are willing to offer our town then I am concerned who I may have to draft into the theater production we will be putting on in August. Frankly, it's becoming an embarrassment to think our people are so uninterested in the community around them."

She was just complaining. Bertie did that a lot. But there was something more to it this time. Almost as if she were actually worried that one of her events would not turn out as awesome as they always did.

Well, except for that first rodeo. That had been a disaster.

It was a strange idea that maybe Bertie, flawless, unflagging, unflappable Bertie might be feeling a little insecure. It was a strange idea that maybe she needed a little encouragement.

"We're not uninterested," I said. "Look at all these people already having a good time and the event hasn't even started. This is going to be amazing, because it's always amazing. There is not a single being in the universe I can think of who puts on better events than you, Bertie. You have set the standard, and no one has come anywhere close to reaching it."

She blinked a couple times, as surprised at what I'd said as I'd been surprised it needed saying.

"You think I'm worried about my standards?"

"No. Nope. That is not what I said."

"I have no doubt of my ability to create the most magnificent events out of nothing but backwoods dust. I have been doing it for a lifetime. I have been doing it long before you were born, Not Little Delaney."

Oh, man. She was really angry. I hadn't heard that name since I was six and insisted going to school meant I was Not Little Delaney any more.

"I know."

"And I would hope that you know I do not rely on you to tell me how good my standards may be."

"I know."

"The standard is where I set it, when I set it, and how I set it. Precisely. No more and no less."

"Robyn is never gonna win this fight," I noted.

She blinked again. Her anger shifting to something that looked a lot more like delight.

"No," she said, as throaty and happy as I'd ever seen her. It was a little frightening, frankly. "She will not."

I grinned at her, and wonder of wonders, she grinned back. "So," she said, back to business, back to being Bertie. "You will speak to Ryder today. I need an answer immediately."

"I will speak to Ryder today. I promise."

"Now would be good, Not Little Delaney. Otherwise, I may be forced to put you on the stage, and we would all prefer to be spared that debacle if possible."

I nodded. "Yep. Now is good. I'll just head that way. To talk to him. I'm sure he's gonna love this idea." I was backing away, smiling for all I was worth, hoping she didn't swoop down and draft me into the production out of spite.

Luckily, she was distracted by the clatter of several metal chairs falling into each other.

The two teens who had been fake sword fighting between the aisles must have felt Bertie's gaze. They looked up from the tangle of chairs, and their faces froze in fear.

I waved my arms, and their eyes ticked to me. "Run!" I shouted through my cupped hands. The boys took off like jackrabbits.

"Delaney," Bertie scolded.

"Can't stay, gotta run. Important police business." I took my own advice and sprinted to the Jeep. I got out of there as quickly as I could, doing a slightly illegal U-turn out onto the main road.

Finding Ryder wasn't the most important thing on my plate, but I had promised Bertie, and if I didn't follow through, she would.

So I drove through town and parked at the Blue

Owl. There were several cars in the lot and a couple semi-trucks. The diner was the only twenty-four-hour place in town, and since it was on the north side of town near the highway, it was a favorite stop for truckers.

It didn't hurt that the food was amazing, or that Piper, one of the main waitresses, was a demigod who had a knack for knowing little bits of the future. She always seemed to know what you were going to order and when you needed your coffee refilled.

The Blue Owl's big windows had booths set in them. From where I parked, I could see some of the patrons. As a matter of fact, I could see Ryder sitting opposite Vivian.

To anyone else he probably seemed relaxed, happy even. But I knew he was very aware he was sitting with a person who would hunt, capture, and maybe torture or kill people who just wanted to live their lives peacefully.

People who just wanted to have a good home, good food, good work, and to spend time with family and friends.

I loved him for standing up for them. Standing up for all of us.

I just didn't like that he was taking this burden on alone. I should walk right in there and invite myself to breakfast.

Or maybe there was a better way to give him a break from Vivian Dunn.

I pulled out my phone and typed: *Hey, handsome. How's that hot scramble?*

I pressed send. He sat up a little straighter and

pulled his phone out of his pocket, still listening to whatever Vivian was saying.

He glanced at the phone. I knew when he'd finished, because he looked up and squinted through the window. I was pretty sure he wouldn't see my Jeep since it was mostly blocked by a delivery van, but just in case, I leaned back so he wouldn't see me in it.

A message buzzed on my phone.

Morning, love

Ah. Heart officially melted.

Need a break? I texted.

From breakfast?

From boring her out of town

There was a pause while he typed, erased and typed. He pressed send and looked out the window again. I scooched down lower, peering over the dash through the steering wheel.

Vivian, of course noticed all this. She must have asked him a question, because he shook his head and took another drink of coffee, squinting over the top of it, still searching for me.

I ducked my head and checked his message.

Why? What would you do to bore her? Talk to her about your top ten running sock preferences?

I grinned.

That would be riveting after hours of your talking about scale rulers and mechanical pencils.

My mechanical pencils are prose worthy

So are my socks

Challenge accepted. Your sock limericks vs my pencil poems

Slam poetry? Bring it. Also, gonna call

He raised one finger when his phone rang, and answered it with his hand over it. I heard him say, "Hang on, this is a work thing," and watched as he stood away from the booth toward the front door and restrooms.

Piper met him halfway, a pot of tea and fresh fruit in each hand. She was bee-lining to Vivian.

It was good to know someone would keep her busy while I checked in with my man.

"Hey," he said. "Sleep well?"

"Until Xtelle and Avnas showed up in our room. You?"

"Like a rock until I realized Vivian's always been an early riser."

I let that go by, not wanting to know how he knew that. She'd said they'd shared a room before, and he'd told me nothing had happened between them. I would believe him a hundred times over her.

"Any idea yet on why she came to town?"

"She said she wasn't on an assignment. There wasn't something about Ordinary that brought her here. But there's a shakeup in the Organization, and she's climbing the ladder. If she found something supernatural, she could wedge her way into a higher position. Oregon was convenient. I think knowing me brought her here. Sorry about that."

"Don't apologize. You didn't know you'd been living among the supers all your life."

"Only because someone wouldn't tell me."

"Weird. I wonder who that was?"

"That was you, Delaney."

"How was I to know you would really be into those kinds of things?"

"My love of fantasy, mythology, science fiction, and monster movies didn't tip you off?"

"Maybe that was a phase."

"I don't do phases. I love what I love. Forever."

I swallowed, my mouth suddenly dry, my chest warm. "Forever, huh?"

"Forever." His voice had gone low and warm. I wanted to kiss him. I wanted to touch him. I wanted to marry him.

I wanted to marry him so much.

"Well," I said, the word coming out too breathy. "Well, that's...well."

He chuckled, and it rolled through me like electricity. I was lit up, alive from just the sound of him. Just the nearness of a simple phone call. And it was this man, only this man who had ever made me feel that way.

"I want to marry you," I blurted out.

There was a slight pause, the click of his breath taken too quickly. "I want to marry you too," he said. I could hear the humor in his voice and also the confusion. "But let's get rid of our monster hunter before she catches wind of it. I am not inviting her to our big day."

"Who would we even seat her next to?"

"Bertie. Because I would trust her to dispose of her body quickly and silently."

I laughed and wished I could see him better though the window. But he was pacing near the wall, and the angle of shadow and sun on the glass hid him from my view.

"Bertie wants you in the Show Off."

"What?"

"She wants you in the talent show."

"What?"

"Did I break you? She wants you to play piano as the closing act of the talent show."

"What?" he sounded a little panicked this time. "Why?"

"She says there haven't been enough entrants, and she wants your gorgeous face up there making people happy."

"She said my face is gorgeous?"

"I might have extrapolated. But yes. It's you she wants."

"I don't… I haven't played piano in years."

"Well, you have until tomorrow to practice."

"That's not going to be enough."

"The armpit farter won last year, Ryder. It's not exactly a high stakes sort of competition."

"She wants me to embarrass myself, doesn't she?"

"You can ask her."

"No."

"When you call her."

"No."

"And tell her you're going to go on stage."

"No."

I let the silence stretch just a second or two. "Right. So that's your other choice. Tell Bertie no."

He groaned. "She'd kill me."

"Maybe."

"She'll make me judge rhubarb contests."

"Or there's the mosquito round up thing I still don't fully understand."

"It's a wetland tour with a rodeo theme. To explain the local wetlands."

"That's right. I think Jean is signed up for that one. I'm sure she'd be happy to swap places with you. Jean has this dance routine with a lamp and a pool noodle that everyone thinks is hilarious."

"I know what you're doing."

"You can tell her no, Ryder. Honestly." I meant that. Bertie might be pushy sometimes, but she was not a tyrant.

"I'll think about it."

"Good. Call her and tell her that."

"I will."

And then we were both quiet, listening to the sound of breathing on the other end of our phones.

"I miss you," I said, stupidly. I'd just been in bed with him a few hours ago. It was silly to miss him. But I thought that was more about the wedding stress, him throwing himself a hundred percent into the planning and management, and me running away from anything even remotely wedding related.

I'd been pulling away from the wedding, and in doing so had been pulling away from him.

"I miss you too," he said simply.

"When is she leaving?"

"I'm pushing for tonight, if possible."

"Good."

Another second ticked by, and Piper glance over

toward Ryder and nodded to Vivian. Obviously offering to go see where he had gotten off to.

"Do you want me to come into work today?" he asked.

"No. No. Take as long as you need to bore her and get her out of here. If you need help with that, let me know. I'll find Than and tell him we need him to work a shift today."

"Okay," he said. "Yeah. Okay. I'll see you tonight."

"I love you," I said.

"Love you too." I heard the shush of his palm over his phone and could just make out him saying something to Piper that sounded like he would be right there.

I knew he was going to end the call. I knew he was going to go back to Vivian and spend the rest of the day explaining why all our manhole covers don't match, or how rotted kelp could be harvested as bait, or all the tedious differences between a ROtring and a Staedtler pencil.

I knew he was going to go on with his day doing this job, looking after Ordinary just like I was going to go on with my day to do the same.

We'd see each other tonight.

But there was something about this good-bye that felt bigger. Felt more permanent.

I didn't like it.

My heart was beating a little too fast, and my thoughts spun. I didn't want Ryder to spend one more moment not knowing how much I really loved him and how much I wanted forever too.

"I want to get married," I said.

There was a small pause. "Okay? You just said that a minute ago, remember?"

"I picked a date. I think we should do Friday."

"A week from now?" He sounded a little panicked. "We don't have the cheese. Think of the cheese."

"No." my mind was still racing, and so was my heart. But it was excitement instead of fear.

"Not a week from now. How about..." I tried to remember the dates Bertie had said the Community Center would be open, even though I didn't know if we'd want the wedding held there. "How about September? Yeah, this September. The second Friday. Do you think we'd have enough time to get everything done? If I help? Really help this time?"

"I..." his voice went out on him, and he had to clear his throat. "Are you sure, Delaney? I know I said I was impatient, and if you want, I want. To wait. If you need time, I want to give you time."

"I know. I do. But I don't. Need more time. I'm ready." I exhaled a laugh. "I'll *be* ready. I want this, Ryder. You're my forever."

"Goddamnit, Delaney Reed. Now you tell me this?" he growled. "When I can't kiss you stupid and drag you off to bed?"

"It's like poetry, the words falling out of your mouth."

"Delaney," he groaned.

"I love you."

I heard the exhale of his breath. "I love you too."

"Good. 'Cause we're getting hitched, Mr. Bailey.

Better stop insulting every cheese manufacturer in the state between now and September."

"I'll see what I can do."

"I expect great cheese. Only the best cheese."

"Only the best," he promised. "Gotta go."

"Good luck boring her. Couldn't think of a better man for the job."

"Hey—"

I ended the call and grinned. My heart was still racing, my breath a little fast. Even my face felt flushed.

I was happy. I was ecstatic.

"I'm getting married," I whispered to myself. Then I swiped my thumb over my phone and called on our very own god of death.

CHAPTER NINETEEN

THE PHONE RANG and clicked over to a computerized voice that told me the mailbox was full. I wondered who could be calling Than so much his voice mail had filled up.

If we weren't short-handed, if we weren't in the middle of a show about to go on, if we didn't have a ghoul and a monster hunter and stolen god weapons messing with our groove, I wouldn't have followed through.

But all those things were happening and we were a small department. Even though Than technically had today off, I needed him on the job.

So I drove to his house, a pretty blue cottage with a white picket fence and a lot of windows that looked over the ocean.

He wasn't there. I knocked, rang the bell, and even peeked in the windows. I tried his phone again, got shuffled to the full mailbox.

Time to try his kite shop.

The good weather drew in the tourists, and traffic was picking up. Bertie would be happy because more people would see the Show Off was going to happen tomorrow and might decide to stay in town for it.

If Than had any kind of business sense, he'd be at the Tailwinds selling the heck out of all those brightly colored wings.

I pulled up next to the shop with the sign painted in a blood red font that looked like a particularly murderous clown had gone to town on it.

The OPEN sign in the door was visible, and the door itself was propped open with a very small stone owl with golden eyes that twinkled in the light.

The owl was new. I stepped past it and into the shop.

The little building was pleasantly cluttered with layers of kites on the ceiling. All of them, if you looked from just the right angle, told a story of hunt and hide, of the wind moving through the natural universe around it.

Which is to say it looked like a craft bazaar had rolled around in neon paint, and exploded into kites of every shape, size, animal, and object you could imagine.

A man and two kids were browsing, the kids looking up at the ceiling with something like awe on their faces. A pre-teen girl was crouched in the corner, digging through a box of what looked like spools of string wound around wooden bobbins.

Behind the counter with its old-fashioned, manual cash register and much more modern card reader, was Death himself.

He had, of course, watched me walk in, his eyes just as twinkly as the little owl at the door.

Those twinkly eyes took me in, from my windbreaker and uniform shirt to my jeans and sneakers. Then he raised an eyebrow.

I grinned. I was happy to see him. I was also still buzzing from the high of finally picking a wedding date.

I didn't know if he could see that on me, that happiness, that joy, but his eyebrows went back to where they belonged and he brought a very delicate tea cup, which Myra had probably given him, to his lips and sipped.

I strolled over to the counter. "Hey, there. Done with your walk early?"

"I finished at exactly the expected time."

"I need you to come into work today."

His gaze lifted past me to take in his shop. "I have done so, as you can see."

"I mean the department. We're short-handed."

"Oh?"

"Things are busier than normal."

He sipped tea.

"*Much* busier."

"In what way?"

I wasn't going to blurt out all of our problems with humans in the room so instead I took out the little notebook I kept on me, stole one of the three pens he had carefully displayed in a small fish-shaped vase, and wrote:

ghoul in town, monster hunter in town, god weapons stolen, mauve really brings out your complexion.

And oh, the look he gave me after reading that last bit. I just smiled with all my teeth.

"As you can see there's a lot of police business we need to attend to. Ryder's dealing with number two on that list, so I need you to help out with the other items."

"This," he said archly plucking the Hawaiian shirt away from his chest. "Is mauve and lime green."

I wrinkled my nose. "I know. I didn't want to point that out."

Both eyebrows rose this time, but the mouth was a straight line. "Point out what, Reed Daughter?"

"Delaney," I said. The bell over the door rang as the dad and kids left the shop. "Mauve is the worst color in the world."

"And yet it brings out my complexion?"

"Did I say that?"

He turned the paper so it faced me.

"Huh," I said, making a big deal out of leaning forward and reading the list. "Look at that."

The girl in the corner came up to the counter and positioned herself behind me. "Oh, you can go ahead," I said. "I'm not buying anything."

"For that comment," Than said, "yes, you are."

I stepped to one side so the girl could put the wooden bobbins of string on the counter.

Than looked down at the two she had chosen. "These are a very fine choice," he said. There was something so overwhelmingly *kind* in his voice, I actually took a moment to really study him.

Than was thin, sallow, his hair combed very carefully into place. Yes, he wore a Hawaiian shirt that looked like sadness and abandoned dreams, but it was neatly pressed and starched within an inch of its life. Behind the counter I expected he was wearing wool trousers and shiny leather shoes because he was classy that way.

He punched the keys on the big clunky cash register and made it ding. "I see. There is a sale. Both of these for only the cost of one. Today only."

"Awesome," the girl breathed. "Can I get two more?"

"If you wish."

She scampered off and he made a big show of drawing out a bright red paper bag, and wrapping thin white paper around each bobbin before placing them in the bag.

"Sale," I said.

"Yes."

"Just those bobbins?"

"Spools."

"Just those spools of string?" I asked.

"Yes." His gaze flicked up to me, and the look he gave me was not nearly as warm as it had been for the girl. "You doubt my ability to peddle my wares?"

"Nope," I said, leaning one elbow on the counter and staring out the windows. "I just didn't notice any SALE sign by the spools."

He hummed.

"Why do you suppose I didn't see any SALE signs by the spools, Than?"

"It may have fallen to the floor."

"Really? May it have?"

He didn't smile, because Than wasn't much of a smiler on the outside. But on the inside I knew he liked it when I teased him.

Or at least he tolerated it.

The girl was back again. Than went through punching the keys on the register, and came up with the new price. Four for the price of free.

The girl looked thrilled. "They're for my friends," she said, bouncing on the toes of her feet.

"Are they?" he asked, as he wrapped another spool.

"We found some old kites but need better string. Geo got his stuck in a tree, and I climbed up and got it for him. The string broke."

"I see." He wrapped the second spool, eyes on his work, but listening to the girl. Hearing, I thought, more than just her words. Hearing, I thought, what I heard.

There either wasn't enough money or there wasn't enough time for her and her friends to have new kites. They were making do with hand-me-downs, and thrilled to have them.

Than dropped one spool, two spools into the bag with the others.

Then a thought came to me. "Where did you find the old kites?"

Than stopped, his hand absolutely still over the open mouth of the red bag. His eyes ticked up to me, held.

It was my turn to raise an eyebrow.

"Oh, out on the beach," she said. "Some were stuck behind rocks. One was just hanging from a tree. Right where we play every day. And they're good kites except for the string we lost."

"Really?" I said. "Did you hear that, Than? There were perfectly good kites scattered out there where the children were playing."

"Fascinating," he intoned.

"Just such a coincidence the kites were left out there after you'd been out on your walkabout. Isn't that a coincidence?"

"There you are," he said to the girl, completely ignoring me. "Have a good day." He folded the top of the bag over once, ran one boney finger along the fold and pushed it gently toward the girl.

She left the shop with a big smile on her face and was already digging through the bag before she'd even cleared the threshold.

"She's happy," I said.

Than moved past me to turn the sign over to CLOSED. "Kites are something to be happy about," he observed.

"You could have just talked to Bertie."

"About?"

"Wanting to donate kites to kids."

He moved past me, and I caught a hint of his cologne, or maybe it was his soap. Something with rosemary and just the slightest hint of jasmine and honey. It seemed like a strange combination, but on him, it was wonderful.

"I am sure I do not know what you are speaking of."

"The coincidence of all those kites showing up right when you were out on your stroll." I nodded toward the window where the girl was already surrounded by three other kids about her age, handing one paper wrapped treasure to each of them.

"Ah," he said, gliding toward the back of the shop where I knew he had a little room with supplies and also a fine selection of tea and reading material. "Some mysteries may forever remain mysteries."

He was through the door then, out of sight. I didn't know if he was activating alarms or just setting the shop to rights for the day. Maybe he kept his reserve uniform back there.

"Have you heard of Vivian Dunn?" I asked.

"I received a message from the Valkyrie about her."

"Ryder's trying to drive her out of town via boredom. I'm not sure it's going to work. She seems…set on something. Like she's caught a scent and isn't going to give up on it."

"She is a hunter. It is their way."

"There are so many things she could find here. So many people." I leaned against the counter and stared out the windows as the girl and her friends ran off toward the beach. A few people were walking this stretch of sidewalk, tourists, mostly.

"Crow thinks the gods' weapons were stolen using a page out of the spell book of the gods."

He stopped making noise for a moment. "That *is* interesting," he admitted. "I haven't heard of it for some time."

"Yeah, I get the feeling no one's been keeping track of it."

He made a sound that might have been agreement,

and I was sure I heard the *thunk* of shoes placed on a mat, then the hissing rasp of laces being tied.

"Changing into those nifty shorts again?"

"I do not own *shorts*." Oh, the disdain.

"You say that, but I saw you in them yesterday. And those socks."

"I do not know what you are speaking of."

"Oh, I think you do."

He made a noise that sounded like he disagreed.

"Bertie's looking for a few people for the Ordinary Show Off."

"The show of talent?"

"Mostly it's an excuse to get out, enjoy the weather, and laugh at your neighbor."

"It sounds delightful."

"Really?"

"No."

I smiled at that and crossed my arms over my chest. "There's a ghoul hiding out in town. It could be anyone."

He was silent.

"Do you know anything about ghouls? I know they're not exactly living or dead, so I don't know how much contact you'd have with them. If Xtelle is to be believed, they're super nice and neighborly with demons."

He still didn't say anything.

"Than?" I pitched my voice a little louder.

I saw Than walk past the window, strolling down the sidewalk. He'd changed out of his Hawaiian shirt and into a plaid I'd never seen him wear. And he'd totally lied about the shorts. He wore them with the same high white socks and sandals. He also had a pair of rather large, red-framed sunglasses balanced on his nose.

"What are you doing?" I yelled through the window. "Where are you going?"

Two things happened very quickly.

Than, outside the shop, turned on his heel and stared at me, his brow pulled down, frowning.

Than, inside the shop, stepped up next to me. "Whatever are you shouting about?"

Okay, three things happened very quickly: I realized I was seeing two Thans even though my brain insisted there was only one god of death and he was standing next to me, smelling of rosemary and jasmine.

"Holy shit, that's the ghoul," I breathed.

I ran to the door, my smile not doing nearly enough to convince the ghoul that I just wanted to talk, if the stark terror on its face were anything to go by.

"I see," Than said, and the chill in those two words could kick off the next ice age.

I reached the door before him and stopped cold. "You, stay."

We didn't need to explain how there were suddenly two identical, slightly odd kite sellers in town.

I slithered through the crack in the door and addressed the Than-ghoul as nicely as possible. "Hi there. Could I talk to you?"

Than-ghoul hesitated, glancing off to the right before back at me. I had the wild thought it was looking for its next fleshy victim to bite.

"It's okay," I said. "I know you're new in town. I'm

Delaney—" I didn't even get the rest of my name out before it shot off like a startled ostrich.

"Gods dammit!" I hauled off after it, thankful I'd put on my running shoes this morning, but mentally cussing up a storm.

I thought it would bolt toward the beach, but instead it followed the sidewalk, running all out to the street corner and turning south into a residential neighborhood.

Luckily, there weren't very many people on the sidewalk. I only had to dodge four and none of them seemed particularly interested in the foot race.

Than, however, was right on my heels, and then he was beside me, his long legs giving him a stride I would die for.

"Don't," I said, "hurt it."

Than didn't even dignify that with an answer. He just put on speed, passed me, and by the next block was almost in reach of the ghoul.

The ghoul risked a look backward, made a startled sound and jumped a wooden fence into a side yard. Death placed one hand on the top rail and flew gracefully over the top after it.

I was almost there. But before I reached the fence I heard an impact, like someone had thrown bricks into a bag of sand.

A soft *oof* was followed by a very loud: "Ah-ha! You think you can just run in here and try to jump on my back? I will murder you in the ear!"

"Xtelle," Than said.

"What? You know I can talk, Old Bones. And that

annoying Delaney isn't even here—Hi, Delaney. I see you're right on the other side of the fence now."

Xtelle was in the small side yard mincing back and forth next to a Than-ghoul sprawled and unconscious on the grass. The other Than stood with his arms crossed over his chest.

CHAPTER TWENTY

I HOPPED THE FENCE. "Keep it down," I said.

Xtelle did lower her voice slightly. "Did you see that? Did you see that kick? Did you see it? Did you see how amazing it was? Hooves. Why would you want squishy feet with toes when you could have hooves? Hooves bring the *hurt*."

Than grunted softly in a way that could have been taken as agreement, then he crouched, one hand extended toward the figure.

"Wait," I said. "I need to know you're you."

Xtelle was still mincing, her little one-two-three, step-step-step thing was going to wear a rut in the yard. Not that I even knew why she was in this yard.

"Of course I'm me," she scoffed. "There is no one as magnificent as a unicorn—"

"—pony," I corrected.

"—*beautiful* as a unicorn pony queen!"

Okay, that's all I needed to hear to know she was the

real Xtelle, but I'd seen too many movies where a bait and switch let the bad guy get away.

"Not you," I said to Xtelle. "You."

Than withdrew his hand and, still in a crouch, looked up at me. "You wish me to prove that I am who you think I am?"

"Yes."

"And who do you think I am?"

"Nope. You're going to answer three questions. If you get them right, I'll believe you're who I think you are."

He sighed and stood. "Begin."

I bit back a smile and squinted at him.

"What is your secret hobby?"

He stilled. "I have many secrets. I have many hobbies."

"The one you hide away inside your house."

The look in his eye was part amusement, but also a little bit of warning. He was willing to play along with this game, but I was going to pay for it.

Worth it.

"I garden."

I nodded, but I couldn't hide my relief. I knew this must be the real Than—for one thing the imposter was wearing different clothes, but I didn't know how quickly a ghoul could transform into another shape. If it were instantaneous, then it was possible Xtelle could have kicked the heck out of the wrong grim reaper.

"What did you spend your recent time off doing?"

"Walking," he said mildly.

"And?"

"Is that your third question?"

"No, it's a modifier of the second."

"Ridding myself of unnecessary inventory."

"Hiding kites for kids."

He just blinked, and waited.

I had a chance to ask him something more, something important. I supposed he could lie to me, but since this was to prove that he was really him, I had a feeling he'd stick pretty close to the truth.

I could ask him if he knew if this war everyone thought was headed our way would mean we would lose people.

I could ask him why he had come to Ordinary, why he stayed. I could ask him when I was going to die, when my friends, my family were going to die. I could ask him if he could bring my father back to life.

From the sudden heaviness in the air, I thought he knew what was going through my mind.

I took a breath and braced myself for his answer. "Do you like Myra more than me?"

That startled him. It was absolutely delightful to see the honest surprise on his face, the almost vulnerable confusion.

It was only a second or two before he took in my grin and pulled his dour expression back into place. "Currently? Yes."

I laughed and nodded. "All right, you're you. Good job. I'm convinced. Let's see who we have here. Do either of you recognize it?"

I bent down next to the ghoul and moved its arms

into a more comfortable position. It groaned, gaining consciousness.

I held on to its wrist for a moment. "You're okay," I said, squeezing gently, "you're safe. But I want you not to run. Can you sit?"

The ghoul groaned, bent both legs, and put its hands underneath it to push upward.

It was strange—really strange—to stare down into the face of a friend, knowing it was not my friend looking back at me.

"Are you okay?" I asked.

That caught it off guard. Its eyes moved between Than and me.

Xtelle just snorted from behind it. When it didn't speak, I tried again.

"I know you're new in town. My name is Delaney Reed. I'm here to help you get settled in, and also to tell you the rules and laws that all the citizens agree to follow here."

Still nothing. It had gone from staring at me to throwing short, slightly panicked looks at Than. The eyes might be moving but the mouth was clamped tight.

"You should talk to her," Xtelle said. "She's the, well, I wouldn't say *leader*, but she has some *small* authority here." Xtelle bent her leg and sort of nudged the ghoul in the shoulder with her knee.

"Gee, thanks," I said.

The ghoul finally twisted to look at Xtelle, and if I thought it looked uncomfortable before, it looked absolutely mortified now.

"Queen Xtelle?" it said, and I had a moment of

vertigo as a sweet tenor voice came out of the not-Than shape.

Weird.

"How could I have not known it was you, Your Majesty? I am honored if you would forgive me?" It executed a pretty good bow considering it was sitting and half twisted around.

"Of course you are honored. Do you hear that, Delaney? *Someone* here is giving me the respect I deserve."

"Super neat," I said just to watch Xtelle's eyes narrow.

"So," I said to the ghoul, "do you have a name and a pronoun you prefer?"

It was interesting that the rest of the world was starting to catch up with us on the whole pronoun thing. We'd been asking that question for generations, since our population was as wide as it was varied. Asking right up front seemed to be the easiest way to keep everyone on the same page.

The ghoul gave one more bow to the ex-queen of demons, then twisted back to look up at me. "I am Artishall the Supple? You may call me Tish? They?"

"Tish." I nodded. "Were you in the car that fell out of the sky yesterday?"

"Yes?"

"How did you take Than's shape?"

"Than?"

I jerked my thumb toward the glowering god of death next to me. "Than."

"Oh?" Tish said. "There was a broken fingernail? On the beach near rocks I was hiding behind?"

Everything the ghoul said came out as a question, but I didn't think it was actually asking me to confirm what it was saying.

I glanced at Than, who held up his left hand. The nail on his forefinger was broken and much shorter than his other nails.

"All right. So that answers that. Good." I smiled, and Tish head-tipped as if not quite sure what to do with approval.

"Why did you come to Ordinary?"

I didn't think Tish was going to answer, but then Xtelle nudged them in the back again.

"I was working? Helping? I was helping a friend?"

"Okay, who's the friend?"

They shook their head.

"What work were you doing?"

Another shake of the head.

"Who were you helping?"

Shake.

"Did you steal the god weapons?" Than asked and his voice dropped the temperature in the surrounding area by twenty degrees.

The ghoul opened and closed their mouth.

"You shall speak now," Than invited, though it sounded more like a command. "I require it."

"But here you cannot, can you, god?" they whispered.

Brave. Stupid, but brave.

"The god may not," I said, "but I can. Where did you get the car?"

They wouldn't look away from Than and even though they were wearing his face, I could see, maybe, the actual shape of the creature beneath it. The eyes were set farther apart, I thought, the mouth wider.

A woman laughed as she strode by with three dogs on leashes, a cell phone pressed to her ear. We were partially hidden from view behind the fence, but there was still a chance someone would look over and see me, two identical twin Reapers, and a talking pony.

Add cell cameras to the mix, and it was a very real possibility Vivian Dunn could find out something odd was going on here by scrolling through social media.

"We're going to need to talk somewhere a little more private," I said. "Come with me please, Tish."

"What about me?" Xtelle asked.

"What about you?"

"Why aren't I going somewhere private to talk to them? I know all the ghoul secrets."

"You told me ghouls are acquaintances. Neighbors."

"And you believed me? Really, Delaney, I thought you had to be clever to be a detective."

"Why are you even here?"

"I ask myself that every day. I signed the contract. You said I had to stay in Ordinary, no backsies."

"I never...no," I said. "Why are you in this yard?"

She looked around as if just noticing she was not at Hogan's house where she belonged. "This isn't my house?"

"One, you don't have a house. Two, no, this isn't the house where you're staying. And three, you know that."

"All these shacks look the same to me. Square, square, square, roof, roof, roof. Someone should put numbers on them so people who are used to living in interesting places like castles, palaces, and fiery volcanic pits, can tell them apart."

"They have numbers." I pointed.

"Well, I ignore those," she said, turning her head to one side.

"Were you spying on me?"

"No."

"Were you meeting up with Tish?"

She snorted. "I discovered Tish at the same moment you did. Well, a few moments earlier than you. And I wasn't spying on Ryder."

I rubbed at my forehead. "I didn't ask you if you were spying on him."

"Good. Because I wasn't."

I knew she was lying. "Ryder's out here?"

"How would I know? I'm not spying on him."

"Xtelle," I warned.

"Fine. He's right over there. For someone who says she's in love, you are shockingly unaware of his presence."

I took a couple steps back to the fence and sure enough, Ryder was out there on the sidewalk at the corner of the block, pointing at a manhole cover.

Next to him stood an aggravated Vivian Dunn. He might not be boring her to death, but he was certainly annoying her.

The look of wholesome sincerity on his face, the way his hands moved like the history of our manhole covers was the most interesting thing in the world, the way Vivian's eyes were glazing over—I couldn't love that man more.

He was, however, between me and my Jeep. Taking Tish out there was a risk. Tish was new to town, and working for someone, and possibly a thief who had access to some very powerful spells. That made Tish a flight risk. Unless I slapped handcuffs on them, which would only draw more attention, I couldn't be sure they wouldn't run for it again.

"Can you take on your normal shape?"

Xtelle gasped, and Tish's eyes flew wide.

"You want me naked?"

"No, not naked, just…the shape you are when you're not something you've eaten."

That all sounded bad, and I was pretty sure I had offended them, but I wasn't sure why.

"Naked?" Tish repeated.

Xtelle cleared her throat. "I'm sure Delaney doesn't want that." She was addressing Tish, but staring straight at me. "No one would ask a ghoul to gadabout in their first skin, because it is incredibly rude and inva-sive. You're not rude and invasive *today* are you, Delaney?"

"I am not," I said. "I'm sorry for the misunderstand-ing, Tish. You're the first ghoul I've met. I'll do better as I learn more about you. Thank you for being patient with me."

Xtelle's mouth dropped open, then she closed it.

The look on her face was something close to grudging respect.

"You are welcome?" Tish replied.

"Plan B. Than, can you take Tish into the station? You can use my Jeep if you want."

"I have a vehicle," he said mildly.

"Okay, is it here?"

"It is not. My house is not far. We will walk."

Like that wasn't going to draw even more attention. "I don't think it's going to be a good idea to see two yous strolling down the streets."

"Then perhaps you would give them a strand of your hair," Than suggested.

"What?" I said a little too loudly. "Are you kidding? You want Tish to be me now?"

The wicked glint in Than's eyes said he wasn't kidding. Also, he was enjoying this. Payback time.

"Artishall, will you don a Delaney skin?" Than asked.

"May I?"

"May he?" Than asked. "Unless you have another letter of the alphabet you would like to use as a plan?"

I narrowed my eyes at him. It didn't bother him in the least.

Because, no. I didn't have another plan.

I could call for back up, but every minute I dithered, was another minute wherein Ryder and Vivian could see us, or Tish might run.

"Dammit," I said. "No, I don't have a better plan." I plucked a hair out of my ponytail, wincing at the tiny sting. "Is this enough?" I held it out for the ghoul.

Tish, who was still sitting on the ground, took the hair from me, and nodded. They stuffed the hair into their mouth, swallowed, and literally between one blink and the next, I was now looking at myself sitting in the grass.

It was uncanny and set off my fight or flight instincts. An awful lot of my brain was agreeing I should be fighting. Fighting the heck outta that Delaney. Or fleeing. Fleeing before Delaney-ghoul caught me and ate me whole.

I inhaled through my nose, exhaled through my mouth, making space for reason. Settling myself with being around this being's nature, this kind of magic.

It wasn't the first time I'd seen someone do something I thought was unsettling, but that was completely normal for them. I'd get used to it if they stayed here. Just the first time seeing myself, a whole living, breathing me right there in the grass was weird as hell.

"Excellent," Than said. "Shall we?" He offered his hand to me, well, to Tish, and I stepped back, nodding and nodding.

"Are you going to give Than any trouble?" I asked.

Tish shook my head, and I wondered if my hair was always that color—more streaks of blonde now that the sun was out, little glints of red. "I don't want to die?"

"He won't kill you."

Than grunted like that was still to be decided. Xtelle snorted like she didn't believe a word coming out of my mouth.

"He won't," I said, glaring at Than, "kill you. He will put handcuffs on you if you try to get away. And as we both just saw, he can outrun you. Even if you're me."

"I am to be tortured?"

That voice coming out of my mouth made my throat close up for a minute. It was the uncanny valley turned up to the max.

"No torture," I assured them. "Just talk. Go with Than. We'll figure this all out. Why you're here, how we can help, what part of the god weapons deliveries you're involved with."

My eyes, well, Tish's eyes went wide. I hoped that was not what surprise looked like on my real face.

"Let me go distract Ryder and Vivian," I said. "Give me about two minutes, then you can head off."

"I'll come with you," Xtelle said.

"No."

"You need back up. Every police show says so."

"I don't need a talking pony for back up."

"Of course you don't. You need a unicorn demon queen."

"No, you're going to go back to Hogan's house where you belong, Xtelle. Unless you want the government taking over Ordinary and starting a war with every single supernatural in town, you will cool your jets, keep a low profile, and go home."

I thought she was going to argue, but she tossed her head, making her mane shine. "Fine. I'll go back to a boring existence in this boring town. When do I get to have fun? When? A nice shopping spree, the theater, a consensual virgin sacrifice?"

"I'm not even going to unpack all that. But if you

want a life that is something more than what a pony is allowed to do, choose a different shape."

"But *responsibilities* come with different shapes."

"Yep. You got this?" I asked Than.

He was a god. The god of death. He had probably met a lot of ghouls before. The ghoul certainly knew him on sight. I didn't think it would be too terribly difficult to keep the ghoul from running.

"If there are problems," Than said. "I will just torpefy them."

The ghoul made a little *eep* sound, and now I wondered if that's what panic looked like on my face.

"Sounds good," I said, not knowing how Than would do that exactly or why the mere mention of torpefying a ghoul would get that kind of reaction out of them.

"But remember to follow the law. No one will be harmed under our watch."

"The ways of Ordinary are clear to me, Reed Daughter." He extended his hand once more to Tish. Finally, Tish accepted.

For a moment I was standing face-to-face with myself. Tish held my gaze, maybe a little fascinated to see me this way too.

"Do you get any more of me besides my shape?" I asked. "Like my thoughts? My memories?"

"I am not a mind reader? Your memories are not mine?"

"So, no?"

"No?" Tish smiled. I knew it was not my smile, because it was shorter, pursed more in the center. And while I thought it was strange to see it on my face, it still was genuine, joyful.

I smiled back, because how could I not, and watched as Tish changed their smile to duplicate mine.

"You're good at this," I said.

Tish nodded quickly. "It is my great pride?"

"I can see why. Okay, Tish, we'll get this all figured out. Go with Than, don't run, or try to escape. If you're hungry or thirsty, let Than know. He'll see that you're taken care of. I'll meet you both there."

"You," I pointed at Xtelle, "go home."

"You can't make me."

"I can," I said.

She rolled her eyes and trotted over to the green space behind the house where the fence was lower. "I do what I want," she said. Then she hopped over the fence and took off at a slow trot.

"The queen is your friend?" Tish said.

"I don't think so, Tish."

Tish-me just smiled back at me and looked smug.

Whatever. I didn't think a ghoul had a very good grasp on the dynamics going on in this town, much less whatever relationship I'd built with the ex-queen of hell.

"Delaney?" a woman's voice called out. "Is that you?"

I glanced over the fence. Vivian Dunn was headed this way, fast, Ryder right on her heels.

CHAPTER TWENTY-ONE

"Go, GO!" I pointed back toward the fence Xtelle had just vaulted, and Than and Tish-me jogged to it.

I got my hands on the fence and hopped up and over it, landing on the sidewalk in front of Vivian, hopefully messing up her line of sight into the yard.

"Hey, hi, you two." I said walking straight at her, which forced her two, three steps back. "Enjoying the weather?"

Vivian oh-so-casually looped her arm through Ryder's. "RyRy has been such a doll," she said, leaning into him. "Taking me around this cute little town and showing me the cutest things."

"Cute?" I said.

"So cute," she stressed.

I flicked a glance at Ryder. His eyes were rolled up toward the sky. I had to clear my throat to cover a laugh.

"So where are you going next?" I took several steps back out toward the main road, and Ryder fell into step next to me, dragging Vivian away from the yard. He didn't ask me why I'd been back there, but I knew he would follow my lead.

"There's a sale on pencils," he said, sounding super excited about it. Which, he might not actually be faking that. "I've asked the store to set aside one of every brand they have. Vivian and I are going to test every one."

"Wow." I couldn't choke out another word, too afraid I'd laugh in his face. "How long do you think that's going to take?"

"Hours," he said with a sigh, like all his dreams had come true.

We'd turned the corner. The kite store and its murder-clown sign were straight ahead. "Well, I'll leave you both to it, then. Good to see you Vivian. Don't stay up all night testing pencils."

Vivian deflated, her shoulders dipping, but her smile set in mortar. "Where are you going, Delaney?" she asked with strained cheer.

"Oh, you know how it is. I'll find something to keep me busy around here. See you later, Babe," I said to Ryder, picking up my pace. "Don't buy all the pencils, I'll need something left to get you for Christmas."

"Let me come with you!" Vivian shouted.

I walked faster and pretended I was too far away to hear her.

"But the pencils," I heard Ryder call out. Just as my hand landed on the Jeep's door, Vivian ran up and grabbed my arm.

"Take me with you," she begged.

"Vivian?" Ryder called out as he strolled over, a fake look of concern on his face. "The pencils?"

She glanced over at him, her eyes wide, and gripped my arm tighter. "Delaney wants to show me around."

"I don't have time—"

"Please," she whispered. "Please get me out of pencil shopping. He spent two hours talking about manhole covers. I don't know what happened to him. He used to be interesting, worldly. But now he thinks counting the barnacles on kelp is high entertainment."

Oh, gods, I was going to kiss the ever-loving face off him.

"I'm working."

"I'm begging you."

"So I'm sensing some reluctance to pencil shopping?" Ryder asked, arriving next to the Jeep and leaning against the hood, his arms crossed.

"They're pencils, Ryder," she said. "Why in the hell would anyone care?"

There it was. The real Vivian. She sounded judgmental and bitter. She sounded like she'd be more than happy to stab Ryder with pencils until he stopped breathing.

I didn't like her much before. I pretty much hated her now.

Ryder's expression barely changed. Just a slight tightening at the edges of his eyes, just a slight clench of his jaw. I had a good feeling he'd seen this side of her before.

"I mean," Vivian said, her laugh falling fat and false

into our shared silence. "I know *you* like them because you are so, so *artistic*. But I want to ride along with Delaney. Ask her some questions for my article."

"You can ask me some questions," Ryder said, sounding a little hurt. "I'm sorry I went overboard on the pencils. There are other things I can show you here. Kelp—"

"No! These are questions only Delaney can answer. What it's like to be a female chief of police. What it's like having your sisters working for you. You promised me you'd answer the questions, remember?"

Vivian turned to me and mouthed, *please*.

I didn't like liars.

I didn't like manipulators.

And I didn't like her.

I opened my mouth to tell her no, when Ryder cut me off. "We'll all go together."

Vivian closed her eyes for a second, her brows pulled tight, her fingers flexing into my arm, really digging deep now like she wanted to punch someone and was only keeping herself from doing so by holding onto me.

I looked up at Ryder, who jabbed his thumb off to the side.

Crow was about a block away, making the "kill it" slice finger sign across his neck.

Something was happening, or about to happen, and we needed to get Vivian out of here.

I jumped immediately into action, opening the back door and all but shoving her inside.

"I'll answer a few questions before I drop you off back at your hotel."

I slammed the door. Ryder had already ducked into the passenger's seat, so I slid into the driver's seat. I started the car, keeping an eye on Crow in my side mirror. Just as I eased out onto the street, I saw me, well, Tish-me running for all they were worth, Death hot on their heels.

I gunned it and turned up the radio, old rock music coming on strong.

"You're staying at the Sand Garden, right?"

"I don't—Can you turn that down?"

Ryder looked away from the side view mirror and turned the music down to a better level. "I know how you love to rock out," he said to me, "but Vivian has questions."

Than caught Tish-me by the back of the shirt and pulled them up short. Tish-me hung their head, and Than leaned in to whisper something in their ear. Tish shivered, and nodded.

Than held onto one of Tish's arms. Crow jogged up on the other side of the ghoul, taking their other arm. Last I saw them, Tish-me was being carefully guided into Crow's car.

So much for promising not to run.

"So, Delaney. Tell me what it's like to be the chief of police?"

"It's good," I said. "Following in my father's foot-steps. I've always known I would go into law enforcement."

"But didn't you get any push-back from the town? I know small towns can be so much more judgmental than big cities."

"In my experience, it isn't towns or cities that are judgmental, it's people. We have a lot of diversity in Ordinary. No one blinked an eye at me taking on these duties. And if they wanted me out of the position, if I weren't doing the best job I could do for them, I'd resign and let someone better qualified take my position."

"You don't really mean that do you?" Ryder asked.

"What?" I said glancing at him as I let a few tourist cross the road. "I do mean that."

"You'd quit?"

I shrugged. "I'd resign. Look." I glanced at Vivian in the rearview. "If I'm doing a good job, if I'm listening to the people in my town and doing everything I can to make sure they're living in a safe and fair community, then I'm happy to be doing that job.

"But if I lose track of what it means to care for people—all people including the ones who make bad choices and mistakes—when I start seeing them as something other than a living, breathing person who deserves to be seen as human before criminal, then someone better tell me so I can resign and let someone with a better sense of ethics, morals, and heart take care of this town."

"That sounds very…correct. Politically," Vivian said with sniff.

"Does it? Good. Because my job is to be strong for people when challenges come storming into their lives. My job is to make sure everyone is going to come out of the storm alive and whole.

"If there has been a crime committed, then I'm going to follow the law and see that fair consequences are handed out for those actions. It's law enforcement, Vivian. But I'm not the judge, jury, and executioner. I never forget that every person who lives in my town, or is just driving through deserves to be treated fairly."

Ryder was watching me while I talked, and I could tell from his small smile that he had not expected me to say that. Which, out of everyone, he should know this about me.

Yes, I handled crime in the town. Yes, I had arrested people, jailed them. I'd pulled my gun before too, though I'd never killed anyone.

Yes, I judged if gods and demons could come into Ordinary, but that mostly came down to whether they agreed to follow the rules. I didn't automatically assume any god, human, demon, or hell, ghoul who looked like me, was up to no good unless they showed me proof those intentions.

Look at Tish. They had come to town in a car that fell out of the sky. They were working for someone. They might have something to do with the theft of god weapons—might even have been the one to steal the weapons.

But until I knew that, until we had facts and proof, I wasn't going to jump to conclusions. I wasn't going to hurt them—ever—if I could help it.

Until proved otherwise, Tish was just another supernatural who had come to town and gotten themselves in a bit of a mess. Plenty of supernaturals did that.

Ryder reached over, and took my hand, his fingers and mine slotting together.

"I don't think you're going to have to resign any time soon," he said.

"I hope not. I like my job. I love it. But if there comes a day when I'm not the best person for it, when I'm not the best *me* on the job, then I'll step away and find another way to help the people in town."

He squeezed my hand gently. "Like they'd ever let you retire."

I gave him a quick grin. "Maybe if I begged?"

"What about moving on to a bigger town? A better town?" Vivian asked. "Move up in the world? Become someone?"

She stared out the window, and I wondered how she saw the place that had always been home to me. From the look on her face, there was nothing special about the weather-worn buildings, the narrow, but clean streets.

I didn't think she saw how Athena's surf shop had new candles displayed in the window, cleverly arranged to mimic an ocean wave. I didn't think she could see how Zeus was still trying to camouflage the lopsided chainsaw statue of a walrus Odin had forced him to carry in his upscale boutique. I didn't think she could see the new tea shop Ganesha, who had returned to town a couple month ago, was going to open, the sign on the window a cheery drawing of an elephant and mouse having tea together.

She didn't see the people here, the lives here, the love here. She saw only the surface of the place.

Which was fine with me. I didn't want anything to draw her attention. Didn't want her interest.

Boring was good. Boring was a shield and a protection.

"I like it here," I said. "I grew up here. I can't imagine living anywhere else."

Traffic was a little slow, so I took a side street, knowing I could cut back through the neighborhoods to the hotel.

"Delaney, you don't want to——" Ryder started, just as I realized I'd turned down a street with the spillover of cars and people heading to the pre-show practice of the Ordinary Show Off.

Traffic slowed to a snail's crawl.

Shit.

The lines of cars on either side of the street perked up Vivian's attention. "Is there an event going on?"

"Just good weather," I lied.

"No, I see something. Is it a festival? How cute."

"Oh, that's a rehearsal, it's not open to the public." I was looking for a turn around, but the streets were narrow and there were cars ahead and behind me. We were at a complete stand still.

"I'm sure they won't mind." Vivian opened the door. She slipped between two parked cars and strode down the sidewalk.

"Shit," I said.

"I'm on her." Ryder shouldered out of the car. A short jog brought him right next to her.

They crossed the street. I wasn't going to catch up to them in the Jeep. Putting on my lights wouldn't do me any good. There was nowhere for the cars around me to move to let me get by.

So I looked for a place I could park. I wedged the Jeep between two other vehicles, blocking a fire hydrant, which—not great—but this was an emergency.

I ducked out of the Jeep and bee-lined to where Ryder and Vivian had disappeared down a cross street.

The air was warmer now, and the smell of popcorn and cherry cotton candy puffed toward me, along with the more savory scents of barbecue.

Because of course Bertie wouldn't let the rehearsal be anything but a show in itself.

Voices rose and fell, the lift of someone really getting a kick out of a joke, the shriek of a child running fast enough it felt like flying.

Hammers banged, out of rhythm, a saw shrilled and stopped, a drill droned.

The Ordinary Show Off wasn't until tomorrow afternoon, so construction of food booths, props, and charity donation stations was still ongoing.

"…many people can get in the way of construction. It's not safe." Ryder said to Vivian. They had stopped on the edge of the little footpath that led to the slight rise of hill overlooking the stage and seating.

"We need to go," I said. "I'm not asking. This," I pointed at the event, "isn't open to the public. It is not safe for you to be here until all of the construction is finished. Let's go."

"But—"

"I can put you in cuffs if you think that would make a better article," I offered flatly.

I was not kidding. She must have figured that out.

"One person all the way up here isn't going to get in the way of the rehearsal," she said.

"Okay, so cuffs it is." I pulled mine out of my pocket and had the great satisfaction of seeing her eyes go wide.

"I don't—"

And then the worst thing happened. Gladys, who ran the Pop Shop popcorn store, and who was also a Siren, got up on stage to sing.

CHAPTER TWENTY-TWO

ORDINARY'S RULES were very clear about god powers—they were to be safely stowed and not used while the god was in Ordinary.

But all the other supernaturals followed different rules.

As long as their powers, magic, or abilities didn't harm anyone, didn't give away the secret of supernaturals in town to the mortals who didn't know their neighbors were the sort of people fairy tales were written about, and didn't break any mortal law, they were free to be who they were, and do what they naturally did.

So when a Siren steps up on a talent show rehearsal stage, there is just one thing that she's going to do: sing.

Gladys started softly at first, almost too low to hear over the construction, nothing more than a sweet cascade of notes as fleeting as birdsong floating in winter snowfall.

Still, there was a tug to that sound, a draw. My breath evened out, quieted without me thinking about it.

I held still, my head bent so I could better catch those notes again.

A second roll of notes rose from the stage. The drill silenced, the saw stopped, the hammering halted.

Even the screaming children and laughing crowd fell still, holding space for the song. To witness it. Waiting.

Gladys began to sing.

The music, the magic in it was blinding. Each note built on the next, climbing, skipping, tumbling, joyous, and free.

A shout of laughter punched out of me, a cheer I couldn't hold back. A cheer echoed by everyone around the stage.

Then we were walking, jogging, running down that hill to be closer to the stage, to worship at the feet of song and promise, woven through with words I didn't understand. My soul craved that sound, my spirit caught in the delicate net of a voice that could bring the world to its knees.

Being the Bridge for Ordinary meant magic didn't hit me as hard as it did others. So while I was running toward the stage, a part of my mind knew this was a bad idea.

I knew I needed to break the Siren's spell and get Vivian out of here before she caught on that there was something otherworldly, that there was something magical about the woman on the stage.

But we weren't the only ones rushing toward the stage. Everyone within four blocks was headed this way, a nearly silent stampede of people desperate to get closer to the song.

This was bad. This was really bad. People could get hurt in crowds like this.

I yelled for Ryder, who was just a few steps ahead of me, and even over the Siren's song, he heard me and spun toward me, his arms open. My momentum threw me into his arms, and he wrapped them around me.

I was found, tethered, harbored against the storm.

"We have to stop her," I said near his ear. "We have to stop Gladys."

His arms tightened, and he nodded. I didn't know if being in contact with me made it easier for him to resist the song, or if it was because he was claimed by a god, and therefore had his own bit of resistance to magic.

But just in case it was contact, I held on to his hand and tugged him sideways to the flow of people, over to the stairs that led to the stage.

I was surprised the crowd hadn't swarmed the stairs, but instead they were pooling out below the front of the stage like an ocean wave fingering out across the sand.

Gladys had control of her song, maybe not of the initial draw, which was especially strong on humans, but definitely of the tone and message of it.

The first notes had tempted, the next notes had drawn people in. But now the song held them, speaking of family and friends and the sorrows and victories of life, of togetherness, of love.

No one rushed the stage, because her song drew them together, cherished them, loved them, and it was enough just to be held in that thrall.

But if she kept it up, things could very easily get out

of hand. I stood on the stage, hidden behind one of the heavy purple curtains.

"Gladys," I called out. "Stop. You need to stop!"

I moved toward her. I didn't want to tackle her, but if it meant ending the song, I was on for it.

The crowd below me gazed up with adoring eyes. Humans, yes, but there were vampires and werewolves, shape shifters and dryads in that crowd. Our town gilman, Chris, was down there, as were several gods— Odin, Frigg, and Athena.

The gods were watching me instead of Gladys, which made sense. They weren't as susceptible to her magic either.

Ryder, who had been right behind me on the stairs, was nowhere to be seen.

I didn't have time to worry about him. Vivian had found the other set of stairs and was walking in a trance toward Gladys.

"Hey, Gladys!" I tapped her on the shoulder. "Good job. That's real good. Show's over folks!"

She stopped singing and looked back at me. "Oh, hello, Delaney. Didn't see you there."

"That was just great," I said, making eyes toward Vivian who stood halfway across the stage, a confused look on her face. "You really have a fantastic set of pipes."

She glanced at Vivian and her eyes went wide. "Oh gods," she whispered. "Is that…?"

I stepped up to the microphone. "That's right. That was just a sneak peek at one of the great acts you're going to see tomorrow, folks."

A groan rolled through the crowd. "I know, I know, but we don't want to give it all away. Buy a ticket, bring a picnic lunch, and you can see all of the acts from start to finish. It's a terrific family-friendly event, and all the ticket money goes toward charities."

The staccato click of a set of heels coming my way fast, told me I was about to get kicked off announcer duty.

"But hey, let's give Gladys a hand." I turned toward the blonde bombshell and started clapping. The crowd joined in with whistles and shouts.

Bertie's heels were still clacking, but she clapped too as Gladys took a bow and waved, then walked backstage.

I stepped back from the microphone, and Bertie stepped up. "Well done," she said as she passed me.

I didn't think I'd ever heard those words out of her mouth before. I almost tripped over my feet.

"Now get rid of the hunter." Bertie put her smile on high beam, spread her arms wide and took the microphone.

"It is wonderful to see you all here, but as our Police Chief Delaney Reed has said, this is just the warm-up. The main event will begin tomorrow at eleven o'clock and will run into the evening. We'll have food, games, plenty of entertainment, and fireworks. You will get to choose this year's Ordinary Show Off! I hope to see you all right back here tomorrow."

She cut the mike, waved to the crowd, then followed Gladys behind the curtain.

I crossed the stage to Vivian. "You're not supposed to be up here on stage," I said. "This is rehearsal."

"Her voice," she said, like she was picking through memories to separate the chaff of reality from the blossoms of dream.

"Oh, Gladys? She's amazing. Was offered a record contract back in the day but decided to settle down here by the ocean instead. You'd think she'd win every one of these Show Offs."

"She doesn't win?" Vivian sounded more like herself, and fell right into step as I walked her toward the stairs again.

"Nope."

She glanced back at the microphone. Bathin was walking toward it, which made me burn with curiosity. He hadn't been in the Show Off before, and I didn't know if Bertie had forced him to perform, or if he really had some kind of talent.

"Who could top that?" Vivian asked.

"There's a guy in town who does armpit music. Bach. Mozart. That sort of thing."

"No," she said sounding slightly horrified. It was probably the first real emotion she'd shown.

"Yep. Small town. You can take the pits to the city, but you're never gonna get the country out of the pits."

She shook her head. "That doesn't even make sense."

"Neither does Phil winning the Show Off two years in a row."

We were almost there, almost down the stairs. The crowd was dispersing now that the Siren call was gone.

About a third of the people remained, kids squealing, the construction sounds banging out through the air.

Bathin cleared his throat, and the microphone whinged with feedback static. "Testing," he said. "Testing. This will be a dramatic reading of *Jabberwocky* by Lewis Carroll."

The audience didn't seem nearly as interested in that statement. Someone shouted, "Do it with your armpits!" and people laughed.

Bathin was unfazed. He took a breath and began in a spooky, quiet bass: "'Twas brillig, and the slithy toves did gyre and gimble in the wabe; all mimsy were the borogoves, and the mome raths outgrabe."

Someone in the audience made an armpit fart, and another person followed. Pretty soon, it was an off-tune chorus of flatulence.

I glanced at Bathin to make sure he wasn't going to get mad about the hecklers, when I saw a shadow behind the curtain move.

The shadow had a sword in one hand and an ax in the other, and my first take was that Bathin was about to turn his boring poetry reading into live-action battle slam poetry.

And honestly, I wanted to see that.

But then the shadow stepped into the light, and I knew this was not a performance. This was not a play.

That was a real sword. That was a real ax.

And the shadow, was a real demon.

A demon I'd only seen once before.

Bathin's brother, Goap was moving faster than my

brain could adjust to the fact he was here, now, in Ordinary.

Or maybe he wasn't really here. The last time he'd shown up and stabbed his brother, Goap had been a projection and the weapon had been nothing but air.

This time, this time details, solid details hit like lightning.

His heavy boot tread. His controlled breathing, the scent of him on the wind—charred wood, basil, and something sharp like whiskey.

He was not a projection.

Goap was here, really here. And he was about to cut off his brother's head with an ax.

I ran.

"Bathin!" I yelled. "Behind!"

Bathin pivoted, but it was late, much too late. I put my hand on my gun, but they were too close together for me to get off a shot without hitting Bathin.

"Stop!" I yelled.

The crowd had caught on that this wasn't a show any more. Someone screamed, Goap swung the ax at Bathin's head, yelling, "Die!" and all hell broke loose.

CHAPTER TWENTY-THREE

EVERYTHING HAPPENED LIGHTNING-FAST. Ryder running the stairs, panic wide and harsh on his face, Bertie practically flying toward us, her speed incredible, the crowd yelling, screaming.

Vivian, slower than me, much slower, but I had the sense she'd drawn a gun out of her purse and was getting ready to squeeze the trigger no matter who took the bullet.

And the worst, the gut-wrenching realization that I'd never get to Bathin, get in front of him before that ax cut off his head.

It didn't stop me from trying though.

I threw myself at Bathin, hoping to knock him sideways away from the main impact point of the blade.

My feet left the stage, and I angled my shoulder to hit Bathin mid-body.

But just as I connected, the ax blade slicing air inches above my ear, my whole body ready to tuck and roll, everything stopped.

Well, I didn't stop. I rammed into a brick wall named Bathin who didn't even grunt from the impact, even though I was pretty sure I'd just dislocated my shoulder.

I fell on my ass and knocked my head so hard on the floor everything blacked out for a second. My shoulder slapped the boards, and pain exploded, bringing me fully awake in a white-hot nebula that burrowed sparks through my muscles.

"Fuck!" I yelled, grabbing my shoulder, trying to blink away enough of the pain that I wouldn't barf.

I was sure I'd see Bathin chopped in half. I was sure I would see Goap smiling his evil villain smile, then probably doing some sort of monolog about how much he'd always hated his brother.

But when I could see, when the pain had faded from a universe of heat to maybe just a small galaxy burning in my shoulder and back of my head, what I saw were both brothers, standing, facing each other.

They were opposites, these demons, Bathin solid and wide as a mountain, Goap lithe and fluid like smoke and oil. But their coloring was the same, and their eyes—one look at their ice-green eyes, and anyone would know they were brothers.

"Are you okay, Delaney?" Bathin asked, not looking away from Goap.

"Yes. What the hell do you think you're doing, Goap? I assume this is the real you this time?" I got my good hand under me and levered myself to a sitting position. The world spun. I swore softly and hung on until the ride came to a full stop.

Goap ignored me. "You have mother's ring."

"It looks like I do," Bathin said. "I'd always supected it could stop time."

I took a quick assessment of the world around us.

Bathin was right, every person was freakishly still, frozen in place. Ryder tilted mid-run to my right, the panic in his eyes burning with fury. Bertie was more than just running—she was actually floating an inch above the ground, her skin gone gold, powerful, nearly invisible wings spread out behind her, wings so large they would block the sun if they were fully solid.

Vivian was in a shooting stance aiming for both the demon's heads.

The crowd below and around were all in various stages of fear and confusion, but no one was fleeing yet, though the children's eyes were being shielded by adult hands.

My stomach rolled for another reason: even the gods in the audience were frozen.

There would be no help there.

There would be no help from anyone.

"Of course it stops time," Goap said. "Mother has always cheated in battle."

"Lucky for me," Bathin said, "and lucky for you."

Goap scoffed. "You were about to be beheaded, brother. This is only a slight delay."

"Let's see, shall we? Kneel."

Goap's eyes narrowed with rage, and every muscle in his body locked up. His face went red from the effort to fight the command, and sweat rolled down his temples.

Bathin pointed downward, like he was telling a dog

to sit. Goap dropped, knees hitting the board with a massive thud that revealed he was much, much heavier than he appeared.

"You've gone soft," Goap said, his hands on his thighs, his face tipped up in a sneer.

"And yet you are the one kneeling," Bathin replied. "Release the weapons."

Goap dropped the sword.

"Both."

He dropped the ax.

Bathin looked over at me. "Are you injured?"

"Shoulder," I said, pushing up to my feet. "I'll be okay." I took an unsteady step toward him.

"Don't," Bathin said. "I'd rather not have him try to take you hostage."

I was going to argue that I could take care of myself against demons just fine, but decided he was right. I was injured, Bathin only had the upper hand here because he had his mother's ring, and I didn't know the range of its powers.

So I stayed put.

"Come closer, Delaney Reed," Goap sing-songed, "I promise not to eat you, my pretty."

Bathin kicked Goap in the face. Goap grunted as his head snapped back. The kick would have knocked my teeth out, but it didn't appear to do any more harm than a love tap to Goap.

He just glared harder at his brother.

"Manners," Bathin chided.

Goap turned his head slightly. It looked like it took

every bit of energy he had to force his head to move. He spit blood onto the wood. "Soft," he repeated.

"I could say the same to you," Bathin said. "You brought the wrong weapons. I cannot imagine that was a mistake."

"I nearly took your head off with Bunny Kisses, the King Killer."

"But I am not a king," Bathin said, glancing at the ax. "Bunny Kisses would not have harmed me."

Goap smiled. "That's why I was going to gut you with Feather Duster, the Brother Stabber."

"Wait," I said, wondering how hard I'd hit my head. "The ax is named Bunny Kisses, and the…sword? That huge blade is Feather Duster?"

"They are demon weapons," Bathin said, like that explained anything.

"Demon weapons. And they aren't named something like Grave Digger or Earth Shaker?"

"Those are monster trucks," Bathin said, while Goap muttered, "Obviously."

"All right, okay," I said, "fine. Why did you try to kill Bathin with something that only kills kings? Why even bring that here?"

Bathin crossed his arms over his wide chest and nudged Goap's knee with his boot.

"Father is coming for you," Goap said. "For you, for mother, for Avnas—who I can't believe just packed bags and is shacking up with her. He is shacking up with her, isn't he?"

"She's keeping her options open." Bathin shrugged.

"Oh." Goap frowned. "Disappointing. I always thought they made a good pair."

Bathin grunted. "So did I. You've told me this before —not about Anvas, but that father wants to kill me. I knew that even before I left his kingdom. Of course he'll want to kill mother for breaking their contract, and Avnas for leaving his service.

"This is obvious. Why are you here? Again. Warning me. Again. What are you up to?"

"Is it so difficult to believe I am just worried about you?"

"You tried to behead me."

"It got your attention, didn't it?"

"Tap…"

"Don't call me that. You left me. You both left me. You don't get to use that name."

Bathin's nostrils flared, but he nodded. "Apologies."

The anger shifted in Goap, settling into stubborn lines. "He is not as you remember him. He is much, much worse. There are some among us who would stand against him."

"Demons are always up for a juicy backstabbing," Bathin said.

"Yes, but it's more. There is a growing rebellion. Change is coming to the kingdom. Brutal change."

"Did you steal the weapons?" I asked.

Surprise crossed his face before it locked down into a sneer again.

"Did you box them up and send them to us?" I asked. "Did you mark them with the red circle and feather?"

"Answer her," Bathin ordered.

I didn't think he'd do it, but maybe he remembered the boot to the face.

"Of course I marked them with a red circle and feather. A simple glance at my Wikipedia page would have told you I carry men between kingdoms."

"The feather," Bathin said, "represents carrying the weapons between kingdoms. From god realm to here."

Goap inclined his head once.

"And the circle?" Bathin asked.

"One of the three primes. You should know this," Goap said.

"I do," Bathin rumbled. "The circle represents salt, or the body. But you didn't use your body to deliver the weapons, did you, brother? You used someone else."

"Wasn't that obvious?"

"Who carried the weapons for you?" Bathin asked.

"A friend."

"A ghoul?"

Goap hesitated, and then pressed his lips together.

I was going to take that as a *yes*.

"Why didn't we see the weapons in the trunk of the car?" I asked.

"My brother's greatest trick is making people and things invisible," Bathin said. "He must have made the god weapons invisible for a short time."

"My greatest trick is breaking locks and stealing from powerful beings," Goap said.

"With the torn page of the god spell book?" I asked.

That got his attention. He turned that glass-green gaze on me. "What do you know of the god spells?"

"I know you have it. I know you must have used it to break into the gods' realms."

"I don't have the page," he said. "I didn't need it."

"Then how did you get into their realms?"

Bathin kicked at his leg again.

"I have seen it. Once. I committed it to memory."

I glanced over at Bathin to see if that was true. Bathin nodded. "He's always had a quick mind. Makes terrible decisions—"

"My decisions are flawless."

"—but I believe he could memorize a spell with one glance."

"Okay," I said. "Why bring the weapons to Ordinary?"

"Did you not hear me say there is a war coming to your border?"

"I heard. Why would you give us weapons? Why would you even risk sending the god weapons here?"

He paused. "It was a favor." He glared up at Bathin. "You're welcome."

"I never asked you for a favor. Nor is it like you to give one, little brother."

Again that pause. And I wondered, just briefly if Goap really was doing us a favor. If he was trying, maybe against his own nature, to help us against his father.

Demons had surprised me before. I didn't see why Goap couldn't have good intentions.

"Perhaps I am not as you remember either, big brother," Goap said. "You have been gone for a very long time."

"Did you send the weapons here because you are offering to join us?" I asked. "In the fight against your father?"

Both brothers wore identical looks of surprise.

Goap shook his head slightly. "Is she always this naive?"

"You'd be surprised at her soul," Bathin said. I didn't know if that was a compliment or an insult.

"Why else would you be here with a king killer ax?" I pressed. "It kills kings."

"Bunny Kisses," Goap corrected. His gaze was locked on Bathin, as if willing him to understand. "I brought Bunny Kisses."

Bathin grunted, and bent to pick up the axe.

It was a short-handled battle ax with a wide, curved edge so bright, it looked like a scrap of the moon had been hammered from toe to heel. The rest of the metal was covered in intricate carvings, spells that tricked and misled the eye.

I could feel the power radiating from it. A heat. A promise. A hollowness that hungered.

"If you kill Father, the throne will be yours," Goap said. Then, in a rush: "I would rather you seated there than him."

Bathin shifted his grip on the ax. "I will never take that throne. This is my home."

Goap nodded. "Then the throne will fall to me. Would you not rather I take up the kingdom than leave it in his hands? Think of all the—"

"Yes," Bathin said simply.

That seemed to catch Goap off guard. "Yes?" he croaked.

Bathin shrugged. "Yes, brother. I'd rather see you on the throne."

"You don't…you wouldn't fight me for it?"

"This is my home," Bathin said again. "If you want the throne, you can fight for it."

"I can't." Goap sighed. "You know I can't kill him directly. I can't. It must be you. The first spawned. Only the first spawned *can* kill him."

"You've been reading the prophecies again. Prophecies very rarely come true."

"Maybe so. But I don't want to risk it. Only a fool would try to bring down the king of demons with a prophecy stating it is the first spawn alone who can take his head. I need…" he cleared his throat. "I need you to fight him."

"You need me to kill him."

"That too."

"A suspicious demon might think you're the one trying to start the war," Bathin mused.

"You know me, brother."

"I did. Once. Now?" Bathin shook his head. "A suspicious demon might pick up Feather Duster and take care of ever having a relative swing an ax at his head again."

Goap rolled his eyes. "You don't frighten me. We both know if we'd wanted each other dead, it would have happened years ago."

"On the spawning grounds," Bathin said.

"You wish. I could have taken you. Even then."

Bathin's mouth curled in a small smile. "Too bad you didn't, because that was your last chance." Bathin lifted his hand. Goap stood stiffly, as if he had been held down by a pile of bricks that were falling away one by one.

"I could kill you," Bathin said.

"You won't."

"If you return to Ordinary uninvited, I will." Those words were harder, colder. Deadly. This Bathin was the man who could kill a king. A man who could crush another demon under his heel. Goap didn't seem bothered by the change.

"Give me your word you will not return uninvited," Bathin ordered.

Goap opened his mouth, closed it, then nodded. "You have my word. If you fight him, if you kill him, you will have no trouble from me."

Bathin grunted. It sounded like he believed him about as much as I did.

"What are you going to do with me?" Goap asked.

Bathin looked my way again. "Delaney?"

Goap's eyebrows went up, but he covered his shock with a frown. "A mortal. A Reed? You're allowing a Reed to decide my fate?"

"I could arrest you," I said. "That way I wouldn't have to wonder when you're going to show up and try to kill someone in my town again."

"No cell will hold me."

"Oh, our cells would. But the last thing I need is a demon who doesn't like my town pacing in my jail. I want you gone, just like Bathin said. I don't think you'd keep a promise to me, but your word means something to him, and his means something to you."

"You are so *wise*," he said with a half bow, and *wise* sounded more like *foolish*.

Yeah, whatever. Impressing demons wasn't ever gonna be on my to-do list. I wanted him out of here. I wanted my town unfrozen. And I never wanted to see him again.

But there was one more thing I needed.

"Give me the page of god spells."

His head jerked up, his jaw tight. "I've told you I don't have it."

"I think you know who does. And that," I said, with a nod toward Bathin, "is worth me locking you up, no matter the consequences.

"The gods are angry, Goap," I said. "They don't like their houses broken into. They don't like their belongings stolen. I'm sure they'll want to discuss the matter with you."

He straightened from that half bow, and folded his hands in front of him. "I don't have the page," he said. "I don't know who has it." He kicked, catching the sword, which had been left on the floor.

It flipped up into the air, helicoptering toward me, fast.

I knew, even as I was moving, that I should hold still. It was nothing but instinct, a knee-jerk reaction driving my actions. I threw up my hands to catch the sword before it hit me in the face, but the pain from my bad shoulder twisted and shortened my reach.

I yelled.

All this happened in the same second Bathin shouted, "No!"

Before I could change course of action, or duck the sword, Bathin's huge hand was there, impossibly grabbing the hilt. He snatched the sword out of the air and away from my head.

"You can't touch this," he panted. "No mortal can."

The world snapped back into motion, the yelling, the pounding footsteps, the swooping Valkyrie all moving again, coming at us fast.

Fire blasted up into the sky in a fountain of sparks, and beyond the pain juddering through me, I registered Goap had disappeared.

"Ow, ow, ow," I said as Ryder collided with me, his arms wrapping me, his breath hot and fast against my cheek. He jerked back, holding me by just his fingertips.

"The ax, the ax," he huffed. "You threw yourself. You threw yourself at the ax. Where are you... How bad.... Are you bleeding?"

"I'm fine, my shoulder. Dislocated, but I'm okay, I'm okay, I'm okay."

He shifted his grip to my uninjured side, sliding into me gently. I felt his heart beating and beating, shaking his muscles, shaking his bones.

"And hast thou slain the Jabberwock?" Bathin called out, raising both weapons above his head. "Come to my arms, my beamish boy! O frabjous day! Callooh! Callay! He chortled in his joy."

I had to give him huge points for continuing with the poem like the whole thing had been a part of the act.

Then Bertie's calm voice washed out over the crowd.

"And that dramatic bit of stage magic will be fine-tuned for tomorrow's show.

"We would have warned you that something exciting was about to happen, but didn't want to rob you of the delightful moment when you realized the boring poetry reading was actually something more. Let us give a hand to our performers."

She clapped, and yes, it took a few seconds before people in the crowd joined in. Those who joined first, from what I could see smushed up against Ryder, were our supernaturals, who knew something had happened in that split second between Goap appearing and taking a swing to Bathin's head, and then disappearing in a gout of flame, the axe and sword now in Bathin's hands.

"Vivian," I said, pushing at Ryder's chest. "Babe." He loosened his arm and I stepped back. "Vivian."

He caught on quick, and pushed me out at arm's length. "Never agree to be part of an act without telling me there are going to be weapons and fireworks involved," he scolded, just loud enough, I knew Vivian would hear him.

"Surprise?" I said with a wide grin. Bathin behind me was taking big, dramatic bows, and the crowd went back to showing their appreciation via armpit farts.

We turned together to face Vivian, who had been smart enough to stow her gun.

"You have a concealed carry permit?" I asked, as we rambled over to her. I thought we were pulling off the ha-ha it-was-all-smoke-and-mirrors pretty well, though my shoulder was killing me and my head throbbed.

Vivian's mouth went hard at the edges, but it was distaste, not suspicion. "Of course I have a permit."

"And you carry because?" I asked.

"I'm a woman traveling alone writing stories about remote areas. A gun was the first thing I purchased."

It was a good cover story. Better than saying she was a monster hunter. I had a feeling those bullets had silver in them.

"You could have gotten a dog," I said. "Protection and someone to snuggle with all in one."

She smiled, and it was the fake everything-is-so-cute smile again. "I am absolutely, miserably allergic to dogs." She pouted.

"Speaking of dogs," Ryder said. "I need to let Spud out. Think you can drop us off, Babe?"

I didn't want her back in my home, didn't want her there with Ryder. Plus, I needed to get to the station to talk to a ghoul, and hey, there were two demon weapons we needed to do something about.

Also, my shoulder wasn't feeling so great, and it was possible I had a concussion. Maybe he should drive me home. Or to the ER.

"Sure," I said. We made it three steps before Bertie called my name.

I winced. "Yes, Bertie?"

"You were late on your cue. I expect you to work that out with your partner before tomorrow night's performance."

She was good. Adding a little extra cover on the fake act might be enough to clear away the rest of Vivian's doubts.

"I'll try. And hey—nice special effects. I thought you were going to cheap out like last year."

"Delaney Reed, I will not tolerate that kind of talk. The special effects in last year's Show Off were adequately spectacular. Even the local website said so." She sounded stern, but there was a twinkle in her eye.

"Thank you for showing up," Bertie said. "Now please leave." She spun on her kitten heels and shouted out orders for the next performer to step up to the mike.

"She's kind of a hard ass, isn't she?" Vivian said.

"Never insult the stage manager," I said, as I started toward the stairs again.

I wasn't at all surprised to see Myra walking our way. Her gaze flicked to Vivian, then Ryder, then the shoulder I was favoring.

"Chief," she said, "you're late for your own departmental meeting."

"Crap," I said, going with Myra's lie. "That was this afternoon, wasn't it? I've got to get Ryder home to let Spud out."

"I can take the Jeep," he said. "You ride with Myra."

"I'd love to sit in on the meeting," Vivian said.

And before I could tell her that wasn't happening, her phone pinged. "Hold on."

I gave Ryder the keys, and mouthed *thank you*, while Vivian frowned down at her phone.

"Problem?" I asked.

"No." She palmed her phone back into her pocket. "Just a spam message." She put on a smile to cover her lie.

"We can take Spud for a walk on the beach," Ryder said. "Nice weather for counting barnacles."

"Sounds great," I said, following Myra as quickly as my aching shoulder would allow. "You two have fun."

"Dislocated?" Myra asked.

"Yep. Also, Goap stopped by to say hi. With an ax."

"I saw. Let's get out of here before Vivian finds an excuse to dump Ryder. Think you can go any faster?"

To get away from Vivian? I discovered I could.

CHAPTER TWENTY-FOUR

A SHORT GAME OF ROCK, paper, scissors won me my sister shining a flashlight in my eyes (which dilated correctly) instead of going into the Emergency Room. Myra also reset my shoulder and followed that up with a painkiller and a brown bag with a peanut butter, strawberry jam sandwich, and some humus and celery.

Even better, was the huge travel mug of coffee she had made just the way I liked.

So by the time we got to the station, and I had filled her in on our on-going demon problem and her boyfriend's place in it, I had plowed through the sandwich, half the coffee, and was feeling a lot steadier.

Jean was manning the front desk, her hair up in one high pony. "Hey. You okay?"

"Word gets around fast. I'm fine."

She nodded. "Bathin too?"

"He's built like a tank," Myra said. "He's fine." Her voice was strong, but I could hear the small doubt behind the words.

"Not a scratch on him," I said. "I promise."

She nodded and dropped the empty, extra-large duffle she was carrying onto the floor by her desk. "How do we want to do this?"

"We need to find out how Tish is mixed up in everything. Goap admitted he was behind the lock picking. But he wouldn't say a ghoul helped him get the weapons out of the realms and into Ordinary."

"You think he's telling the truth?" Jean asked, bringing her strawberry milkshake with her as she sat on the edge of my desk.

"I don't know why he'd need to lie about it. He wants Bathin to fight the King of the Underworld for him. He thought arming the gods would give us an advantage when the king decides to go after Ordinary."

"Huh."

"And the god spells?" Myra asked. "Does he have the missing page?"

"He says he doesn't."

"Helpful," she said. "So how do you want to handle our ghoul?"

"Have they said anything?"

"Not a peep," Jean said. "Also, it's super weird to see you sitting in there."

"Yeah, okay, so that's a thing we need to figure out. Myra, do you know what ghouls eat for sustenance?"

"I did some asking around. Anything but meat. I packed an extra lunch."

Of course she had.

"Get that. Let's bring them out here so they don't feel as constrained behind bars. Right now the only thing we can hold them on is trespassing, and frankly, that yard they were in is a vacation rental. No one has been there for months."

"I'll get them," Myra said.

She sauntered back to the small jail cell behind the doors at the far end of the station. Jean slurped her milkshake.

"What about the monster hunter?" she asked.

"I don't know. I'm taking it one disaster at a time."

My phone buzzed. I checked the messages. A text from Rossi said: *you're welcome* and was followed by three bat emojis and a cow.

"What did Rossi do?" I asked Jean.

She shook her head. "Other than have a game night without inviting me?"

"You're as bad as Crow."

She grinned. "I heard you picked a date," she said. "Good job."

"Is Ryder texting you behind my back?"

"Maybe."

"Jean."

"He's going to be my brother-in-law. A little friendly gossip session now and then only makes our relationship stronger."

I pushed her knee hard enough, she had to plant her foot to keep from falling off my desk.

"Go sit in a chair," I groused.

She laughed and got off the desk, choosing to stand instead.

The door opened. Bathin strode in, carrying a black-wrapped bundle about the size of an ax and sword.

313

"Is Myra here?"

"Yep. Those the weapons?"

"Yes. The cloaking cloth should make it easier to handle them."

"Can I see?" Jean asked.

Bathin shot me a quick look.

"Please?" she begged. "C'mon, Delaney. Let me see the shinies."

"Go ahead," I said. "She'll bug me forever if you don't."

Bathin placed the bundle on the counter and flipped back the cloth.

"Holy shit, those are gorgeous," Jean said. "And look at you all Conan the Barbarian in those tight jeans and T-shirt. If I weren't dating someone, I might chat you up."

Bathin gave her a killer smile and shifted his stance. "You like?"

"Oh, gods. You're posing," I said.

He flexed his arms, making his biceps pop. "I don't know what you're talking about."

"Hey, handsome," Myra said, leading Tish-me into the room. She'd left Tish in handcuffs, which was prudent. "Who are you posing for?"

"You, babe," he said. "Only you."

Jean cooed and fluttered her eyelashes at him and Myra. Myra guided Tish to sit in front of my desk. Tish's eyes, well, mine, were wide and their face was slack with awe.

"My Prince?" Tish breathed. "I am not worthy?" Tish bent forward, gaze on the floor.

"Tish," Bathin said, as he rewrapped the weapons. "I hear you've been working with my brother."

"Yes, my Prince?"

I raised an eyebrow. That was more than I'd been able to get out of them.

"Lift your head, Tish." Bathin tucked the weapons under his arm again. "You are going to answer the Reed sisters' questions now."

"Yes, my Prince?"

"You will tell them the truth."

Tish hesitated.

"Tish. That was not a request," Bathin said.

I knew Bathin. He rarely took this stance, this…command.

Bathin was a prince of hell: royalty. It was impossible to miss the power behind his words.

"I will gift you with a skin," Bathin said.

Tish's eyes flew up to meet Bathin's gaze.

"Truly, my Prince?"

"If you answer the Reed sisters truthfully."

Tish swallowed. "I will? Yes? I will?"

"Good."

Bathin handed the bundle to Myra. "They're heavy," he noted before letting go of the full weight of the weapons.

She braced for it, and nodded. "No kidding. You okay?" she asked him quietly.

"Wholly." He cupped the side of her face. She leaned into his palm, closing her eyes. It was just a moment, a second or two, then she eased away and carried the bundle to the big duffle by her desk.

"Now for your gift, Tish," Bathin moved around the counter and stopped next to the ghoul. "Open your mouth."

Tish did so. Bathin placed a small pebble on their tongue. "Swallow."

Tish did that too. Bathin pressed his fingertips on Tish's forehead. "Become," he intoned.

Tish shivered and was no longer me. Tish was now a young person, maybe fifteen? Brown hair long enough they had to tuck it behind their ears but it still stuck up a little.

Tish's eyes were soft brown, their skin several shades darker than my own fish-belly white complexion. Their chin cut a hard straight line and angled up to a killer jawline, their lips wide and rosy.

This Tish was of medium build, and if I were to think of them as an athlete, I would place them in wrestling or gymnastics.

"Is it comfortable?" Bathin asked.

Tish nodded and nodded, the glisten of unshed tears in their eyes.

"Good. Now do not disappoint me, or I will take what I have given."

Tish swallowed, then turned their attention to me. "I will answer your questions now?"

"All right. Here's the first one. Are you hungry?"

Tish's short dark eyebrows ticked up.

"Truth," Bathin reminded.

"Yes?"

Myra put a peanut butter and jam sandwich on the flattened brown paper bag in front of them.

They threw a quick look at Bathin, then lifted the sandwich and shoved half of it into their mouth in one go.

"Dang, dude," Jean said, "That's pretty impressive. Oh, and when I say "dude" I'm using it as a term of non-gender affection."

Tish chewed twice, smiled, then shoved the other half sandwich after the first. Two more chews and that was that.

"Are you working for Goap?" I asked.

"I was?"

"Did you deliver the god weapons?"

Tish nodded. "I did?"

"Did you deliver the Queen's ring?"

"Yes?" Here they glanced up at Bathin again. I could see the trepidation on their face.

"Did you steal the god weapons?" I asked.

"I...helped? I held? I put the boxes in the right places?"

Apparently ghouls were pretty round about in their speech patterns.

The door opened again. Odin, Frigg, and Crow strolled in. "How's it going?" Crow asked. "Got any news to share?"

Tish bit their bottom lip and kept their eyes resolutely on me.

"Why did you all decide to drop by?" I asked.

Odin shrugged those massive shoulders of his. "Crow told us you found the ghoul. Tish, is that right?"

Tish held still, only the sweat that had broken out to cover their forehead indicating they had heard.

"That's right," I said. "Tish is being very helpful right now."

"Sounds good," Frigg said. "Carry on."

They all stood in the small lobby, hands in pockets or on hips, waiting. It would be intimidating if you didn't know they were gods. It certainly must have been intimidating to Tish who knew they were gods.

"Tell us how you helped." Myra touched Tish's shoulder to bring their focus back to us.

"Prince Goap called upon my service? To walk where he told me, stand where he told me, take what he told me?"

"Did that involve you walking into god realms?" I asked.

Tish nodded.

"And how did you do that?" I asked.

"Did Goap have a spell?" Jean asked. "A paper with a magic spell he used to get you into the god realms and get you out?" She wiggled her fingers like she was doing magic.

Tish's shoulders drooped. They nodded again.

My heartbeat picked up the pace. Goap had lied. He had used the page to pick the godly locks.

"I am not alive? Dead?" Tish mumbled. "The spell allows no living or unliving to cross into their realm? Me? I am not dead or alive, am I?"

Crow swore, then chuckled.

"Smooth," Frigg said.

"How did you miss that loophole?" Odin demanded, smacking Crow on the back of the head.

"It's been awhile," Crow protested. "I bet neither of you remember the exact wording of your spells."

I looked over at them. They were both frowning.

Terrific. But that wasn't a problem we could tackle right now.

"Do you have the spell?" I asked.

Tish shook their head.

"Do you know where it is?" Myra asked.

A pause, then Tish nodded.

Jean exhaled, and her breath smelled like strawberry. "Wow, dude. That's great. That's really great. Do you have it with you?"

Again the head shake.

"Where is it?" I asked.

"Buried? In the flowers and birds?"

I looked over at Myra. "There's a lot of flowers in town. A lot of birds."

"Penguins?" Tish asked.

"You buried it in Mrs. Yate's yard with her penguin?" I asked.

Tish tipped their head toward Crow. "Penguin and flowers maybe?"

Crow groaned. "You have got to be kidding me. You? You were the one who broke my penguin statue? You buried the spell I've been looking for for *centuries* in my flower box? Holy shit that is ballsy. And brilliant. Respect."

Tish offered a very small smile.

"We need to put that in the vault, pronto," Myra said.

"If you'll excuse me," Crow said, "I'm going to go dig up an old spell."

"Not without me." Myra tugged the duffle up and settled the strap on her shoulder.

Crow was already out the door, and Odin followed. Frigg tapped the counter with her knuckles. "I'll keep an eye on them. Make sure Crow actually hands it over."

"Thanks," I said. "Good luck."

She left with a quick wave over her shoulder.

"Okay, now what are we going to do with you?"

Tish gave me the same little smile. "Keep me?"

"That's complicated. No, don't get all mopey looking. You came here because a demon wanted you to deliver stolen items. That's a lot to deal with. The gods could charge you with theft. They'd be legally in the right to do so.

"And I think you knew exactly what you were doing —no, wait for me to finish—but you were also doing what you were ordered to do by your prince."

Tish bit their lip and nodded.

"You've let demons into town before," Bathin noted mildly, leaning against the wall, his hands stuffed in his back pockets. "Demons are a lot more conniving and dangerous than ghouls."

"Demons sign a contract agreeing not to break the laws."

"Tish can sign the contract."

"Tish isn't a demon. There's a reason we make demons sign a contract. Demons are very contract motivated. I don't think that's the same for ghouls."

Bathin hummed in agreement.

My phone buzzed, and I looked at the screen. A text from Ryder.

All good

I sent him a thumb's up icon, even though I wasn't sure exactly what good he was talking about.

"If someone hosted Tish, maybe," Jean suggested. "Take them under their wing and show them the ropes."

"It would have to be someone with strong boundaries and communication skills," I said, thinking through all the people in town.

The thing I wasn't saying is that it would also have to be someone who could deal with Tish's natural quirks—mainly eating things and turning into them.

Tish had the potential of getting into a lot of trouble with a skill like that. They needed someone who could see through any shenanigans they might pull.

Bertie shoved her way into the building. "What was that hunter doing on my stage?" she demanded. "I thought you were keeping her away from my event. But there she was, with a gun. A *gun* on my stage. Do you know how much I have on my plate without dealing with an armed confrontation? Do you know how many details are falling to the wayside, Delaney? Do you know how difficult you have made my life?"

Wow, Bertie was furious.

Tish shrank down in their seat, trying to be as small as possible.

But I was used to Bertie. "Sorry," I said. I meant it. "It was the best I could do under the circumstances."

"Circumstances?"

"I was trying to make sure Tish here was brought to

the station, which meant taking Vivian in the other direction."

Bertie walked around the front counter and leaned to one side to get a look at Tish who was dodging her line of sight.

"The ghoul? I see. Sit up straight, Tish, posture is important for a first impression."

Bathin snorted. Bertie ignored him, all her attention on Tish, who did as they were told and straightened up.

"Very good," Bertie observed. "The weapons are vaulted?"

"Myra has them. They're digging up the god spell which, if Tish is telling the truth, is buried in Crow's flower beds."

"I see. The hunter?"

"I haven't solved that problem yet."

"And why not?"

"Because we're trying to decide what to do with Tish. They want to stay in Ordinary, but they can't stay without someone taking on guardianship, at least for a few years."

"Bertie, you should adopt them," Jean said.

"What?" I asked.

"What?" Bertie echoed. "Why would I do that?"

"You need an assistant," Jean said. "You were just saying how much work you have to do. Tish is really good at following directions and following through. Aren't you, Tish?"

"Yes?"

"It's not a bad idea," I said. "You'd need to do more than employ them, though. They'd need a place to stay.

Someone to show them what it means to live in Ordinary."

"Of course, of course," Bertie said, dismissively. "Tish, dear. Do you act? There are several parts in our upcoming play that I am still looking to cast."

"No?"

"No matter." Bertie held out her hand. "Come with me. We have much to do."

Tish stood, looked at me. I nodded.

Tish looked at Bathin. He inclined his head.

Then Tish took Bertie's hand and smiled.

"First, let's get you proper shoes. We have a lot to do before the show tomorrow, and we will not be slowed down by blisters."

They walked out of the building, Bertie's expression stern, but not unkind, Tish smiling that small smile.

"I am a genius," Jean said. "Did you see that? Bertie has an assistant. Finally! Do you know how many events we're going to get out of?"

"None of them?" I leaned back in my chair. "You know how she is."

Jean lifted her chin. "Nope. You can't ruin my dreams. Tish will be such a good assistant we'll get out of two, maybe three whole events this year."

"Maybe this decade."

"I'll take it," she said.

"Thanks for the assist, Bathin. With Tish just now, and with Goap."

He was typing on his phone, pressed it one more time, then dropped it in his pocket. "Goap will be back."

"I know."

"My father will bring war to our borders."

"Ooooo," Jean said rubbing her arms. "Say that again. It was so fantasy-hero, I got chills."

Bathin grinned. "He's gonna want a fight."

"I know. Do you think he has the book of god spells?"

"No. We would know. The entire world would know if my father had that power in his hands."

"Well, there's one plus on our side."

"You're doing the math wrong, Delaney." Bathin pushed off the wall, and started toward out door.

"Oh?"

"We have all the pluses. And we always will." He winked before the door closed behind him.

"Think he's going to see that Myra gets the weapons stowed?" Jean asked.

"Yes. Where's Hogan?"

"Waiting for my shift to be over. I'm making dinner tonight. Bibimbap."

"Sounds cozy."

"Where's your man, Delaney?"

"Walking the beach with a monster hunter."

"Bummer." Jean slurped the last of the milkshake out of the cup and tossed it in the trashcan. "But at least you know he's coming home to *you* tonight, not her."

The door swung open again. This time it was our other officers, Hatter and Shoe, who came in, laughing and wiping their faces.

"Hey boys," Jean called out. "Nothing new except Bertie adopted our ghoul, Tish, Crow's digging up an ancient god spell and handing it over to Myra so she can lock it away with the Hell weapons Bathin's brother used to nearly take off Bathin's head and stab Delaney."

"So it's just another run-of-the-mill Friday," Shoe said in his low grumble.

"Ain't that the truth?" Hatter drawled in his fake accent that was leaning a lot more Texas lately.

"Hey boss," Shoe said. "Heard you put on quite the show today."

"Demons," I said. "Just a head's up? Xtelle's ring can stop time."

"Well, ho-lee shit," Hatter said. "I don't suppose she'd loan that out? I have a three-day weekend coming up."

"No," I said.

Jean winked at Hatter, and kept winking. "No. Totally no. We aren't allowed to commandeer demon weapons for private use." She strolled over to him. "I totally wouldn't bribe it off of Bathin and pass it around."

Hatter gave her a low five.

I pointed at her. "You know better." I pointed at Hatter next. "You should know better."

He grinned. "Never hurts to ask. You okay? I mean besides the attempted fratricide."

"Yeah, I'll write the report. Basically Goap wanted to get Bathin's attention so he swung Bunny Kisses at him, which didn't leave a scratch because he's not a king."

"You hit your head, boss?" Shoe asked.

My hand went to the back of my head, and I winced. "Once, why?"

"That sounded like a concussion talking."

"Ha-ha. Would you like a cup of fresh coffee?"

"Yes?" he asked with a frown, sensing a trap.

"Good. Get me one too."

Hatter laughed. Shoe might have grumbled about it, but he strolled to the coffee station and poured two cups.

"Shouldn't you go home?" Jean asked. "Your head? Your shoulder?"

I couldn't bring myself to dealing with Vivian again. Not yet. "First I'm going to write up my report."

"In that case," Shoe said from the coffee station, "I'll brew a new pot."

CHAPTER TWENTY-FIVE

THE REPORT TOOK SOME TIME, as I had to write one that didn't have any of the supernatural or magic in it, and then write the other with all the supernatural happenings that had gone down today, which would be stored in the library.

I'd sipped my way through the mug of coffee Shoe gave me, and kept drinking it when it got cold. Shoe had some kind of magic touch when it came to making a pot of drip coffee. I had asked if he put vanilla in it or cinnamon or something and he'd looked at me like I'd lost my mind.

I'd watched him make it. Several times. Nothing fancy, just water, filter, grounds. But when I did the exact same thing in the exact same order with the exact same measurements, it didn't turn out nearly as smooth as his brews.

By the time the coffee was gone, and both reports were done, all the adrenalin of the day had worn off. I wanted to go home and face-plant in my bed. But

Vivian would be there. Well, maybe not in my bed. Hopefully not in my bed.

But she'd probably be on our deck, curled up on our couch, maybe even drinking a glass of our wine.

I was exhausted just gathering my stuff, but I put on my game face. Ryder had had to deal with her a lot longer than I had. I could do my part to try to bore her too.

I dug around in my desk drawer looking for my keys, patted my jeans, then remembered Ryder had my Jeep.

I sighed. "Shoe, could you give me a lift home?"

He looked up from one of the cold cases we were still working—someone had been walking through the grocery store and crunching all the cookies in the bags and leaving them there for people to buy. It was only the one brand, but we still hadn't caught them in the act.

"Thank gods, yes," he said. "Anything's better than this."

I smiled. "You know how to make a girl feel special."

He chuckled as he pulled keys from his pocket. "I am one smooth-talking bastard. All the ladies say so."

Hatter laughed so much he choked, and was still laughing when Shoe slammed the door hard enough to test the strength of hinges.

Shoe was in such a crappy mood for the short drive to our house on the lake, that I just let him grumble and grouse.

If I'd thought any of those things he was accusing Hatter of were true, I'd have reassigned them new partners. But they'd come down from Tillamook, veteran

police officers even my dad had trusted with the supernatural happenings in town.

They were peas in a pod, even if one of those peas
currently wanted to smother the other one in his sleep,
and also had detailed plans of how he'd carry that out
without getting caught.

We pulled up to the house. Lights on in the living
room and over the porch, but none on the deck.

"Thanks, Shoe."

"What? Oh. Sure. Hey, boss?"

I looked over at him.

"Do we need to start planning for the final show
down?"

I nodded. "I'll get the gods together and find out
how they want to handle it if Ordinary is attacked. We'll
pull the old covenants and see if there are any provisions
on whether or not the gods can actually stand in Ordinary to defend it against foes."

He was nodding and nodding. "I was talking about
the wedding."

"Final battle?"

"Should I have said blessed event?"

"Sorry about your raise." I opened the door.

"I already got my raise."

"I'm docking your pay for smartassery."

He laughed. I slammed the door and watched him
drive away while wondering how I got so lucky to have
such annoying employees who still made me like them
so much.

"Delaney! Delaney!" a voice called out from the
bushes on one side of the house.

Even without looking over, I knew it was Xtelle. I thought about ignoring her, but she'd probably barge into the house after me. If Vivian was still in there, it would be a disaster.

I strode over to the bush, which was doing a fairly good job of hiding her in the shadows.

"Hey, Xtelle. You can't be here tonight."

"We'll be brief," a second voice said from another bush. I squinted, and could just make out Avnas' dark form.

"You both need to leave."

"But we have intel. On the spell book thing," Xtelle whined. "You promised you would reward us."

I shouldn't. I really shouldn't stand out here talking to the bushes. Just my luck Vivian would look out and see me acting like a total weirdo.

"Tell me tomorrow."

"But the reward," Xtelle said.

"Tomorrow." I rubbed my sore shoulder. "It's been a really long day, Xtelle. This can wait until then."

I turned to leave but the branches of the bush shook and Xtelle pushed her head through them. Luckily, she was in pony form.

"The book has been found and lost again," she said out of the side of her mouth as if somehow that would make it look like she wasn't talking. "Several creatures are trying to hunt it down, including a god."

"Really. I'm going inside. Let's pick this up tomorrow…"

"Cupid," Xtelle said. "Cupid wants the book."

Tired as I was, my mind spun with possibilities.

Cupid had briefly stopped by Ordinary not too long ago, but hadn't been back since. I wondered why he was so interested in the spell book now. I wondered if finding it would be made easier or harder now that we had the missing page.

I wondered what part Ordinary would play in his hunt for it.

"Now, I really must be going," Xtelle said. "I can *not* believe you forced me to hide my magnificence in a bush. I shall expect my reward in diamonds, rubies, and gold. A crown would be appropriate, a tiara sufficient."

She unstuck herself from the brush, made a couple wet kissy sounds, then she and Avnas trotted off into the night.

Telling me a god was looking for the god spell book wasn't really the intel I'd wanted. I didn't even know how reliable her sources were. She could be making it all up, just to see if I'd actually give her a crown.

She was going to be so disappointed.

I pushed the whole thing out of my mind to deal with tomorrow. Tonight, I needed to face the monster hunter in my home.

Game face: on. Shoulders: still sore. Determination: ready to rumble.

I opened the door.

The soft swaying blues of *The Sky is Crying* flowed through the house.

I walked in, my shoulders dropping, my feet moving to the rhythm of the song as I dropped my bag at the door.

The lights were low, but I didn't hear laughter, didn't hear voices.

I walked into the space between the kitchen and the living room, and just stood there.

The sky was dark, a twinkle of lights across the lake winking through the window. The flames in the fireplace twisted and hissed. Dragon pig slept with its feet straight up in the air, an empty roll of tin foil across its round little belly.

Spud looked up from where he lay beside his buddy, and tapped his tail on the floor before putting his head back down on his paws and closing his eyes.

I didn't see Ryder in the living room, didn't see him on the patio, didn't see him in the kitchen.

Then the floorboards in the upstairs bathroom creaked, water shut off, and I closed my eyes. I tracked him from the sounds he made. That twisting pivot on the ball of his foot as he shifted around the bathroom door like he was navigating an obstacle course instead of just walking down the hall.

The double step he took outside our bedroom door, so he could three-point shot something onto the dresser, the pat of his palm on the newel post at the top of the stairs.

All of that was Ryder. Every movement, every sound a part of him filling my life.

I breathed it in, this awareness of him in my life. The space he took up in it. The space he took up in me.

I loved it.

I loved him.

He thundered down the stairs like a spilled bag of rocks and hit the bottom almost silently.

"Delaney," he said. "Damn it."

I opened my eyes. "It's like poetry when I'm with you."

He rubbed his hand over his hair, messing it up, and grinned at me. "Yeah?"

He was barefoot, and wore a pair of old sweats that hung low on his hips, and a Pink Floyd T-shirt that had holes all the way around the collar.

It was a good look on him. Relaxed. Loose. Comfortable. He fit here. In this house, with me.

I wanted to touch him, hold him, be held by him. So I walked toward him.

"I was going to have a glass of wine waiting for you," he said.

"Yeah?"

"I was going to light some candles."

"I don't need candles."

"Huh. What do you need?"

I pressed my fingertips to the space just below his collar bone, feeling the steady beating of his heart like an echo of my own. I flattened my hand, and ran my palm down his chest until I could cup the heel of my palm against his hip bone. "You."

His breathing had gone thready but that was all the invitation he needed.

He bent, I lifted. Warm arms wrapped around me. I tucked one foot behind his ankle, pressing into all the spaces of him where I fit.

His lips lowered to mine as the song cried out about seeing his baby in the morning.

"What about Vivian?" I asked.

He paused, his lips so close they brushed mine when he spoke. "Gone."

"Hotel?"

He pulled back a little and looked down at me. "You want to talk about her right now?"

"Just trying to keep track of loose ends. It's been a day."

He tightened his arms once, then eased up on the pressure, and took me by the hand.

"Wait," I said. "No. I thought there was going to be kissing. What about the kissing?"

"Buried under loose ends," he said. But he smiled. "I put a blanket and pillows on the couch. Let me pour the wine."

I protested and tugged on his hand, and almost got him wrestled down on the couch with me, but he was flexible and strong and got out of my hold.

"That better be good wine," I grumbled as I kicked off my shoes with a groan and crawled up the couch, messing with the bed pillows he'd stacked there and pulling my favorite blanket down around me.

"So where is she?" I asked.

"Spokane, I think." He poured thick red port into small glasses. "She got a tip from *Under the Oregon Moon*. It's a Facebook blog that follows supernatural sightings in the area. Wouldn't tell me what it was, but I ran the police reports from the area. Wanna guess what showed up?"

"Aliens?"

"Close." He brought both glasses over, handed me mine, then eased onto the couch with me. It took some finagling, but we both managed to get comfortable, my head on his shoulder, both of our glasses of wine forgotten on the floor.

"What did you find?"

"Reports that cows in the area are being drained of their blood. But the only wound they can find are two punctures on their necks. They're not saying they look like vampire bites."

"But they totally look like vampire bites," I finished for him. The text Rossi had sent earlier suddenly made more sense. "Well, hell," I said.

"Mmmm?"

"I don't think we can have our wedding in a church now that he's called in that favor for us."

"Rossi?"

"Yeah. Such a meddler."

"I don't care. He got Vivian out of our hair. So no church wedding it is."

"Bertie wants us at the Community Center."

He hummed again, his fingers running softly over my shoulder.

"We're gonna need some place bigger than that, I think," I said.

He didn't say anything, but his breathing was becoming more rhythmic, lengthening.

"You asked me. Yesterday. How many gods I invited."

"Okay," he mumbled.

"I invited all the gods," I said. "All of them. Even the ones who aren't in Ordinary."

He grunted and then chuckled. "We're definitely going to need something bigger than the Community Center. Beach?"

"Too cliché?"

"Forest?"

"Maybe."

"We could do it here on the lake," he said softly, his words a little fuzzy.

The song ended, and the tick of the clock I'd hung in the laundry room tacked down the edges of the darkness. I knew I didn't have to decide right now. I knew Ryder was almost asleep.

But it was important. To be a part of this. To let him know.

"Anywhere," I said. "Anywhere there's you, I'll be there. Just let me be with you. Never let me go."

I wove my fingers into his, and he was just awake enough to slot them together the way that worked best. Our way.

"Love you, Laney."

"Love you, Ryder."

His hand stilled on my shoulder, and beneath my ear, his heart—my world—beat strong and steady.

ACKNOWLEDGMENTS

I'd like to thank the amazing people who have helped me bring this installment of Ordinary, Oregon, and all its rascally citizens, to life.

To my cover artist, Lou Harper of Cover Affairs: thank you for the inspiration of a car dropping out of the sky. You are the best, and I truly appreciate all your work, patience, and talent.

Big shout out to my intrepid copy editor Sharon Elaine Thompson, who always makes my sentences shine. Thank you bunches to my brilliant beta reader, Dejsha Knight, who keeps me hopeful. Ladies, you saved my bacon on this one. Thank you.

I'd also like to give a heap of gratitude to author, publisher, and founder of Rainforest Writers Retreat, Patrick Swenson. This book began during the three day word count battle at the (virtual) retreat this year. I needed the push, and Rainforest Writers Retreat (the event, the people, and that darn word count whiteboard) never disappoints.

To my husband, Russ, and my sons, Kameron and Konner, I love you, always. Thank you for being the best part of my life and for sharing your lives with me.

And finally, to you, dear readers: Thank you for visiting Oregon's most magical vacation destination. I hope you enjoyed hanging out with the gods, ghouls, and people who call the town their home.

Oh! One last thing. There are some exciting things coming up right around the corner for our Ordinarians (Ordinariites? Ordinariers?) including (or so I've heard) a big wedding. Rumor is they're going to serve the really good cheese. I hope to see you then!

ABOUT THE AUTHOR

DEVON MONK is a USA Today bestselling fantasy author. Her series include Ordinary Magic, Souls of the Road, West Hell Magic, House Immortal, Allie Beckstrom, Broken Magic and the Age of Steam steampunk series. She also writes all sorts of short stories which can be found in various anthologies and in her collection: A Cup of Normal.

She lives happily beneath the lovely, rainy skies of Oregon. When not writing, Devon can be found drinking too much coffee, watching hockey, and knitting silly things.

Want to read more from Devon?

Follow her blog, or sign up for her newsletter at www.devonmonk.com, or find her at the social media sites listed below.

ALSO BY DEVON MONK

ORDINARY MAGIC

Death and Relaxation

Devils and Details

Gods and Ends

Rock Paper Scissors

Dime a Demon

Hells Spells

Sealed with a Tryst

Nobody's Ghoul

Brute of All Evil

SOULS OF THE ROAD

Wayward Souls

Wayward Moon

Wayward Sky

WEST HELL MAGIC

Hazard

Spark

AGE OF STEAM

Dead Iron

Tin Swift

Cold Copper

Hang Fire (short story)

SHORT STORIES

A Cup of Normal (collection)

Yarrow, Sturdy and Bright (Once Upon a Curse anthology)

A Small Magic (Once Upon a Kiss anthology)

Little Flame (Once Upon a Ghost anthology)

Wish Upon A Star (Once Upon a Wish anthology)

Made in the USA
Coppell, TX
21 July 2021